Shaken

Pamela Beason

WildWing Press
Bellingham, Washington, USA

ISBN 978-0-9798768-7-5

Published in the United States of America by:

WildWing Press
3301 Brandywine Ct
Bellingham, WA 98226

**Other Books
by
PAMELA BEASON**

Mystery/Suspense

ENDANGERED
First of the new Summer Westin mystery series

THE ONLY WITNESS
Free excerpt at the end of this book

Romantic Adventure

CALL OF THE JAGUAR
Available in ebook stores everywhere

To keep up with Pam, visit:
http://www.pamelabeason.com

Chapter 1

When the first ripple of earth surged toward her, Elisa Langston stood up and stared, not trusting her eyes. The field around her was quiet; all she heard was the rasp of rubbing branches overhead. Even after the wave had lifted her and set her back down, then rolled on toward wherever it was going, she didn't quite believe it. Was she hallucinating?

But then a second wave, this one more malevolent, roared through the ground, driving her to her knees. Ridge after ridge of earth rolled through her field like breakers surging toward the beach. Car alarms sounded in distant parking lots. Increasing in speed and size, undulations of soil rose and fell around her, tearing landscape fabric, noisily tossing her neat rows of potted plants into mangled piles. Overhead, branches cracked and popped as the taller trees around her shimmied and swayed like crazed hula dancers, showering her with red and gold leaves.

A streak of black-and-white fur flashed past.

"Simon!" she shouted, but the panicked cat was gone. She didn't blame him. If she had four legs, she'd be running, too.

This was the biggest earthquake she'd ever experienced. And the weirdest. It felt as if the planet had suddenly returned to its ocean origins, and the whole world was liquid again. A large wave swelled up beneath her, toppling her backwards, and she was nearly buried by a sudden deluge of rainbow-colored foliage. A tremendous ripping sound came from the north, followed by a thundering crash that reverberated through the ground and rattled her teeth. The old homestead!

Elisa dug her fingernails into the dirt, trying desperately to regain her feet and turn toward the noise. Snapping sounds erupted all around her. A sweet gum crash-landed a few feet away, its impact jolting every bone in her body. She flailed wildly, struggling to find purchase in the roiling soil. A rush of cold air blasted her face, and then she felt a crushing blow to her legs and chest. After a brief close-up of speckled bark, her world went black.

When Elisa opened her eyes again, it was dark. How long had she been lying here? Her eyes wouldn't focus on the numbers on her wristwatch. The first stars were out, weak pinpoints of light barely visible among scattered clouds. A gust of wind blew leaves and dirt into her face. Rain would follow soon.

The uneven soil beneath her was cold, and its dampness had soaked through her clothing and hair. Waves of shivering rippled through her. Her head pounded so badly that she would have sworn a freight train rumbled somewhere nearby.

The tree trunk pinning her to the ground was no more than eight inches thick. She was strong, even if she was small. If she could get proper leverage, she should be able to shift it off her body. When her shivering subsided for a few seconds, she tried to move her legs. A lightning bolt of pain shot through her, white hot, then icy, leaving her breathless.

Giving up for the moment on her lower limbs, she fingered the wetness at the back of her head. She'd landed on a rock. When she stretched her hand in front of her face, it was dark with sticky fluid. Groaning, she managed to squeeze her fingers into her front jeans pocket and slide out the penlight she habitually carried. Its tiny beam confirmed the blood on her hand.

She wrapped her arms around the trunk again, pressing the stinging heat of her scratched cheek against the cool bark of the American sweet gum that had nearly killed her. The tree was one of the Festival variety, prized for its brilliant foliage in an area dominated by evergreens.

"I'm never forgiving you," she hissed into a cluster of orange leaves. "I babied you for years, and this is how you pay me back?"

A thin wail drifted on the breeze. A cat crying? "Simon?" she whimpered. "Go for help, bud. Run to the office. Get Gerald."

Right. As if a cat could rescue her. Her business partner, Gerald, usually left the nursery promptly at five, and for all she knew, Simon needed to be rescued himself. It was an unbearable thought, that her pet might be lying nearby, in pain, waiting for *her* to make things right.

"Anyone! I'm out here!" She slashed her penlight through the air. "Hey!"

Sirens wailed, nearing, then receding. How bad was it out there? A fresh surge of shivers gripped her. She gritted her teeth, picturing buildings reduced to rubble, fires raging from broken gas lines, streets made impassable by wide crevasses and upthrust chunks of pavement.

Her stepmother worked thirty miles away, in Seattle. Had she been on the Evergreen Point floating bridge when the quake hit? Elisa shut her eyes, tried to blank out the sudden, unwanted vision of a giant wave sweeping Gail and hundreds of other hapless commuters into the frigid depths of Lake Washington.

"Hey!" Her shout sounded insignificant, even to her own ears. The sixty-five acres of Langston Green were hardly a wilderness, but they felt like one now. How many times had Gerald begged her to carry a cell phone? If she'd only given in, she could dial nine-one-one now. But instead, she lay here—trapped—clutching only a fading penlight. Her pockets held nothing more than a pair of sharp-edged cutters and a small ball of twine. At best, she could snip twigs away from her face and entertain herself with string games until help arrived.

If help arrived.

How long would it be before someone thought to look for her out here? They'd check her apartment first, then the office and greenhouse. When they didn't find her, they'd probably think she'd walked the few blocks to the coffee shop or grocery store as she often did in the evenings. Only Timo knew her plans. She chewed on her lower lip, fretting. Did anyone know where *he* was? Was he all right?

Two fat raindrops spattered her cheek, warning her of what was to come. The nighttime temperatures now dipped into the low fifties. Odds were good that she'd expire from hypothermia before dawn. "Anyone out there? Help!"

She wasn't prepared to die. What could anyone say about Elisa Maria Langston in an obituary? Hers was a pathetic life to review. Finding a lost kid on a mountain as a teenager had been her only accomplishment worth noting. She'd peaked at sixteen. How mortifying. No adventures. No great achievements.

Who would miss her? A stepmother and stepsister, an aunt, a handful of colleagues and friends. No Significant Other would cry at her graveside. She always imagined that by now she'd be married, have a child or two. What the heck had happened to that plan? Sure, she'd had dates and even a few torrid sexual liaisons. But embarrassingly few of them, now that she stopped to count. Most men were put off by an assertive Latina who drove a backhoe.

Over the years, she'd been proud of managing by herself. She was strong, self-reliant, and independent. But at the moment, she simply felt alone.

Clouds swirled in the dark skies overhead. Their movement made her nauseous. Closing her eyes, she clenched her jaw to silence her chattering teeth. She couldn't feel her left foot anymore.

~

Twelve miles away, Jake Street held up one hand to halt traffic in the lane behind the accident, then motioned for the vehicles on the other side to come through. The drivers slowed as they passed, taking in the tragic spectacle of a minivan flattened by a fallen tree. While two firefighters wielded the jaws of life on a van door, another held a woman screaming for her baby. Jake swallowed hard and turned his gaze back to the traffic. A trickle of rain slid down his neck.

A squad car pulled onto the shoulder behind the minivan, and an overweight officer climbed out. He extracted an orange safety vest and hand-held stop sign from the trunk, then approached Jake. "You look like you've done this a few times."

"Plenty." More times than Jake cared to think about. But at least he was just directing traffic this time. The smashed vehicle, the EMTs, and the flashing lights brought back memories of another night that ended with a lot of blood and death and guilt.

"I'll take it from here. Thank you, sir."

"No problem." Jake returned to his Land Rover. His cell rang just as he slid into the seat.

"Where are you, Jake? Are you okay?" It was the secretary at Atlas Security.

"I'm fine. I'm in Kirkland. I was on my way to Langston Green when the quake hit."

"Oh yeah, Langston. Our latest scammer."

Scammer? He flinched at the word, especially as applied to Elisa Langston. His heart had nearly stopped when he'd spotted her name on his list of possible fraud cases.

"Reports are coming in from all over," the secretary said. "I guess it's pretty bad down south. Bill's working on getting the helicopter up. He'll want you to ride along."

Like many insurance companies, Atlas Security had emergency procedures in place to check on their clients and speed recovery in any way possible. It was good for the customers and good for Atlas's bottom line. But if the situation in Seattle was as chaotic as it was here, it could take a while to get a chopper into the air.

"The floating bridges are closed, traffic lights are out all over, and trees are down everywhere. No way I can make it back to Seattle now," he told her. "I'm going to continue on to Langston Green; I can at least see how that client is doing. Call on my cell when you need me."

He stuck the phone in his pocket and pulled away from the accident scene, glad to be gone before the firemen extracted the infant. The only wails he heard had come from the mother.

Elisa closed her eyes against the rain and tried to marshal her thoughts. She had to figure a way out of this. She was a problem solver. The tree that pinned her was simply the biggest obstacle she'd had to tackle so far. Not to mention the heaviest.

She moved her legs just to feel the pain, to bring back some focus. It was becoming harder and harder to think. Hypothermia was taking over. With numb fingers, she dug the penlight into the soft dirt at her side, angled the bulb toward the old homestead building in the faint hope that someone might spot the dim glow.

This was ridiculous. She had hidden out here to trap her vandal, her Gremlin; not to get trapped herself. She couldn't die shivering in the mud, pinned under one of her own trees. Shoving the heels of her hands into the dirt, she pushed hard. A black wash of pain rolled through her, so strong that for a few seconds she thought it was an aftershock from the earthquake. After catching her breath, she tried again. This time a dark fog surged up from the agony in her leg to wrap around her head. Her vision dissolved into a swarm of buzzing gnats.

After nearly an hour of detours on back roads, Jake Street finally pulled his Land Rover into the parking lot of the Langston Green nursery. The property was pitch black. He drove slowly toward the remodeled farmhouse that served as the nursery's headquarters. He stared in surprise as his headlights illuminated the enormous root ball of a Douglas fir. The tree's equally massive trunk lay in the crevice it had plowed into the upper story of the building. From a nearby pole, a snapped power line swung in the wind, showering comet-tails of glowing sparks.

Switching on the overhead light, he quickly flipped through the property description attached to his clipboard and found what he was looking for. Gas. The place used natural gas for heat. Crap. He thumbed through the pages, scanning the information for the location of the shut-off valve. Offices downstairs, a one-bedroom apartment on top. Oh God. *Resident: Elisa Langston.* He knew she was the nursery manager, but she lived here, too? He hastily retrieved his all-in-one tool from the glove box, switched on his flashlight, and stuck one leg out into the rain.

His cell phone chirped. He impatiently shook it out of his pocket. "Street here."

"The 'copter's warming up at Boeing Field," the secretary told him. "Bill wants you with them to document damage and secure the sites. They could pick you up at three locations on the east side." She rattled them off.

He chose the closest one. "Hayward Playfield. I'll be there in an hour."

"Bill said thirty min—"

"Tell Bill to go without me if he needs to. I've got to deal with a situation here first." He disconnected before she could object, pulled up the hood of his windbreaker, and ran toward the ruins of Langston Green.

The front door of the old house was locked. The gate in the wooden fence was also locked, but thankfully it was only six feet high and had no barbed wire on top. He managed to climb over it with little difficulty. No guard dogs rushed him from the darkness beyond the sidewalk. He found the gas meter by the back door and turned off the flow.

The door was unlatched. He stepped in. "Hello? Anyone here? Elisa?"

He made a quick sweep through the first floor. Offices, a small kitchen and bath. This story was not too badly wrecked by the tree, but the floor was littered with debris. Rainwater steadily dripped in through the huge hole punched in the ceiling.

He played his flashlight beam on the steep, rain-slick stairs that rose to the second story. The groaning of the downed tree against the house's splintered timbers was ominous. He gritted his teeth. Stable or not, he had no choice but to go up. He grabbed the railing and climbed the steps.

He knocked on the door at the top of the stairs. No answer. He pushed it open. "Elisa?"

The apartment was tiny—and ruined. The tree had taken out most of the roof. He had to crawl under the dripping limbs to shine his light into the kitchen. He quickly scrambled out, avoiding the ragged hole ripped into the floor, and headed for the bedroom. "Elisa?"

His flashlight illuminated the emptiness of the place. She lived alone, judging by the lack of male paraphernalia in the rooms. Her taste was uncluttered: no doodads littered the bookshelves or the dresser, but the bright quilt on the bed and flamboyant art on the walls spoke of a passion for the exotic. Her open closet door revealed jeans, flannel shirts, boots, coats of varying weights. He measured a small jacket against his six-foot frame. Tiny and tough, that's how he remembered her.

Where was she? He looked out her bedroom window. The wind gusted and tree limbs scraped the walls behind him, reminding him that he needed to get out of here. The file said Langston Green covered sixty-five acres. His gaze roamed the fields to the south. Pitch black out there, except for a dim yellow ember of light in a far corner. What the heck was that?

A voice penetrated the cold fog that claimed her. "Elisa?"

She opened her eyes to the harsh glare of the moon shining directly into her eyes. But then, in a startling maneuver, it retreated upward, its light forming a smoky halo around a man's silhouette. It had been a flashlight, then. But who—?

The Gremlin! Her heart leapt into flight mode. Her fingers dug trenches in the dirt. The pepper spray she'd carried for just this moment lay out of reach somewhere near her right foot. She was a trembling bug on a pin, completely at his mercy.

She held her breath as he bent closer. Although she couldn't quite bring him into focus, he didn't fit the image of how she'd imagined her tormentor would look. The glow of the flashlight turned his hair red. His jaw was square; his eyes, when the light caught them, intense. Blue? She couldn't tell for sure. He gently pushed her hair away from her forehead and peeled a leaf away from her scraped and bloody cheek. His fingers left trails of warmth across her icy skin. "Elisa."

That red hair, that caress. It couldn't be.

"Dad?" Her uncertain whisper was lost in the loud chatter of her teeth. "I'm sorry." Sorry for the way she'd managed the nursery, sorry for letting this dang tree get the best of her. Sorry for letting the whole family down.

"Hang in there, sweetheart." Although the words were something her father might have said, the voice was all wrong. The stranger took off his jacket, knelt beside her, and draped it over her quivering form. The windbreaker smelled faintly of lime, and the flannel lining radiated the warmth of his body.

"I know you're strong, Elisa." Large fingers, dispersing a luxurious heat, enfolded her small trembling ones. "You've always been strong."

It was wonderful not to be alone any more. He bent close

again. Masculine lips, soft and warm, brushed her forehead. "Help's on the way. You're going to be just fine."

Strobes of red and blue flickered across the landscape. He let go of her hand and pushed himself to his feet.

No! Don't go! But before she could make her lips form the words, her angel disappeared into the blackness.

Chapter 2

Elisa's dream took her back to the nursery in the hours before the earthquake.

Simon rubbed hard against a sweet gum.

"There's no point in marking them," Elisa told him. "These trees are leaving." She lifted him to her shoulder. Purring, he dug his claws into her canvas jacket and swiped his soft head across her cheek. "You're hopeless," she told him. "A typical male. Oblivious to reality."

"*Cómo?*" A dark-skinned teen stood beside her, a half-smoked cigarette between his fingers.

"Timo!" she exclaimed, startled. The kid moved so quietly she hadn't noticed his arrival. "Just talking to Simon." She inclined her head to indicate the cat, then, switching to Spanish, said, "You shouldn't smoke."

"I know." He avoided her eyes as he took another puff. Was he particularly prickly today? Maybe it was her imagination; Timo was a young man of hard work and few words.

Elisa resisted the urge to brush a lock of black hair out of the teen's eyes. According to his employment application, Timo was nineteen years old. He looked more like fifteen; at most, sixteen. But maybe at thirty-two, Elisa herself was too far away from nineteen to recognize that age when she saw it.

He gestured toward the canister of pepper spray and the small penlight sticking out of her back jeans pocket. "You expect *el demonio*?"

"I'm going to hide out here and watch for him after dark." She couldn't bring herself to call her vandal a demon, as Timo did. His acts so far had been destructive and annoying, but not particularly frightening. Certainly not *demonic*. She thought of him as the Gremlin.

"Good idea to see who he is," Timo agreed. "But maybe not to catch him." He flicked a concerned glance her way. "Maybe I stay with you."

"Don't worry, he probably won't even show up. Besides, you're going to need your sleep. Somehow we've got to deliver these tomorrow."

Elisa nudged the toe of her boot into a hillock of soil. The sweet gums had been heeled into soft dirt on top of the native glacial till; their roots shouldn't have grown too deep in the years she had coddled them. Using the pincers with the backhoe, she should be able to load them into the delivery truck without too much trouble. Unfortunately, the summer workers had gone back to school weeks ago. Langston Green was down to its skeleton staff for the off season, and she'd been unable to find laborers through the temp agencies. The outdoor crew currently consisted of herself and Timo.

"I know six men," Timo said. "*Hombres muy fuertes.*" He flexed his own biceps to make sure she understood his Spanish, then translated anyway. "Strong."

Although he'd worked for her only a few months, Elisa felt a special kinship with Timo. The angular planes of his face were similar to her own features. His accent was familiar, too. In his words she heard an echo from her past: Spanish spoken to the rhythm of the ancient Mayan language.

"*Bueno*, I want to hire your six men," she said. "They must bring green cards or proof they are U.S. citizens."

"Of course."

"And they have to be at least as big as you are, okay?" Even in his cowboy boots, Timo stood only two inches taller than she. And she was five-foot-one.

His eyes narrowed to slits. "They will be strong."

"Tell them ten dollars an hour." She pulled a wad of bills from the pocket of her jeans. "Now, I'm giving you ten dollars apiece for a big breakfast at the Valley Café. Okay?" She waited for his nod. "I'll pick the whole crew up there at seven-thirty tomorrow morning." She handed him seven ten-dollar bills.

"And please go to Lindman's Hardware and tell them to set aside six new..." What was the Spanish for *shovel*? She made a shoveling motion with her hands.

"*Palas*," Timo supplied. "Shovels."

She was embarrassed that Timo's English was so much better than her Spanish. "Yes, six shovels. The good ones, with reinforced handles. And two new wheelbarrows." She pushed another three hundred into his hands.

With care bordering on reverence, Timo folded the bills and pushed them deep into a pocket of his grubby jeans. "You may trust me, Señorita Langston."

"Call me Elisa. 'Señorita Langston' sounds old enough to be your mother."

The boy's expression went dark.

"Something wrong, Timo?" she prodded. He shook his head. "Is your mother okay?"

He studied the toes of his boots and shrugged in that annoying way adolescents had of dismissing a question.

"Your father?"

Timo drew his index finger in a slashing gesture across his throat. "*Muerto*. More than two years ago."

A chill ran up her spine. The loss of a father, another thing she shared with him.

"I'm so sorry, Timo." She raised a hand, but he moved away to avoid her touch.

He tilted his head toward the street. "I go now, before it grows dark? To find the six men?"

She nodded. He ground out the cigarette butt under his boot and headed for his old bicycle. She watched him pedal away, his inky hair ruffled by the breeze, his worn jean jacket flapping open, his legs slightly bowed because they were a little too long for the small bike.

The earth shifted under her.

"Timo!" Elisa wailed, opening her eyes into a room that was much too bright.

"Sorry. I didn't mean to bump you."

Elisa turned toward her sister's soft murmur. The room was a blur of stainless steel and white tile. "Oh, no," she groaned.

Charlie bent over her, a fragrant long-stemmed yellow rose clutched in one of her slender hands. "Are you awake for real?"

"I was *so* hoping this was a bad dream."

"Nope, you're in the hospital." Charlie thrust the rose into a bouquet on the bedside table, then turned back to study her. "Is Timo a new cat?"

"No, Simon's the only cat." Her breath caught in her chest at the memory of him running amid the falling trees. "Did you find him?"

Charlie shook her head. "We're leaving food out for him. It's gone, so I'm sure he's okay."

Elisa squirmed at the blithe reassurance. Simon might be eating the cat chow, but it could also be Roberta, the opossum, or one of the many raccoons that haunted Langston Green. She needed to climb out of this bed, find Simon and Timo. But she wasn't sure she could even sit up, let alone stand. She felt like she'd been on a three-day bender. Or how she imagined she'd feel if she'd ever actually gone on one.

Her left leg, encased in bandages from toes to hip, was hoisted into the air in some sort of traction device. She stared at the disaster. "Have I been screwed?"

"What?" Charlie sounded shocked.

"Get your mind out of the gutter, Sis. Did they put screws in my leg? Look at this! How am I 'sposed to drive the backhoe?"

Charlie placed a hand on Elisa's arm, just above the strip of tape anchoring her IV line. "Elle, I don't think you'll be driving that backhoe for a while. You could work in the shop."

Elisa Langston, behind a florist's counter? She wasn't big enough to be a bull in a china shop. She'd be more like a donkey, backing into delicate bouquets. Toppling crystal vases with an awkward touch. She squinted to bring her sister's face into focus. Was Charlie trying to be kind? They'd been at odds since the day they'd met, the day her father had introduced Elisa to her new mother and sister.

She hadn't wanted a new mother; she wanted her old one to come back. And she didn't want a sister, either, especially not one exactly the same age as she, and half a head taller, with golden curls and pink dresses.

But Charlie had been thrilled. She'd told everyone that she *loved* her new sister, who looked like an Indian princess, and promised that she and Elisa would be best friends forever. Ever since that day, Charlie had cheerfully dragged Elisa everywhere, showing her off like she was some sort of clever pet. People often remarked how wonderful it was that they were so close.

Now, here they were again: Charlie, the beautiful blond stepsister unscathed by the biggest geologic disaster to hit the Pacific Northwest in a hundred years, and little dark Elisa, laid low by her own inventory. She whimpered, "I don't have time for this. I have to get those sweet gums planted!"

"Are you talking about the trees that fell on you?"

"*Liquidambar styraciflua.*"

"If you say so, Elle."

Elisa panicked. "They aren't *all* ruined, aren't they? Those trees?"

"Calm down. Gerald's taking stock now. He'll drop by later."

"Give me the phone. I've got to call Timo."

Her sister placed a hand on her hip. "Are you coherent

enough to be making phone calls? You were speaking in tongues just a second ago. And who is this Timo?"

"That was a Latin botanical name, as you very well know," she said. "Timo's my best field hand. He's only a kid, and I need to make sure he's okay." She held out her free hand. "The phone, Charlie."

Squinting hard to bring the numbers into focus, Elisa tapped in Timo's number. After three rings, a female voice with a Spanish accent responded.

"This is Elisa Langston. May I speak with Timo?"

"Timo?" Something crashed in the background. A baby started crying.

"Timoteo Martinez." Elisa spoke loudly so the woman could hear over the din.

"No Timo here. *No conozco ningún Martinez.*" The woman hung up. Elisa stared in confusion at the receiver.

"No luck?"

"Never heard of him." Elisa frowned. Had things gone as terribly wrong in Timo's world as they had in her own? She remembered the tears in his eyes before the earthquake.

"You probably dialed the wrong number."

"I don't think so." Jeez, her head ached. She rubbed her brow with the back of her hand and found the left side of her forehead covered with sticky gauze. The way the room refused to come into sharp focus made her woozy. It was like viewing the world through a haze of petroleum jelly. "What time is it?"

"Seven-thirty. P.M."

Too late to call the office. She handed the receiver back to Charlie.

Gail Langston, slim and elegant as usual, came in carrying two cups of coffee. She handed one to Charlie.

"Where's mine?" asked Elisa.

Gail turned. "You're awake! I'm so relieved, sweetheart. How are you feeling?"

Charlie moved her index finger in a spiraling motion near her right ear.

"I am *not* crazy." Elisa studied the hazy image of her stepmother and suddenly remembered her vision of a disaster befalling Gail during the earthquake. "Did the bridge sink?"

"Must be the pain medication," Charlie told her mother.

"Don't talk about me like I'm not here! Where *were* you last night, Mom?"

"It took me hours to get here." Gail said. "They closed the floating bridges right after the quake. Do you have any idea how long it takes to drive around Lake Washington at rush hour?"

Elisa closed her eyes to focus on the question. There were so many variables. Her thoughts swirled like clouds in the wind. She couldn't stop fretting about Timo. And Simon. The nursery.

"No," she groaned in frustration. "I can't do the equation. I don't know how long it takes to drive around Lake Washington at rush hour."

Gail's fingers patted her shoulder gently. "Sweetheart, you don't have to do any equations. It took me more than three hours to get home after the quake." She nodded at Charlie. "Definitely the medication. Or maybe the concussion. How's your vision, honey?" Gail fluttered her manicured fingertips in front of Elisa's face.

A wave of nausea rose to Elisa's esophagus. She squeezed her eyes shut and gripped the sheets in her fists until it passed.

"Look, Elisa," Charlie said. "Visitors."

Even before she opened her eyes, Elisa could tell from Charlie's syrupy tone that the visitors were men. They wore fire department uniforms, and looked vaguely familiar.

"Hi there," the taller one said. "We were dropping off another patient, so we decided to stop by and see how our tree-hugger is doing."

"Don't pay any attention to my partner's rotten jokes." The dark one inclined his head toward her. "You might not remember us. We're the emergency medical technicians who brought you in. He's Leon, and I'm Jon. And you're Elisa, right?"

"That's right," Charlie answered for her. "Elisa's raving a little tonight. She claims she's been screwed."

The EMTs exchanged an uncertain look, as if fearing an imminent charge of sexual harassment.

An impish grin crossed Charlie's face. She held out her hand. "Charlene Langston. My friends call me—"

"Charlie!" the two men chorused.

Leon, his cheeks red with embarrassment, cleared his throat. "You came in just as we were packing up yesterday. The resident told us your name."

"This is my mother, Gail Langston."

Gail delicately offered her hand to the tall man. "Delighted to meet the heroes who rescued my daughter."

The dark EMT bent close to the bed. "Hang in there, Elisa."

Blue-black hair. Dark, almond-shaped eyes.

"I am *not* raving," she assured him, smoothing out the ripples in her hospital gown. Oh, jeez, were those blue blobs stamped across the cloth really teddy bears? She quickly turned her focus back to him. "I'm fine."

She tried to push herself into a more dignified position. A pulley shifted, rocking her injured leg and launching a shockwave of pain through her body. It took all her willpower to keep from screaming. So much for dignity.

When she trusted her voice again, she asked, "Was there another man with you last night?"

Jon shook his head. "Just the two of us."

"A tall man, with reddish hair and a square jaw?" asked Elisa. *And a kind voice. And a gentle touch.*

Gail Langston raised her eyebrows. Charlie gave her mother

an I-told-you-she's-crazy look.

Leon said, "You were very disoriented. That happens a lot with head injuries."

Jon snapped his fingers. "The guy who dialed nine-one-one," he said. "That's who you're thinking of. He met us in the parking lot, and he left his flashlight with you so we could find you."

Thank God. Her rescuer was real; she hadn't just conjured him up. "What was his name?"

The EMTs glanced at each other and shrugged simultaneously.

"We didn't get it," Leon said. "He took off as soon as we got there, said something about meeting a helicopter."

If that wasn't typical of her luck. The only man in ages who was kind to her had just been passing through. She hadn't even had the chance to thank him.

Leon said, "Get well, Elisa."

They turned to leave.

"Thank you!" Charlie and Gail called as the men went out the door.

"Charlie." Elisa motioned her sister to lean close. "Take the tall one."

"Leon Maxwell? He's got to be Mom's age. He has silver hair."

Silver? Through Elisa's blurred gaze, it had looked ash blond, like Gail's. But she knew black when she saw it, and the other EMT had black hair. "I like the Latino."

"Latino?"

"The dark one."

"Jonathan Park?" Charlie laughed. "Sounds Korean to me, not Latino. Station Eleven. That's just down the street from us, isn't it, Mom?"

Gail nodded. She smoothed the pillowcase next to Elisa's cheek. "I'm so glad you're better. You never quite woke up after they brought you back from surgery last night. I've never seen you so ... still ... for so long. I was worried."

"I wasn't," Charlie said.

"You were crying," Gail reminded her daughter.

"Something was in my eye," Charlie said. "No measly tree could kill Elisa. I mean, remember the canoe accident in junior high? I thought I was going to drown."

"You had on a perfectly good life preserver," Elisa said. "And then you grabbed *mine*, too, and floated downstream with it."

"Exactly." Charlie stabbed the air with one finger. "See, Mom, even without a life preserver, Elisa survived death-defying rapids. Then there was that famous incident where she slogged through ten-foot snow drifts to save the twin babies—"

Elisa couldn't stop a snort of incredulity, which made her head ache even worse. It rarely snowed more than a few inches on Tiger Mountain, and those 'babies' had been just one three-year-old boy.

"Enough, Charlie," Gail said.

"Just checking her memory," Charlie said. "The long-term seems okay, but the short-term is mashed potatoes."

"Ignore her." Gail tucked the sheet around Elisa like she had when she was a little girl. "Rest, sweetheart. Try to sleep."

Elisa shut her eyes. Her brain did feel like it had tangled with a potato masher. She'd lost nearly twenty-four hours. The blond guy was gray and the Latino was Korean. She *was* raving. The woman who answered Timo's number didn't know him, and her guardian angel flew away in a helicopter. Nothing made sense. She was a blurry-eyed, metal-encased lunatic. With a whale of a headache. Her leg throbbed, too. Every part of her was scratched and bruised, and her back felt like she'd been tortured on a rack.

Gail's voice, now barely above a whisper, intruded through her misery. "Oh, hello, Gerald. Elisa's much better today."

Oh, jeez, not Gerald. Could she feign sleep?

"She was awake just a second ago." Charlie poked her in the shoulder.

"Charlie!" Gail admonished. "Leave her alone."

"Howdy, pardner," Gerald Donaldson said in a hokey accent. His lips briefly bussed her cheek. "Tiffany's here, too."

He thrust his chin toward his fiancée, who waited in the doorway, arms folded across her chest, tapping the pointed toe of her high-heeled boot on the tile floor.

"Hi, Tiffany," Elisa croaked. "Pardon me for not getting up."

The young woman crinkled her lips in what was probably intended to be a smile. From a pocket, she extracted a pack of cigarettes, then registered the No Smoking sign on the wall and slid them back into her jacket. Her eyes fixed on Gerald, flashing a signal of impatience that could not be misread, even through Elisa's blurred vision.

"I found these on the office porch." Gerald held up a flashlight and a black windbreaker. He tossed the jacket onto the bed. "Any idea who they belong to?"

She recognized the jacket. "They're my—" She'd almost said *my guardian angel's.* "They belong to the man who found me."

She pulled the windbreaker up to her nose, and inhaled. Citrusy, just like she remembered. Had his smile, the broad shoulders, and his gentle touch been real, too? Had he actually kissed her forehead?

"Does it smell like him?" Charlie grabbed it and sniffed. "A manly smell." She held the jacket up by the shoulders. "And it's a nice, manly size. Definitely a hero's jacket. He'll come back for it." She looked at Elisa. "He'll come back for *you.*"

Fat chance. The EMTs came back for Charlie, not for Elisa. Heck, her own mother hadn't even come back for her. Why would a handsome stranger? Elisa banished the uncertain memory of him and tried to focus on her business partner. "Gerald, have you heard from Timo?"

"The Martinez kid?" He shook his head.

Elisa fretted. Timo was as dependable as the Northwest rain. He'd never even been late for work.

"Have you seen Simon?"

Gerald clutched the bed rail. "You're worrying about a cat? We've got much bigger problems. The nurse said I've only got five minutes, so I'll make it short and sweet. Well, not so sweet. You thought the Gremlin was a problem? This is worse. It looks bad out there. Real bad. I think we're ruined."

Elisa's vision had cleared by the time Gerald returned the next morning. Without Tiffany in tow, he pulled up the guest chair to describe in detail the devastation at the nursery. He started by telling her about the big Douglas fir that had fallen on the main building.

Elisa took a deep breath, struggling to control her sorrow. That tree was at least three feet thick and close to two hundred years old. She'd never see another one like it. And the old house! It had been her grandparents' home, briefly her father's, and now hers. The tree had shaded the north windows. From her dining room table, she often watched cedar waxwings among the branches. Now the place would never be the same.

He removed his eyeglasses and pulled a folded handkerchief from his pocket. "We lost a lot of greenhouse glass. Nguyen was out there all day yesterday, covering the roof with plastic."

"Oh, no." She gulped and wadded the sheet between her fingers. "We need that stock for Thanksgiving and Christmas!"

"Well, not everything bit the dust. Some of the carnations and orchids survived. And the poinsettias."

So maybe the damage wasn't *that* bad. As soon as Gerald left, she'd call Peter Nguyen, her greenhouse manager, and get a thorough report on their inventory.

Gerald steamed his lenses with a breath, then wiped them

with his handkerchief. "The irrigation system is in pieces."

"Again?" The Gremlin had sabotaged the pipes twice during the summer.

"I turned off the water. All the trees came down."

She pictured delicate root systems exposed to the raw night air. "Did you cover the roots?"

He looked up. "What?"

Elisa gritted her teeth. The man might know how to sell plants, but he knew virtually nothing about how to take care of them. "Most of the stock will survive if you cover the roots and keep them watered. Just throw dirt over them. Timo will know what to do."

Gerald made a face. "I tried to call that kid. His number's out of service."

First the woman who'd answered the phone said she didn't know Timo, and now his number was out of service? Had the earthquake scrambled the phone lines? "Maybe you could drive by his house."

"If he wanted to work, he would have shown up by now. Wouldn't he?"

Elisa felt like throwing something at her business partner. Instead, she said evenly, "See if you can get the summer kids back to help after school. Hire some temps."

Gerald slid his glasses back on. "Elisa, I'm trying to tell you. It's a disaster area. There's not much worth saving. As for temporary help of any kind, believe me, it's all booked up. Everyone is paying top dollar for cleanup crews right now."

That was so like Gerald. If a problem couldn't be fixed with a phone call or two, it couldn't be fixed at all. Why had her father ever made him a shareholder?

Changing the subject, she asked, "Have you found Simon?"

"I haven't seen him."

"Could you put out some of his favorite food? It's the chopped fish in the little green cans in my apartment."

"I'll buy some at the market. I'm not going in that building. The roof could collapse any minute, or the whole place could catch fire or explode. The utility company shut off the gas, but there could be a pocket of fumes in there somewhere."

Elisa's stomach spasmed. Her most precious possessions were in her apartment. A photo of her mother and father and herself when they'd been a family, a quilt made by her grandmother, an embroidered Guatemalan *huipil* dress left by her mother.

But it wasn't fair to ask Gerald to risk his life for her mementos. And if the building was as bad as he said, she couldn't ask Gail or Charlie to look for them, either. "There's a sack of Simon's favorite dry food out in the tool shed. Please tell me that's still standing."

Confusion settled over Gerald's regular features.

"The shed with the red door?" She failed to stifle the sarcasm in her voice. "With the giant yellow backhoe parked in the carport?"

"No need to get testy," he said. "I'll get the food the next day I'm there. Or better yet, I'll get Nguyen to do it."

The next day I'm there? Gerald wasn't planning on working today?

He anticipated her question. "I called our regular customers and told them we would be shut down for a while." He pushed his glasses up on his aquiline nose with his index finger. "But," he gave her a tentative smile, "All is not lost. As a matter of fact, this earthquake could be the best thing that ever happened to us. "Walt Baker called this morning."

She frowned.

"Walter Baker, Tiffany's brother-in-law. The CEO of Baker Development?"

Of course she remembered. Baker was a swift-talking man in snakeskin boots and a suede jacket that cost more than most people's monthly wages.

Grinning, Gerald leaned forward. "He upped the offer he made four months ago. Three million dollars for sixty acres. You can keep the five in the corner with the barn and the greenhouse."

Her jaw clenched in anger. "That jackal!"

The smile disappeared from Gerald's face.

"The Langstons have owned that property forever." She struggled to push herself up higher in the bed. "He thinks just because we're down that he can swoop in for the kill."

Gerald wrapped his fingers around the bed rail. "Did you hear what I said? Three million dollars."

"If he thinks I'm going to sell out just because of an earthquake, he doesn't know me. Langston Green is not going to become another tacky condo-golf course development."

"Think about this." Gerald scrubbed his head with his knuckles. "Think hard. Three million! Even after clearing up all our debts, that would be something like seven hundred thousand for me. And your father left the rest to you girls, didn't he? That would be more than two million for you three."

Actually, Terrence Langston had willed his seventy-five percent of Langston Green to Elisa. Gail and Charlie had inherited the florist shops. But Gerald didn't need to know that. "We'd both be out of a job," she said.

"With that much money in the bank, who cares?"

"Peter Nguyen would be out of a job. As would Beth and the field workers. And Timo."

Gerald looked at the ceiling and combed his fingers through his straight brown hair. Elisa could almost hear him mentally counting ...*eight, nine, ten.* After taking a deep breath, he lowered his gaze to hers. "You'd still have the florist shops. You could fix the greenhouse, use the barn or raze it. There'd still be jobs for all your strays."

Strays? What the heck did he mean by that? "Langston Green was my great-grandparents' homestead. Langstons have always farmed those sixty-five acres. I won't sell out to a tape-worm like Baker. Not while there's still hope."

A plump, gray-haired nurse came in and told Gerald that morning visiting hours were over. To Elisa, she said, "For you, it's bath time. The doctor will come by shortly to check on you."

Elisa grimaced. No doubt the doctor would stop by for a lengthy discussion while she was wearing only soap suds. But at least she could ask him to take the traction device off her leg. She had to get out of here.

"Elisa, you don't understand." Gerald sought her attention again. "There *is* no hope. Langston Green is a disaster area." He buttoned his coat. "Please think about it. Three … million … dollars." He punctuated each word with his index finger as if coaxing her to follow the bouncing ball.

The nurse glanced up at that, and studied Gerald's back as he exited. When she turned to Elisa, her gaze telegraphed the question: *you're* worth millions? Elisa narrowed her eyes. *Maybe you should have given me silk pajamas instead of a teddy bear gown*, she telepathically retorted.

Eighteen miles away, Timo Martinez crouched outside the packing shed and pulled up the collar of his denim jacket against the brisk wind. Through a crack in the old wooden walls, he watched a few workers sorting apples in the dimly lit interior. He waited until Señor Vales, the supervisor, came out for a smoke. Once the mustachioed man had taken his first puff, Timo emerged from the shadows.

Vales swore and nearly dropped his cigarette. "*Hombre*, you scared the piss out of me."

Timo apologized.

"We have no need for pickers now. The apple harvest is fi-nished."

"I'm not looking for work. I'm Veda Martinez's son," Timo

said in Spanish. "She hasn't been home since before the *tem-blor*. I came here yesterday and the day before, but everything was locked." He'd lain awake in the apartment for three nights now, imagining the worst. A woman had been crushed when a wall had fallen in downtown Seattle: he'd seen it on the news. And in Kirkland, just a few miles down the road, a tree had flattened a van, killing a baby in a car seat. His own mother, however, had disappeared the day *before* the earthquake. It made no sense.

The man grasped Timo's shoulder with strong fingers. "I'm sorry. I thought you knew. I thought someone would tell you." He took another puff on his cigarette.

An explosion, a building collapsing, a truck running off the road, mowing down pedestrians on the sidewalk. Timo pictured his mother's limp body. That was the only way she would have left him in this fix. "She's dead!" he gasped, at last giving voice to the horrible word that was running through his thoughts. *Muerta.*

Vales dropped the cigarette to the dirt and ground it out with his shoe. "No, no, son. It happened the day before the earthquake. They got her."

Timo blinked, then swallowed against the lump in his throat. At least his mother was alive. This was not the worst thing, but close to it. They'd be after him now.

Elisa studied the man who sat in the hospital guest chair by the window. A most attractive man, with an intelligent face, strong features. His slightly wavy hair was tinged red by the afternoon sun streaming in the window behind him. He raised a pen, teased it along his jaw line, then lowered it and jotted something on the newsprint lying atop a clipboard in his lap.

He was doing the crossword puzzle on the back page of the *Seattle Times*. Her father had done that crossword every morning.

The man went through the motions again, but this time, after he'd filled in the squares, he glanced up. Any resemblance to her father suddenly dissolved and Elisa could breathe again. Her father's eyes had been gray; his narrow face sprinkled with freckles. This man was much more striking, with a direct blue-eyed gaze, evenly tanned skin stretched across high cheekbones, and a square jaw. His hair was actually a reddish-brown, more mahogany than a true auburn.

And he was staring at her. Embarrassed, she moved her uncertain gaze away from his steady one, focused on the wall clock, and tried to blink away her grogginess. Although she'd told the doctor she wanted no more pain medication, the nursing staff must have put something in her juice, because she'd been dead to the world for nearly three hours now.

"Aha," he said. "Sleeping Beauty awakes." His voice was deep, smooth and warm. Just the way she remembered it.

He rose. Tossing the newspaper on the chair, he tucked the clipboard under his arm and walked toward her. "You're looking much better than the last time I saw you."

Elisa self-consciously smoothed her hospital gown and swallowed against the dryness in her throat. She croaked, "It was *you*, then."

"Water?" He picked up a plastic water container from her bedside table and crooked the straw for her.

The cool liquid soothed her parched throat, but she found it unwieldy to drink while lying on her back. And the tall stranger made the situation even more uncomfortable by keeping his eyes fixed on her, as if he were memorizing her face. When she handed him back the cup, his fingers briefly brushed hers. Her cheek and forehead tingled at the memory of that same warm touch on the night of the earthquake.

"If you hadn't left your jacket behind"—she gestured at the black windbreaker hanging from the chair—"I'd think I had imagined you."

He gave her a curious look. "So you remember me?"

"Of course I do." Her face burned at the memory of his lips on her forehead. "Although my memory of that night is kind of hazy. I thought you were my guardian angel."

"I'm hardly an angel." He grinned, displaying a dimple previously hidden in his right cheek. "I'm Jake Street."

He paused a moment, as if his name should mean something to her. Close up, she could tell he was about her age, and more solid and muscular than her father had been. He was also much more handsome, although his rugged face was marred by an odd horizontal scar that started near his left eye and blazed back across his temple to disappear into his hairline.

"I'm from your insurance company—Atlas Security." He dug into the pocket of his sports jacket, then pressed a business card into her hand.

Embarrassed that in her concussed and hypothermic state, she might have confused a business associate for her father or an angel, she lowered her eyes to the card. What else had she imagined during that encounter? Had this man really touched her, called her sweetheart, told her she was strong?

She was drugged, bandaged and braced. It was so unfair to also have to deal with strange men who had no qualms about stopping by unannounced. Doctors, the virile Fire Department medics, now dapper Jake Street of Atlas Security Insurance. At least she'd managed to talk the orthopedist into releasing her from the traction device this morning, so her foot wasn't in his face. But no doubt her hair was kinked up in its usual post-sleep haystack formation, and she had gauze and adhesive tape stuck to her face. She said, "Angel or insurance man, I have you to thank for my life."

"I don't know about that. You strike me as a pretty tough woman."

She inhaled. The man's scent, a mixture of soap and lime aftershave, mingled with the bleach odor of the bed linens. "How did you find me?"

He shifted his weight from one foot to the other. "Actually, I was on my way to meet you that evening when the earthquake struck."

She didn't remember expecting anyone. Had the tree wiped out her memory as Charlie had claimed? "We had an appointment?"

"No." He looked a little guilty as he admitted, "I'd planned to just drop by."

"I don't care if you were burglarizing the place. You called 9-1-1."

He laughed. She liked the way his eyes crinkled at the corners. "Why did you come to see me?" she asked.

His expression turned serious. "To discuss Langston Green's recent claim history."

For the first time, the title on Mr. Street's business card registered in her sluggish brain. *Investigator.* Her heartbeat quickened. Why had the company sent an *investigator* to talk to her?

He thumbed through the stack of papers attached to his clipboard. "I see here irrigation system breakage. Stolen tools." He raised his eyes to hers. "Sabotage of a backhoe?"

The Gremlin's handiwork. "Your company already paid those claims."

"True," he said. "But this number of claims in a narrow time frame automatically triggers an investigation. It's a computer thing. And now that I've reviewed your paperwork, I have to say that I am concerned. There seems to be a problem of escalating destruction at Langston Green."

Elisa winced at his choice of words. "We've had a spate of vandalism, but we're getting it under control." Even as she said the words, she knew it was more wishful thinking than reality.

"We'll talk more about that later." He thumped his fingers against the top sheet of paper. "Yesterday, your partner, Gerald

Donaldson, filed a claim for nearly a million dollars due to the earthquake."

Oh jeez, the damage had to be terrible then. Sudden doubt gripped her. "Langston Green is insured for that much, isn't it?"

Street flipped through his papers again, raising an eyebrow at the last page. "As a matter of fact, you increased your insurance from $900 thousand to $1.75 million ... only four months ago." Letting the page drop, he scribbled something on it.

Score one for Gerald. She regretted the harsh thoughts she'd had about her partner this morning. Yet Street's pen was still poised in the air, and his brow had crinkled with an expression of disapproval. She stared at him. "You think we increased our coverage because we expected an earthquake?"

Jake Street smiled again, but this time the expression didn't quite reach his eyes. "Of course not. But this latest claim—nine-hundred-and-fifty thousand dollars—is a very large amount. I've taken a quick look at your main office and the greenhouse. While the damage to both is extensive, it looks to me like they can be salvaged with basic repairs."

"Then the rest must be for lost inventory," she told him.

He looked skeptical. Elisa bristled. While it was true that she spent her time tending plants instead of studying the books, she knew her business. This was humiliating, being forced to hold a business meeting while flat on her back. Had Street planned it this way, when she was at a disadvantage? She fumbled among the sheets for the bed control.

"Langston Green is a thriving concern, Mr. Street. We are the principal suppliers for two florist shops. In addition, we do a large volume of sales to landscapers and to the general public. Our average yearly gross is more than two million dollars." She wasn't about to tell him that their expenses often whittled the total income down to only a modest profit. Especially in the past two years; even with insurance reimbursement, the evil pranks of the mysterious Gremlin were proving costly. "So, Mr. Street, a nine-hundred-and-fifty-thousand-dollar claim does not sound excessive to me."

"I see." His tone implied just the opposite. He let the words hang in the air for a painful moment, then said, "Your claim would be easier to justify if you had suffered heavy property damage, or if you had larger buildings and had lost a lot of valuable equipment." He folded back the page to study another beneath it before looking up again. "However, as I understand it, your property is mostly just raw land."

"Correction: it's cultivated land. It's a nursery, remember?" She fumbled with the sheets again. Where was that dang control?

"And your inventory is mostly ... plants?"

"So?" His Detective-Columbo-just-let-me-get-this-straight tone grated on her nerves. "You were there, Mr. Street. Surely you could see the damage for yourself."

"It was dark." He quickly flipped through the pages on his clipboard. "Your partner didn't submit a detailed inventory. I'll need paperwork to document the initial value of the plants."

"You don't think our inventory is worth that much? When was the last time you visited a florist shop? Or landscaped an acre? Or purchased a potted plant? I have one grove of trees worth nearly a hundred thousand dollars." She grimaced at the memory of the precious sweet gums toppling. "At least I *had* a grove of trees—"

He was suddenly charming again. "I'm sure you can easily find the records I need."

"I'm sure I can. They're on our computers." Gerald's description of rain inside the building flashed into her thoughts. "Assuming our computers are working."

He continued in an even tone. "I'll check on that. As I said, this is only a routine investigation. Once we've documented the initial value of your inventory, we'll document the damage.

Plants, in an earthquake—"

"Fall over, break their stems, lose their leaves, snap their roots..." Finally, her fingers located the bed control next to her pillow. She jammed her thumb against the Up button.

"But they grow back, don't they?" His eyebrows lifted in an expectant pose.

The bed halted when the back was nearly vertical. Although the pressure on her broken leg was painful, at least she felt more dignified. She fixed a stern gaze on him. A strand of red-brown hair had slipped onto his forehead, making him look like the boy next door instead of the professional pain in the neck he was proving to be.

"If you can sell broken plants and trees with no limbs, then please let me in on your secret, Mr. Street."

Gail Langston strode in, elegant in a lilac-colored shirt and designer jeans. She held her now-habitual cappuccino from the espresso stand on the hospital's main level. "Elisa!" she scolded. "I heard you all the way down the hall."

Charlie, clutching a similar foamy concoction, breezed in behind Gail. She wore a form-fitting turquoise turtleneck and chunky Navajo earrings and necklace. She tossed a hard look in Elisa's direction before turning to Street. Looking him over, her expression brightened. "I hope we're not interrupting anything important, Mr. ..."

Jake Street introduced himself. "Ms. Langston and I have just concluded our meeting."

"We have?" Elisa asked.

His gaze met hers. Such piercing eyes. *Interrogator's eyes.* "Our initial meeting," he said. "Since you're incapacitated, I'll contact your partner, Mr. Donaldson, to get a detailed inventory list. We'll walk through the property to verify the damage."

"Gerald can't tell a beautyberry from a Himalayan honeysuckle. Can *you*, Mr. Street?"

He gave her a blank look.

"I thought not. You'll have to wait for me."

"That makes sense." A glint of emotion—irritation, amusement?—flashed in his eyes, but disappeared before she could identify it. "We'll postpone proceeding with the claim until you're available to help. I'm sure we can work this all out in due time." He tucked the clipboard under his arm.

Postpone? Due time? What kind of insurance mumbo-jumbo was that?

After snatching the flashlight from the bedside table, he grabbed the windbreaker from the back of the chair, hefted his briefcase, and left.

"He took your flashlight and jacket." Charlie looked as if she might bolt after him.

"*His* flashlight and jacket."

"*He's* your guardian angel?" Charlie stared through the open door.

Elisa groaned. "He is most definitely *not* an angel."

"He's drop-dead gorgeous. Can I have him?"

"Charlene Langston!" Gail scowled at her daughter.

The aroma of freshly brewed coffee and steamed milk wafted over the sheets. Snatching Charlie's cup from her hand, Elisa drank half the latté in a few quick gulps while her sister's mind was fixed on Jake Street.

"Weren't there some boys named Street in high school?" Charlie tapped a finger on her chin.

The only Street Elisa remembered was a nerdy guy with glasses in her Explorers Club. He hadn't been any taller than Timo. "I don't remember anyone who looked like *that*."

"True. This one is *very* good-looking." Charlie turned her gaze toward Elisa, and finally had the grace to put on a slightly embarrassed smile. "I mean, I wouldn't presume, but you two didn't appear to be exactly hitting it off. It seemed like you had already alienated him."

"The alienation was mutual. He's all yours." She took

another swallow of Charlie's latté as a nurse entered with a wheelchair.

"Now what?" Elisa barked. She handed the half-empty cup back to Charlie, who stared into it in annoyed confusion. "I had a bath, the doctor's been here, I've had lunch—and I've had way too many visitors."

"We have to take the staff as they become available, don't we?" The nurse smiled. "You growled at the doctor this morning. Now you can growl at the ortho techs while they put the cast on your leg. You do want a walking cast so you can go home, don't you?"

Elisa couldn't wait to start repairing the nursery, find Timo and Simon. She'd show Jake Street that Elisa Langston was never *incapacitated*. He'd soon discover that his 'due time' was going to be *tomorrow*. She eagerly threw off the sheets. "Can I get a running cast instead?"

Jake cursed his luck as he strode down the stairs to the hospital's ground floor. When he'd first seen Langston Green on his investigation list, he'd been nervous about having to tangle with Elisa. Now he could see their interaction was going to be just as thorny as he'd feared.

The sight of her trapped beneath that tree, so small and fragile-looking, had nearly undone him. He'd never seen Elisa helpless before. He'd called the hospital at least ten times to check on her. He'd had trouble sleeping the last two nights for worrying about her. How many times had he dreamed of caressing her smooth olive cheek, running his fingers through that silky raven hair, kissing her full lips? And she had such incredible eyes. Her irises were not an opaque cocoa, but a startling liquid brown so clear they seemed bottomless. Even with the bruises and bandages, Elisa was more beautiful than ever. He would have known her anywhere.

But she hadn't recognized him. He jerked open the exit door

harder than he had intended. The elderly woman at his elbow gave him an odd look. He forced a smile and gestured for her to precede him through the door, then made himself walk to his SUV at a more sedate pace. His resentment was unfounded, he reminded himself. He'd changed a lot over the years. And even back then she'd paid no attention to him.

Actually, it was a good thing she didn't remember what he'd said to her as she lay trapped beneath the tree. He'd lost his professionalism, something he rarely did. He was relieved to see the fire back in her eyes, but now that she was on the mend, she was acting just as stubborn and arrogant as she always had.

If his career had taught him anything, it was that anyone could turn to crime under the right circumstances. The increase in Langston Green's coverage, the barrage of ever more expensive claims, the vandal that nobody had ever seen: these were definitely suspicious. His colleagues in the insurance business tended toward the "guilty until proven innocent" theory, and unfortunately, most of the time, they were right. He'd give Elisa a fair shake. He really hoped she was an innocent victim. But if Elisa Langston thought she could get the best of him these days, she had a surprise coming.

Chapter 3

When Elisa was finally released from the hospital, it was nearly dusk. With her new cast thrust out in front of her, she sprawled across the back seat of Gail's Lexus. As they passed through neighborhoods on the way from Bellevue back to Woodinville, Elisa saw fallen trees, cracked driveways, tumbled rock walls and brick facades.

"Seattle took the brunt of the quake," Charlie said. "The east side only got that weird wave action; no shaking. The house has a couple of new cracks and we can't shut the laundry room door, but that's it. We were lucky."

Through the borrowed cotton hospital scrubs, Elisa massaged her thigh above her cast. She hoped that Timo and Simon had been luckier than she.

"It'll be like old times, having you at home," Gail said over her shoulder. "You'll love the way we've redecorated your room."

Elisa groaned inwardly at the thought of being cooped up in the family home again. "This is just temporary. Until I fix up my old apartment." As they passed a familiar landmark, she perked up. "Can we stop by the nursery?"

"Not a good idea," Gail said.

"Just for a minute?" Elisa begged. She needed to see the devastation Gerald had described. Maybe she could coax Simon out of wherever he was hiding, or find some sign of Timo, or at least rescue her treasures from her apartment.

Charlie took her right hand off the wheel and reached back between the seats to pat Elisa's good leg. "Too depressing," she said cheerily. "And it's almost dark. You shouldn't even be thinking about work; the doctor said to take it easy. Besides, Gerald's looking after everything; you don't need to worry."

Certain her words would set Elisa's mind at rest, Charlie drove past the turn that would have taken them to Langston Green. Her gaze met Elisa's in the rear view mirror. She smiled. "This is going to be such fun, all the Langston women in the same house again."

If the back of Charlie's neck hadn't been protected by the headrest, Elisa would have thwacked her sister with a crutch.

Elisa's childhood bedroom, which she'd painted a rich terra cotta, was now lavender and silvery gray, colors that, in her opinion, reflected the Pacific Northwest's cloudy environment rather than complementing it. She favored vibrant hues: reds, yellows, blue-greens.

The bedroom wall held an array of photos, ranging from before Elisa was born to the present. One photo, a gathering of the Langston clan at a Memorial Day picnic, dramatically documented the differences in color preferences. In scarlet trousers and turquoise jacket, Maria Elena Langston's small figure stood out like an exotic bird among the subdued beiges and pastels favored by the extended Langston family. Elisa stood in front of her mother, a dark-haired toddler in a gold sweater and orange leggings. Two parrots trying to blend into the local flock.

"And then the mama parrot flew away," Elisa murmured, "Leaving her parrot chick behind."

She joined Gail and Charlie in the kitchen, noticing that they'd gone out of their way to prepare her favorites for dinner: a fruit salad full of mangos, strawberries, and crunchy jicama; chicken enchiladas with fresh cotija cheese and green tomatillo sauce; crusty homemade bread.

The traditional pitcher of red wine punch was missing. "Where's the *sangría*?" she asked.

Gail set the table with gaily colored placemats and napkins. "You can't have wine. You're on painkillers."

"*Sangría* is the best painkiller I know. What's the point in surviving an attempt on my life if I can't have *sangría*?" Elisa regarded the table. "Five places?"

"We invited Gerald and Tiffany," Gail said.

Great. Just what she needed, her business partner who was convinced that the nursery was a total loss, and his fiancée who despised her.

Noting the look on her sister's face, Charlie added, "But Gerald said they had to be somewhere else tonight."

"They are such a cute couple." Gail positioned a fork on a napkin. "Especially Tiffany. That girl has such exquisite taste. I've never understood why she didn't aim higher, career-wise."

"She seems like the perfect restaurant hostess to me," Elisa said. "But if they're not coming, why five plates?"

Charlie grinned. "You'll see."

The doorbell rang. Charlie came back with two men whom she and Gail made a fuss of welcoming. The tall silver-haired man handed a bouquet of red and white carnations to Gail, who exclaimed over the flowers as if she didn't see hundreds each day at work.

Leon Maxwell. And Jonathan Park. The two EMTs who had treated her. Out of uniform and out of context, but finally in sharp visual focus for Elisa. Instead of Fire Department blues, tonight Jonathan was dressed in a black-and-red cotton sweater and Leon wore a corduroy jacket over an open-collared shirt.

"I would have invited your friend, too," Charlie said to Elisa. "But he was in such a hurry that I never got his number."

"Friend?" Who the heck was she talking about?

Her sister turned to Jonathan. "Jake Street. Elisa's guardian angel."

"Mr. Street is our insurance rep," Gail told Leon.

"*Their* insurance *investigator*," Elisa corrected. Despite flashing those beautiful eyes and his on-again off-again charming smile, he'd treated her more like a suspect than a client.

"Ah. The plot thickens." Jonathan smiled.

Charlie chuckled and laid her hand on his. The throbbing moved up from Elisa's leg into her head. Over everyone's protests, she pushed herself to her feet, shooting a look at Charlie. "Either you make *sangría* or I will."

During dinner, both men made a special effort to include Elisa, asking her questions about the nursery and various plants. Jon had an infectious smile; no one could observe the twinkle in those deep brown eyes and that friendly grin without smiling back.

So he wasn't Latino. He was only of medium height, maybe even shorter than Charlie. And he was olive-skinned, black-haired, surely more her type than her sister's. But Jon's eyes remained fixed on Charlie. Elisa sighed morosely. It was the story of her life.

Gail laughed too heartily at Leon's stories about EMT calls to assist victims in odd situations. Big toes stuck in bathtub spouts, people pinned beneath their own cars in their own driveways. Elisa drank too much *sangría*, trying to dull the memory of her tree-hugging humiliation along with the ache in her leg. Nine-thirty was the end of the evening for her.

Hours later, Elisa abruptly sat up, drenched in sweat and expecting to find the contents of the room tossed and broken. The earthquake had felt so real. The echoes of Timo's screams and Simon's piercing meows of terror still rang in her ears. She reached for pillow beside her, expecting to feel Simon in his usual place, and touched only cool linen instead of warm fur. She switched on the lamp and took a deep breath, dragging her mind out of the nightmare. The clock by the bed read 1:12 A.M.

Simon. Timo. She could no longer stand not knowing what

had happened to them. Charlie and Gail seemed determined to keep her away from Langston Green. Awkwardly dragging her plaster-encased leg, she crawled to the edge of the bed, found her new crutches stashed beside it, and hauled herself upright.

She remembered Jon and Charlie helping her to bed. She prayed that it was Charlie, and only Charlie, who had changed her clothes: she wore a pajama top, floppy shorts, and cotton socks. They would have to do; it was too much trouble to struggle into anything else. In the closet she found a nylon windbreaker that belonged to Charlie. She pushed her right foot into the leather boot she'd been wearing when the tree attacked. Charlie's size ten jacket could be bunched up on her size six frame, but there was no way Elisa could keep on her sister's shoes.

The rubber tips of her crutches squeaked on the hardwood floors of the hall and front room. True to the nurse's promise, the technician had given her a walking cast, but he'd also warned her not to put any actual weight on her leg for a week. Elisa carefully negotiated around the throw rugs, afraid to test her uncertain skills. In a shell-shaped dish on the table in the entry hall, she found two sets of keys. The pink rose keychain would be Charlie's, she was certain.

The door leading into the garage creaked. She stopped, listened. No sounds from the bedrooms. She pulled the door shut behind her and flipped on the lights, hobbled to Charlie's Toyota 4-Runner. It hurt like hell, but she managed to wedge her cast between the front seat and the floorboard. Thank heavens the SUV had automatic transmission.

After the garage door went up, she pressed the unfamiliar gas pedal a little too hard, and rocketed backward onto the street. Rain sheeted down the windshield. No lights came on inside the house. So far, so good. She drove a few blocks and turned down Willow Road, Timo's street, looking for his home address, 3521. The area was a low-rent district of small clapboard apartments that had once been World War II military housing. When she reached the address, she stopped the SUV and stared in disbelief. 3521 was a tennis court.

Through the rain-streaked windshield, she studied the neighborhood. It looked like the sort of modest area an agricultural worker would live in. Maybe he'd written down the wrong address, transposed numbers or something? But then there was that telephone business. She'd checked it out herself. Sure enough, Timo's number, the same one she'd dialed in the hospital, had been disconnected. And the tears in his eyes, she hadn't imagined those. She pounded a fist on the steering wheel in frustration. Then she headed for Langston Green.

A CLOSED FOR REPAIRS sign barred the parking lot. Determined not to get in and out of the vehicle any more than she had to, Elisa drove forward until the rope that held the sign stretched across the Toyota's grill. She slowly depressed the accelerator until the rope broke loose from its side post. It whipped across the front of the SUV, flinging the sign into the gravel.

At first it was hard to make sense of the black mass that had erupted in front of the old farmhouse. After a moment she understood that she was looking at the unearthed root ball of the giant Douglas fir. It was too dark to see beyond the roofline, but judging by the incline of the tree, the fir had taken out at least a third of Elisa's upstairs apartment.

She clenched her jaw against an onslaught of emotions. This had been her great-grandparents' homestead a hundred years ago, then briefly, her grandparents' and father's home, until they'd moved to more modern premises in Bellevue. The building was a turn-of-the-century farmhouse, tall and austere. Its exterior had until now remained unchanged, painted barn-red with white trim for as long as Elisa could remember.

Elisa left the SUV in the middle of the lot and lurched

through the darkness to the scene. She laid a palm against the giant fir's rough bark, swallowing hard against a lump in her throat. "I'm going to miss you so much, old friend. And the birds and tree frogs will miss you even more."

She was glad that nobody was here to make fun of her sorrow over a tree. Lifting her face toward the sky, she let the rain wash away her tears before moving on. Moving clumsily on the crutches, she made her way up the homestead's broad steps in the dark, skidding a little on a damp patch at the top where the rain had blown in across the wide painted planks.

She tipped up a potted chrysanthemum on the railing and extracted a key from beneath it. The rain beat a gentle patter on the roof. The sound of home. Simon loved this wide covered front porch as much as she did. In winter, he prowled for mice in the crawlspace beneath the planking. In summer, he sprawled across the swinging chair.

She leaned on the crutches, peering into the dimness of the yard and parking lot. "Simon? Come here, boy. Simon?"

Only the gentle night breeze responded, rustling the alders that fronted Langston Green. She limped to the front door and turned the key in the lock, reflecting that this security measure was now of little use. Any burglar could simply scramble up the trunk of the fallen fir to get in.

The light switch didn't work. She stuck her head back outside the doorframe. Sure enough, a short section of the main line dangled loosely from the juncture where it met the building. She rubbed a hand across her forehead in frustration. Why hadn't Gerald hired someone to cut away the tree, cover the roof, restore the electricity? There were tarps in the sheds, an extension ladder in the barn in back of the greenhouse. Maybe she could just climb up and cover the whole mess, tree and all.

Get a grip, an inner voice told her. It was almost two A.M. and she was on crutches. She took a deep breath. The only light in the building was spillover through the windows from the distant streetlights out front. Why hadn't she brought a flashlight? She kept one upstairs, under her kitchen sink, although she wasn't too sure about the age of its batteries.

Maybe Gerald kept a flashlight in his desk drawer? Leaving the front door wide open for the additional illumination it offered, she moved slowly in that direction, testing each placement of the crutches for stability before swinging forward. Debris littered the floor: office supplies scattered by the quake or the wind, bits of bark, clumps of fir needles.

Easing herself into Gerald's leather chair, she rested her head against the high cushioned back for a moment, letting her eyes adjust to the dimness. The smooth padded arms, although a bit damp, were silky under her touch.

This chair and desk had belonged to Terrence Langston before Gerald inherited them. By rights, they should have been hers. But the proportions of her father's furniture were all wrong for her. The chair seat was too deep, the backrest too high. The desktop was too far across; she couldn't reach the other side without prostrating herself on its shiny mahogany surface. In the days after his death, it had been one more slap in the face to discover that she was literally too small to fill her father's space at Langston Green.

She leaned forward, ran her fingers around the black cubbyhole beneath the huge desk. No flashlight there. The center drawer was locked. The two file drawers on the left, locked as well. Same story for the right. She had no idea Gerald was so secretive. Or maybe, as her father might have suggested, expedient? She was careless in her office work, leaving papers piled on her desk. Another of her many shortcomings.

She heaved herself to her feet and lurched toward the office kitchen. The small utilitarian room was slightly brighter than the office, thanks to a branch that had punched through the ceiling above the sink. Rainwater dripped steadily onto the countertop.

In the silverware drawer, Elisa found a penlight that cast a tiny circle of brightness. It would have to do. As she closed the drawer, a board creaked overhead.

Would nine pounds of cat make the floorboards in her apartment creak? "Simon?" The noise overhead stopped. "Simon?" She listened for an answering meow, but heard only the tapping of raindrops spilling onto the counter beside her.

"Timo?" He'd been in her apartment before. Maybe, if he were in trouble, he'd go there. "Timo? It's me, Elisa."

She maneuvered herself to the narrow stairs, whose steep pitch and short steps would never pass modern building codes. Did she really hear movement up there? "Simon? Timo?" She felt silly, shouting in the dark. "Whoever it is, come on down." *Please*, she added in her thoughts, *and bring my huipil and photo with you.*

The sagging wooden steps, worn down by generations of Langston feet, glistened with moisture. She laid the crutches next to the railing. It would be easiest to sit on her buttocks and lever her way upstairs. Nobody was here to see. Heave, heave, heave, haul up the crutches. Halfway up, she stopped. Was that a thud?

"Simon?" The cat considered her apartment his own; maybe he was there now, trapped somewhere. "Simon, is that you?" A series of scratching noises. "Simon? Hold on, I'm coming."

Beneath the nylon jacket, sweat filmed her body. She had no idea that fifteen steps could be so much work. Finally gaining the top landing, she pushed open her apartment door. No cat spilled out to meet her. The palms of her hands were black with grime. She wiped them on her shorts and then pulled herself painfully up onto her crutches.

She surveyed the scene inside. The apartment that had been her home for nearly ten years was a wreck. A wet breeze engulfed her. Along with damp night air, an acrid odor emanated from the kitchen, which had taken the main impact of the fir. A broken bottle of vinegar, ammonia? Her thoughts flashed to Gerald's fear of pockets of gas lingering after the main valve had been turned off. Surely that was just paranoia, wasn't it? It had been days since the quake.

Balancing on one crutch, she flicked her miniscule beam around the small apartment. Ridiculous. The massive hole in the ceiling and north wall provided more light, even under cloud cover, than the penlight. The couch held neither boy nor cat, only a puddle of rainwater. A branch had stabbed her small antique dining table, neatly halving the oak top. One of her two chairs had suffered a similar fate and now lay in several pieces next to the ruin of the table.

"Damn it!" Anxiously, she checked the living room wall. Her beloved family photo and the Guatemalan *huipil* in its shadowbox frame still hung there. The brightly colored embroidery on the native blouse glowed in the flashlight beam. Although the frames hung askew, the cover glass was intact. She breathed a sigh of relief.

Maybe her bedroom closet had been spared as well; maybe she still had clothes of her own. Could she carry a few things under an arm? Lowering the penlight, she took hold of the crutches. Around the partition, in the kitchen, she heard something move. Intruding branches obscured the dark corners of the far walls; she couldn't see where the noise was coming from. "Simon?"

Five quick, light taps, moving away. Footsteps? The back of her neck prickled. "Timo? If you're here, answer me!"

Hobbling through soggy clumps of Douglas fir bark and needles, scraps of wallboard and cedar roof shingles, she plowed a course toward the kitchen, ducking branches that hung low. What little light there was shone more brightly here, reflected from the white porcelain tiles on the counters and walls. The black-and-white pattern of the floor was spattered with debris.

"Hello? Anybody here?" The tang in the air burned her eyes. Had Timo been smoking in here? Was he now shimmying down the fir outside? "Timo? Is that you? Answer me!"

Surely, if he heard her, Timo would respond. Could it have been a burglar, or a vagrant coming in out of the rain? Or ... the Gremlin? Had he progressed from skulking around the fields to skulking around her apartment? Was she standing in the spot he had occupied only a moment ago? Or maybe he was nearby, cloaked in the shadows, watching.

She swatted dangling fir branches out of her way and pried open the doors to the sink cabinet, lowered herself to the floor and nervously felt among the bottles and sponges.

Aha! Finally, a decent-sized flashlight. The switch ignited a strong beam. She quickly highlighted the dark corners of the kitchen and dining area. Nobody was hiding in the shadows. The hole in the floor was definitely creepy, though.

The breeze whined. The intruding branches dipped in response, scratching across the battered dinette set. Raindrops spattered around her with a tapping sound. The knot between her shoulder blades eased. The noises she'd heard had only been these.

Dish soap slowly dripped from an overturned bottle onto the floor tiles nearby, forming a small pink pond. Various cans and broken jars, along with their gooey contents, littered the floor, spilled from an open cabinet above. No wonder the place smelled. In one corner of the dining area, next to a damp dishtowel, lay another bottle on its side, along with half of a brightly painted platter. The other half was splintered into tiny shards like confetti. Her mother had brought that platter from Guatemala.

She uprighted the bottle of dish soap. She switched off the flashlight, took a deep breath of foul air. The apartment didn't seem so dark now that her eyes had adjusted. The hole in the roof let in a surprising amount of light, even through cloud cover. This room had always been too dark: maybe she should put in a skylight. It would be nice to see the moon at night.

Suddenly reality hit her like a meteorite. Install a skylight? She had to rebuild the office, restore the apartment. Buy new furniture. And that was just *this* building. She'd need to fix the greenhouse and the irrigation system, buy new stock to replace dead plants.

Thank God for insurance. She hoped Atlas Security would be efficient and generous. But the way Jake Street's brow furrowed when discussing the earthquake damage did not promise an easy settlement. Although his intense blue eyes had not seemed completely hostile, had they?

Now how had the investigator's eyes crept into her brain? She gave herself a mental slap and reached for her crutches. At the edge of her peripheral vision, she caught a flash of movement. The Gremlin? Her fear flared up again. She hurriedly grabbed the flashlight.

"Rrrow." Simon switched his tail. The cat's fur was wet and filthy. He looked miserable. But he was alive!

"Simon! Come here, boy," she crooned. Leaping into her lap, Simon placed his front paws on her chest and rubbed his head across her chin. She hugged him, spitting out a few hairs that stuck to her lower lip. "I'm so glad to see you, buddy!"

She kissed the top of his wet head. Purring mightily, the cat dug his claws into her thighs. She didn't care. She'd gladly wear cat tracks all over her body the rest of her life. "Our home is ruined, partner." She stroked his damp fur. "But we're still here, aren't we? Down but not out?"

The cat sneezed, then gazed at her with mournful eyes. "I know, it stinks in here."

Was it her imagination, or had the acrid scent grown stronger? She flashed the light around the room again, finally settling on the bottle next to the broken platter.

"Stay here." She set Simon down on the floor and crawled

over to the bottle, bumping the flashlight and her cast along the filthy tile. According to the label, the container had been filled with Goddard's Lamp Oil. Pine-scented kerosene, purchased for a camping lamp. A shining river of the liquid stretched along the baseboard, running under a dangling branch, out to—

Another movement caught her eye, this one slow and swirling. In the dim light near the broken wall, gray spectral wisps crawled along the baseboard. Throwing down the flashlight, she grabbed the damp dishtowel and crawled toward the smoke. She was only about two feet away when the ghostly tendrils burst into flames.

"No!" This couldn't be happening. Awkwardly wedged under the fallen tree trunk, she beat at the fire. Burning debris flew in all directions. The dishtowel burst into flames in her hands. She threw it away from her and dragged herself back to her crutches. Simon hissed from inside the sink cabinet.

She hurriedly pushed herself to her feet, swinging her crutches into her armpits. "Simon!" How could she carry the cat? "C'mon, boy, we've got to get out of here." She dragged him out of the cabinet and hoisted him to her shoulder. "Hold on."

A dangling tree branch caught fire, suddenly lighting up like a torch. Simon leapt from her shoulder and disappeared into the darkness.

"No! No! Simon! Simon, come here!" The breeze gusted. The flames surged toward the roof. "Simon!" An orange tongue of fire licked across the living room carpet. The century-old lumber of the building would burn hot and fast. She turned, dashing for the stairs. Still screaming for Simon, she tore the photo and the framed *huipil* from the wall. At the top of the landing, she hurled the crutches to the floor below, sat with the mementos in her arms, and slid, jolting down each step. It hurt like hell.

Something crashed overhead. The ceiling was shrouded in smoke now. "Simon!"

The sprinkler system was useless. Gerald had turned off the water. "Simon! Simon!"

Two steps from the bottom of the stairs, she heard a whoosh, a giant intake of air. Cringing, she braced for an explosion that never came. Instead, a brilliant light engulfed her, followed by a sudden rush of hot wind. Bits of white-hot debris rained down on her as she crawled to the back door. The crutches! She glanced back. Flames rose from the steps behind her, and overhead, liquid fire flowed over the ceiling. "Simon!"

Then she was outside, dragging herself through mud and downed fir branches. Where was the alarm? They had smoke alarms in the building, wired into the— Of course! No electricity, no alarms. A series of loud pops exploded somewhere in the burning building. Wrapping the frames of the photo and *huipil* inside her jacket as best she could, she propped herself against a stack of potting soil bags, shivering with cold and damp.

"Simon!" She frantically searched the darkness for a glimpse of black and white fur. No amount of insurance money could replace the warmth of the cat's small body, the soothing vibration of his purr. She'd found him, then a starving kitten, her first summer at Langston Green. She'd cried into his fur when her father died. He'd listened to her rants about the Gremlin, to her money worries. That old cat was her best friend.

She rubbed her eyes with the back of her hand. The building was fully engulfed now, the orange flames against the ebony sky an image that would be forever etched onto her retinas. Her father had been born in that house. Her business headquarters and her home would soon be nothing but ashes. Langston history was going up in flames.

"Simon!" she screamed into the night. Her shouts seemed

faint amid the cackle and hiss of flames, the crash of structural beams. "Simon!" He was an outdoor cat. Surely he'd gotten out. Surely he'd head for the furthest acre, away from the fire. Her leg throbbed like the bass reverb from a cheap speaker. Her crutches were feeding the flames, just when she needed them most.

"Damn it!" She brushed at the tears on her cheeks. Her fingers came away black with soot.

Where was the Fire Department, for God's sake? Langston Green was surrounded by a crowded commercial and residential district. Did nobody call in fires anymore? Or was the Fire Department still sifting through earthquake rubble, too busy looking for the missing to be bothered with a few errant flames?

The missing. A beloved cat. "Simon!" she yelled over the crackling flames.

The missing. A boy with no phone and no address. "Timo, where are *you*?"

The bathroom window in her apartment exploded, followed by one from the office below. Flames licked out through the new openings, hungrily eating at the sides of the building. Something hot brushed her elbow. She recoiled, slapped at the cinder in panic. But her fingers smacked into fur, not flames.

"Rrrrooowww?" Simon's black and white coat was mostly gray now.

"Simon! Thank God!" Letting the frames she clutched tumble to the ground, she buried her face in his filthy, wet fur. He smelled like a soaked sheep, like an abandoned dog that had slept in a smoky garbage dump. When the roof collapsed with a crash, the cat dug his claws into her abdomen and struggled to be free, but she wrapped her jacket around him and clung to him. Even if Simon ripped her to shreds, she was not going to let him go.

She pulled herself up the stack of potting soil bags and tentatively touched her cast to the ground. Pain shot up her leg and fireflies danced in front of her eyes. But after a few seconds they faded. It was bearable. She picked up the frames she'd discarded and hobbled to the parking lot, cursing with each step. Simon's claws dug into her neck and shoulder.

Charlie's SUV, thankfully, was marred only by a dark covering of ashes. Shortly after she exited the parking lot, Elisa passed the engine and aid truck from Station 11, speeding down the empty street with lights flashing and sirens blaring.

"Fat lot of good you'll be now," she growled as the vehicles zoomed by. She thought about turning around. But what for? Simon wailed his distress from beneath the passenger seat.

"I know exactly how you feel," she told him. "Let's go to Mom's."

The house was dark when she returned at three forty-nine A.M. Amazing. She'd had no idea that her mother and sister were such heavy sleepers. Simon clung to her shoulder, his claws firmly embedded in nylon and flesh, frozen into catatonia by the strange surroundings. When she peeled him off in the bedroom, he disappeared into the open closet.

There was nothing to hold onto between the doorway and the bed and she couldn't stand the weight on her injured leg any longer. Lowering herself to the carpet, she crawled. Upon reaching the bed, she stripped off her sodden jacket, her boot and sopping wet socks, and then collapsed onto the mattress. Her entire body throbbed. Oh, for the painkillers on the counter in the bathroom. Along with some leftover *sangría.*

But it was too much of an effort to get to the bathroom. To get anywhere. In the clean, quiet bedroom, her nocturnal expedition seemed surreal. She hadn't really watched the old homestead building go up in flames, had she? Maybe it was all just a bad dream. Except for Simon, of course. He was really here, wasn't he? Hiding in the closet, for now.

The bed still smelled of lavender. She smelled of kerosene.

And smoke. She remembered the tendrils of smoke in the apartment, the smell of cigarettes. The creaking boards. The sense of someone there with her. Exhaustion overtook her before she could sort it out.

Chapter 4

"You've got to be kidding." Jake Street groaned into the phone. He had been looking forward to sorting out inventory with Elisa, and now this? More evidence against her?

"No joke. The main building burned to the ground. And she was there."

How could he be so attracted to a criminal? Should he admit to his past history with Elisa and remove himself from the case? No. His past history with her was decades ago. The romance was only in his imagination. He had to find the truth. "I'll check it out," he told his colleague.

"What the heck happened here?"

She awoke to find Charlie's carefully made-up face only inches from hers. "Were you sleepwalking?" the lipsticked mouth asked. "Did you drag yourself around the back yard? I think this level of filth is a new record, even for you."

Elisa craned her head around her sister to see the clock. Eight fifteen A.M. "Shouldn't you be leaving for work?" she croaked.

"Our Woodinville shop doesn't open until ten A.M., remember?" Charlie said. "You're lucky that Mom left fifteen minutes ago. I, however, have plenty of time to grill you. But it appears that I'm going to have to get in line."

Elisa pushed herself upright. And was immediately sorry. Her back hurt. Both legs hurt. Her buttocks felt like she'd been dumped from a bucking bronco. Her scalp and face burned. The pastel sheets were streaked with black, and the clothing she'd tossed onto the floor was soggy and soot-covered. So the fire wasn't just a bad dream after all. Her heart sank. "Oh, Charlie," she moaned.

Then her sister's words finally registered. "Get in line?" Elisa's tonsils were raw. She coughed, sucked in a deep breath, started coughing again.

Charlie brought her a glass of water from the bathroom. "Your admirer from the hospital is here."

She had an admirer? Oh, no. "You don't mean Jake Street."

"He's drinking a cup of coffee in the kitchen right now."

The man had already intimated that the insurance claim from the earthquake was too high, and now she had to explain her building burning to the ground? She was in no shape to face him. Elisa grabbed Charlie's arm with both hands. "Throw him out."

"Do you really think that would be wise?" Charlie cocked an eyebrow. She knelt on the floor, peered under the bed. "Where are your crutches?"

"Uh, I might have ... misplaced ... them." Elisa sipped at the water, letting it trickle down her burning throat as she sought to martial some rational thoughts.

Charlie came up dangling the string of keys on the rose keychain. "Are these *my* keys?"

"How did those get there?" Elisa sputtered.

Tossing an angry glance over her shoulder, Charlie stalked out, keys in hand. She slammed the door behind her.

"Wait!" Elisa yelped. "Help me to the bathroom!"

Groaning, she levered herself out of bed and lurched to the bathroom. When she was halfway there, Simon emerged from the closet. He stared at her, switching his tail. A smudge of soot over his right eye lent him an ironic expression.

"I don't want to hear anything out of you," Elisa muttered. But she couldn't help grinning at the sight of him.

She brushed her teeth and washed her face. Gingerly, trying

to avoid the constellation of sore spots on her scalp, she parted her long hair on the side and swept it across her forehead in an attempt to cover the blisters there. In a drawer, she found a couple of paper clips. She criss-crossed them in her hair, fashioning a makeshift barrette to hold the heavy tresses out of her face.

Elisa managed to pull on a pair of Charlie's pajama bottoms over her cast. They would be pink, of course. But topped with one of her sister's cream colored sweaters that dangled halfway down her thighs, they didn't look half-bad. Relatively speaking.

Jeez, it was hard work hauling around non-functional body parts. And this was only one leg. Paraplegics deserved medals for just getting through each day. Bracing herself against the hallway walls with both arms outstretched, she lurched to the kitchen.

Jake Street occupied one of the chairs at the kitchen table, his face softened by a smile. But then, his eyes were focused on Charlie, and all men smiled at Charlie. The minute he spotted Elisa, his expression changed to one of dour caution.

"Good morning," she said. Thank heavens a chair was within reach. She lowered herself into the seat.

"Nice to see you up and about." His cool blue eyes examined her slowly from head to foot. "Didn't they give you crutches?"

She waved a hand. "Oh, you know how those folks are. Insurance red tape or something silly like that. Charlie, do you think I could get a cup of coffee?"

"Well, you probably could, but you'd spill it." Charlie rose, poured, and then thunked a cup down in front of Elisa. The liquid slopped over the lip, and Elisa had to take her first sip holding the dripping cup over the saucer. She gazed at Street through lowered lashes. This morning he wore a blue sweater beneath his charcoal sports jacket. On the table in front of him was his clipboard.

He leaned forward. "I heard there was some excitement at

Langston Green last night." His face gave no hint of what he was thinking. "I heard that a fire burned your main office building to the ground. And according to the report, the responding firefighters saw you fleeing the scene."

"What?" Charlie straightened in her chair, her eyes wide with surprise. She turned to Elisa. "The homestead building burned? You were in a fire?"

Elisa wondered what sort of expression was on her own face. The way Street said it sounded really bad. How could she explain?

Charlie stared at Elisa for a second. "Well, obviously you survived. Are you crazy? And you took *my* Toyota?" She leapt out of her chair and disappeared in the direction of the garage.

Elisa tried to keep her voice calm as she faced the investigator. "I was not 'fleeing the scene.' The place was already a lost cause because they were so late; what was the point of going back?"

He regarded her coolly. "Your apartment has not been habitable since the earthquake. So what were you doing at Langston Green in the middle of the night?"

"Good question." Charlie chimed in, having returned just in time to hear Street's last comment. She carried Elisa's treasures, which she deposited on the kitchen counter. Crossing her arms, she waited for an answer.

Of course Charlie would side with a virile insurance investigator instead of her own sister, Elisa thought with irritation. Street couldn't actually think that she'd had something to do with the fire, could he? She studied his face. Yes, he suspected her. It was written in his eyes.

It looked very bad, she saw that now. Anything she said would sound like an excuse. Stalling for time, she sipped her coffee. The bitter brew needed more milk, but she was not going to hop to the refrigerator to get it. And Charlie looked in no mood to be accommodating.

Finally, she said, "I don't think you'd understand."

Street casually folded his hands together on the table top. "You need to explain it to me, Ms. Langston. If you expect Atlas Security to pay your claim."

Charlie gave a little gasp. A strange reaction to Street's statement. Following her sister's gaze, Elisa swiveled. Simon, his fur only slightly cleaner than last night, stood uncertainly in the kitchen doorway, switching his tail.

"It's only Simon, Charlie." Elisa patted her lap, glad for the distraction. "Come here, boy."

Instead of accepting her invitation, the cat strolled to Jake Street and rubbed against his shins. Street withdrew his legs under his seat. Simon made a second pass, leaving a trail of white hairs across the dark fabric of his trousers, then stood up on his hind feet and placed his front paws on the man's thighs, meowing.

Elisa smiled. "He's hungry."

"He's filthy." Charlie wrinkled her nose. If left to her own devices, Elisa suspected her sister would deliver the cat to the nearest dry cleaner.

As was his habit when he demanded attention, Simon extended his claws. "Yow!" Street yelped and batted the cat away.

Elisa suppressed a chuckle. "Charlie, do you have any tuna? Or chicken or something?"

Charlie turned to inspect the cupboards.

Elisa scooped up the cat and settled him on her lap. "Simon lives at Langston Green. He's been missing since the quake. I had to go look for him." The cat purred and rubbed his head against the underside of her chin.

"How much could you see at three in the morning?"

She raised her chin and looked at him. "Haven't you ever loved a pet, Mr. Street? I've spent three days wondering if Simon was dead or injured. I couldn't sleep, and I had to see if

I could find him. He won't come for just anyone. He's semi-wild."

Street rubbed his thigh. "No kidding." He slid his chair back under the table and turned his attention to the clipboard. "Tell me about the fire."

Where should she start? He extended his hand and gently lifted her hair to reveal the blisters on her forehead. "That is where you got these, right?"

Disconcerted, she leaned back out of his reach. "I went into the building to look for Simon and retrieve a few things from my apartment," she said. "Gerald told me about the tree and the water damage. I wanted to save what I could." She coughed. "It was dark and wet and there was stuff broken and spilled everywhere. I had a feeling that I might not be alone. Then all of a sudden, everything was in flames, so then I grabbed a couple of things and got out of there."

"And what did you bring out?" He poised his pen over his clipboard, ready to write.

Items retrieved, value. Her brain must have sustained smoke damage, because it was certainly processing much more slowly this morning than Jake Street's was. Naturally his mind was on money. With the fire, they'd have to file yet *another* insurance claim.

"Other than Simon, I didn't have time to retrieve anything of real value, if that's what you need to know. Just sentimental items. An old photo. And a *huipil*."

"A what?"

"These." Charlie interrupted the task of dishing up tuna to place Elisa's mementos on the table in front of Street.

He picked up the framed *huipil* and studied the bright embroidery. Elisa noted with dismay that the glass on top had cracked, no doubt from her violent descent of the stairs. Street shifted it to one hand, balancing it on his palm. "It's heavy.

What did you call it? A weepo?"

"*Huipil*," Elisa corrected, pronouncing it carefully, *wee-pill.* "It's a traditional Guatemalan garment, a long cotton blouse, woven and embroidered by hand. There's a skirt in there, too. My father made that frame so the whole costume could be stored inside."

"This looks like hundreds of hours of work." He traced a finger lightly over the glass, following a zigzag pattern that bordered the square neckline.

She was surprised. Most men were oblivious to the artistry of embroidery and weaving. "It is. Each village makes their own distinctive patterns. In Guatemala, a huipil like this would be worn for special occasions, like festivals and weddings." This had been the garment her mother had worn to marry her father.

"A collector's item, then?" he asked.

"Sort of." Pulling the frame close, she inspected the cracked glass. The fabric beneath, fortunately, appeared clean and dry. She made a mental note to take the frame apart soon and inspect the garment to be sure it wasn't damaged.

Street shifted his attention to the photo. "Your father, I presume." His finger hovered above the figure of Terrence Langston. "And ... the woman?"

"My mother." Elisa took the photo from him. The picture had been taken at Reflection Lake at Mount Rainier. Leggy and thin at five years old with dark braids streaming over her shoulders, Elisa leaned against her mother. Maria Elena's ebony hair was a sleek American chin-length bob, but her dark skin and the sharp planes of her face revealed her Mayan origins. She was laughing, her black eyes shining in the sun. Terry Langston was laughing, too, looking down at his young wife. The three of them looked like a happy family. How deceiving appearances could be.

Street brought her back to the present. "I see that your

father took out the original insurance policy on Langston Green. Is he retired now?"

"My father died two years ago," Elisa answered.

"In a car accident," Charlie added. "A pileup on Highway 405, in the rain."

Elisa exchanged a sorrowful glance with her sister. Terry Langston had been on his way back from a funeral home, where he'd been making arrangements for *his* father's service and burial. The double loss had been almost unbearable.

"I'm sorry," Street said. He leaned toward Elisa and gently touched her fingers where they clutched the frame. "And your mother?"

"She's—" Elisa stopped. This was too personal. "My mother's not an owner or a beneficiary, so what business is it of yours, Mr. Street?"

He removed his hand and leaned back. "Just curious." After an awkward pause, he said, "Let's get back to the fire. How did it start?"

"I don't know," she said honestly. "There was an acrid odor and all kinds of things were spilled on the floor. Suddenly there was a whoosh and the whole place lit up."

He stared at her for a long time, his eyes inscrutable as he rubbed a finger across the scar on his left temple. Finally, he asked, "You *saw* this?"

He sounded like a prosecuting attorney trying to trap her into an admission. "Of course I noticed the flames. What are you trying to imply?"

He raised an eyebrow. "Why do you think I'm trying to imply anything?"

Now he sounded like a psychiatrist. *She* was the injured party, he was supposed to be helping her, not playing mind games. He worked for the insurance company, for heaven's sake, and Langston Green had dutifully paid the premiums for twenty years now. Was Atlas Security going to stiff them now when they most needed the protection? She studied him. Friend or foe?

He smiled back.

Charlie stood at his elbow with the pot. "More coffee, Jake?"

"Thanks; I've got to go." He rose and then turned back to Elisa. "But we're not done, Ms. Langston. I still need you to walk me around Langston Green. When would be convenient? Since you're obviously ambulatory."

She wanted to get on with it as soon as possible. "This afternoon? Say, one-thirty?"

"Let's make it two." He headed for the door.

"You'll need to wear outdoor clothes and boots," she told him. "It's not a city park."

"And you'll need crutches." He glanced over his shoulder. "Unless you expect me to carry you." He flashed her a wink, then shut the door behind him.

"Very cool, our Jake," Charlie noted. She sat down in the chair Street had vacated. "The old homestead really burned down last night?"

Elisa cradled her head in her hands. Her life was sliding downhill. First the Gremlin with all the nonstop destructive incidents, then the earthquake. And now the fire. Her father would be mortified at how she'd destroyed the family business.

"Oh, Elisa, the office! Your apartment! All your things!" Charlie wailed, patting her arm. Then, after a brief pause, she added, "Although it's not like you had really nice clothes or furniture or anything."

Elisa raised her head to glare at her sister.

Charlie stuttered, "I mean, there could be a bright side to this, couldn't there? Nobody got hurt in the fire. There's insurance. And you can buy a whole new wardrobe. New furniture. For a whole new place."

"What a lucky break!" Elisa said sarcastically.

Charlie sobered. "You're right. I'm sorry. First the earthquake, now this. But Langstons are tough, right?" Doubling her fist, she gave Elisa a playful punch on the arm. When Elisa didn't respond, she asked, "And the business will be okay. Won't it?"

Elisa wearily rubbed her forehead. She'd never told Charlie and Gail about all the vandalism, about the Gremlin that had been haunting Langston Green. As far as they knew, all of the nursery's problems were earthquake-related. "We'll have to rebuild. Gerald will have to see what's left of the records." Suddenly, she was so tired.

Setting her coffee cup down on the table, Charlie patted Elisa's shoulder. "It's a good thing we have our hunky insurance man looking out for us, isn't it?"

"*Looking out for us?*" Sometimes Elisa felt the urge to smack Charlie's natural optimism right out of her. Hadn't Charlie observed Jake Street's skepticism?

"He smiled at both of us. And he winked at *you*."

"He's trying to trap me."

"Into what? I wouldn't mind being trapped by him. Did you notice how that sweater matched his eyes?"

Trust Charlie to zero in on a man's appearance even while the world was crashing down around her. "My office is in ashes, Charlie. Along with my apartment and everything I own," Elisa reminded her. "And no matter how good-looking or charming Mr. Street may be, he's not 'our insurance man,' I don't think he's here to protect us, and he's hardly 'our Jake.' He's more like 'our headache'."

But yes, of course she had noticed that his sweater was the exact same shade of blue as those piercing eyes. Just like she'd noticed the tingle of electricity when his fingers touched her.

As he drove toward Woodinville Police headquarters, Jake mulled over the quandary of Elisa Langston. He'd always assumed that she was adopted, since she was petite and brunette and the rest of the family was tall and fair. But no, Terrence Langston was her real father. Why didn't she want to talk about her biological mother? Her reticence made him more curious about that piece of her history.

In high school, Elisa had been famous for her lightning-fast tongue, her ability to cut down anyone with a sharp retort. When they'd let girls into Explorer Scouts, she'd been the first to join the Search and Rescue Unit. She always had to be the toughest and the best, whether it was on the history exam or on the soccer field. She rarely had a date because she was Cold with a capital C, all the boys said. But he hadn't bought it. Smoldering, he would have described her, cool on the surface but hot at the core. She sat home alone on Saturday nights because the boys were afraid to ask her out. He ought to know.

The light in front of him turned red, and he braked to a stop. Did Elisa still spend her Saturday nights alone? Surely not. How could any adult male ignore that lush figure, those flashing eyes, those full lips... The light turned green. Why were his thoughts trotting down this road? He abruptly reined them in. Elisa Langston was a fraud suspect. He truly hoped she was telling the truth. But smart and sexy didn't necessarily equal upstanding and honest.

As a youth, he'd always supposed the Langstons were rolling in dough. It was a natural assumption: two florist shops and a huge nursery bore the Langston name. But their house was distinctly middle class. All three women worked. And if the tax records attached to his clipboard were accurate, the Langston Green nursery was barely squeaking by.

The insurance record showed a pattern of claims that began twenty months ago, shortly after Elisa had started running the place. Then, the exorbitant claim from earthquake damage. And now, only a few days later, Elisa Langston just happened to be on the property in the wee hours of the morning when the place burned to the ground?

He parked in the lot of the police department, and sat making a few notes about what he needed to find out. About what he was legally entitled to ask for, since he wasn't law enforcement now. His job as an insurance investigator was more frustrating than rewarding, more about finance than about justice. The process seemed designed to keep the money in the company's accounts as long as possible. Nobody was ever happy to see an insurance investigator. Some days he felt like a con man.

On the other hand, there were *real* cons—the frauds who had engineered their losses. He got satisfaction out of exposing those cheats; that was almost like the good old days. Nabbing a perp was always balm for his soul. He stared at the notes he had written on his pad. He never imagined that Elisa Langston might end up being one of the perpetrators he snared.

But there was still the chance that she was innocent. And she wasn't snared yet. What he knew about the plant business could be etched on the head of a pin. For years now, he hadn't even bought flowers for a woman, other than for his mom and grandmothers on Mother's Day. Dinner, maybe a play, or in the winter, downhill skiing and a drink at the ski lodge: that was usually as far as his imagination for dating extended. As little socialization as possible prior to maneuvering a woman into his bed. And there hadn't been much socialization *or* maneuvering in recent years, now that he thought about it. What the heck had he been doing with his life?

He'd been working, he reminded himself. Trying to rescue something out of the morass of his career. This insurance investigation job was only a stepping stone on the way back to who he wanted to be. He locked his Rover and headed for the police station. Flowers and Elisa Langston. He never knew where a case was going to take him.

Gail and Charlene Langston—Elisa's stepmother and stepsister, he now knew—were like hothouse orchids, pretty things that needed pampering. But Elisa was tough enough to bloom in harsh environments. Maybe she'd be a wild rose or an alpine lily? No. Remembering her fiery brown-eyed gaze, he dismissed that mental image. What the heck had she been wearing in her hair this morning—paper clips? Elisa Langston was not a blossom at all, but more like a Jalapeño pepper. Small, packing a punch that could make you gasp. He wasn't sure what she was up to, but it was going to be interesting finding out.

Chapter 5

"You're not leaving that beast here, are you?" One arm through the sleeve of her trench coat, Charlie paused to stare at Simon, who sat on the kitchen floor looking hopefully at the saucer that had held tuna only a few minutes ago.

"I can't take him back to the nursery yet," Elisa said. "He'll stay in my bedroom."

She fervently hoped the cat would be on his best behavior. Simon wasn't used to captivity. Without dirt to dig in and trees to sharpen his claws on, he was capable of shredding that beautiful lavender comforter, reducing the immaculate silver carpet to piles of gray lint.

"I'll take him out this morning and bring a litter box home with me this afternoon," she promised.

"Yuck." Charlie wrinkled her nose as she finished pulling on her coat. She checked her hair and makeup in the hallway mirror. "If I send you over some new crutches, you promise not to 'lose' them?"

Elisa gestured a "cross-my-heart" motion that made her sister smile.

"At least you'll be seeing Jake again," Charlie said. "Yummy."

"Right." Seeing him would mean a treat for her eyes, no doubt, but talking to him was another matter. Could mean a noose for her neck.

"The old homestead really burned down?" Charlie asked one last time.

Elisa nodded sadly.

"It's so hard to get used to the idea." Charlie was still shaking her head as she closed the door behind her.

Elisa pulled herself together, grabbed Simon and hobbled to the back yard. She hovered over the cat as he scratched up the flowerbed. As she limped to the back door, he struggled in her arms, and when she dumped him on the kitchen floor after shutting the door behind her, he yowled to express his outrage. "I know," she told him. "I'm not exactly happy to be cooped up here, either. But you've got to behave yourself."

As she ate a bowl of cereal, the cat watched every spoonful. She gave him the leftover milk. When the doorbell rang, Simon skidded over the hardwood floors as he fled for the safety of the bedroom closet. The bell continued to ring for the three minutes it took for her to lurch like Frankenstein from kitchen to front door. "For heaven's sake, I'm coming!"

A pimple-faced delivery boy from Langston Florists stood on the step. He handed her a pair of crutches.

"Better than flowers. Thanks." She pushed them under her arms and leaned forward. Much better than balancing on one leg.

The delivery boy made no move to leave. "If I had any money in my pajama bottoms, I'd give you a tip."

His face turned crimson as he backed away. "That's not necessary, Miss Langston. I'm sorry..." He galloped down the steps back to the van.

Teenage boys. So easy to embarrass. She thought about how Timo had made a face when she'd told him that the six temporary workers needed to be at least as tall as he.

She sure needed her best field worker now. Heck, she'd settle for just seeing the boy again, just knowing he was okay. If luck was with her, maybe he'd show up at the nursery today.

As if she'd been blessed with good luck recently. Cursed was more like it. Was someone really out to bring her down? Her thoughts flitted aimlessly from one acquaintance to another for a moment, then she shook her head. The Gremlin had to be some kid having a little malicious fun; he couldn't be anyone she knew. He certainly hadn't caused the earthquake. And surely the fire had been an accident, the result of broken branches rubbing against kerosene-soaked timbers. She couldn't blame some anonymous entity. But she sure could use some help.

"Langstons make their own luck," her father had been fond of saying. Along with "Langstons never give up," and "I'm counting on you, Elisa, to take care of things."

"I'm on it, Dad," she responded to his voice in her head.

The police sergeant smoothed his beard with a finger as he considered the papers in front of him. "Langston Green. Tough case. Sporadic vandalism, no real pattern."

"Do you think the manager has been working to end it?" Jake asked.

"Elisa Langston?" The sergeant considered for a moment. "After several incidents, she wired the place with motion-sensor alarms. It must have cost a fortune, but it didn't work out too well." He chuckled. "Raccoons, possums, even deer kept setting them off right and left, especially after dark. The neighbors complained. We told her we couldn't keep responding to the false alarms, so she finally disconnected them."

Jake made a note for the Langston Green file. "How about surveillance cameras?"

"Yep, she's got several out there. Never recorded anything of use as far as I know. She even hired security guards—couple of our off-duties—but nothing ever happened on their watch."

"Sounds like the vandal's keeping track."

The sergeant leaned back in his chair. "Would be a piece of cake to scope out," he said, "Langston Green is open to the public." He shook his head. "As you know, there's not a lot we can do about this kind of hit-and-run vandalism. And so far, all these incidents"—he thumbed through the stack of reports— "are more nuisances than real threats."

"Until last night."

"If that fire was arson, then of course we'll put more legwork into this." The sergeant tapped the papers into a neat stack. "You know, you may be right to take a hard look at Elisa Langston. Nothing like this ever happened while her father was in charge."

By the time Elisa had washed again and talked Peter Nguyen into driving over to pick her up, it was nearly noon. Raiding her sister's bureau, she exchanged the pink pajama bottoms for a pair of charcoal gray designer sweats, rolling the extra six inches of fabric into unfashionable folds around her ankles. Socks, one boot, the long cream sweater, and her old stained canvas coat completed her ensemble. She looked like a waif in a TV charity campaign.

"I just can't believe it," Peter told her as he backed the Langston Green delivery van out of the driveway. "How could the main building catch on fire?"

Tears instantly blurred her vision. "I don't want to talk about it."

Peter turned his eyes back to the road. "You're the boss."

Now she'd insulted her greenhouse manager. As if she had so many allies that she could afford to alienate one. "I'm sorry, Peter," she said, her voice cracking. "I'm feeling a little overwhelmed right now."

The tense lines of his face softened. "Of course. I understand."

"Let me know what I can do to help." He hesitated a moment, then said, "Gerald and I, well, we feel pretty bad that we didn't come back to the nursery after the earthquake."

"Don't worry about it. It was a hectic time for everyone."

Peter Nguyen was somewhere around her father's age. He'd

come from Vietnam as a youth accompanied by a one-armed older brother and a shy younger sister with ugly burn marks on her face. He refused to talk about what had happened to his parents. Comparing her losses to his, she experienced a ripple of guilt. What a wimp she was.

They turned into Langston Green. Elisa stared grimly at the devastation, so brutally evident in daylight. Where the stately old Langston farmhouse had demarcated the center of the property, there was now only a pile of blackened debris. Ironically, a good deal of the Douglas fir had survived the fire: the horizontal ebony column of its trunk dominated the scene. Yellow tape stretched between stakes formed a flimsy border around the ruins. A patrol car from the Woodinville Police Department was parked at an angle before the ruins.

"What's the cop doing?" Elisa asked.

"She was here when I arrived. Keeping people away from the ruins, she said. She told me it's the normal routine." Peter parked the van in front of the greenhouse. He pulled open the passenger door and gave her a shoulder to lean on as she lowered herself to the ground. "Ready?"

"As ready as I'll ever be." She lumbered beside him into the greenhouse, now Langston Green's principal building.

Many of the roof panels had fallen and shattered. Glass shards glittered among the pots on the tables. She stared at the roof fifteen feet overhead, now filmy with clear plastic. "How did you manage to cover that by yourself?"

"Gerald helped."

That surprised her. She'd never known her partner to willfully get his hands dirty, let alone wrestle with ladders and giant sheets of plastic.

"Some of the others came in, too: Marty, Jim and Sarah." Peter named the summer employees, all local teenagers. "They just stopped by to help out."

A lump formed in Elisa's throat at the thought of such

unexpected generosity. But the fact that Timo had not been among the other teens worried her even more.

"Gerald told them we'd be closed awhile due to damage," Peter continued. "I suppose now they're back in school."

Her mental gears shifted from blessing Gerald for his help with the greenhouse to cursing him for not hiring the kids to restore the place during the hours they were not in school. If everyone had worked while she'd been in the hospital, maybe Langston Green could be open now. Maybe the old homestead building would still be standing.

In one corner of the greenhouse, Peter had set up what he called his 'clinic tables,' where he nursed broken plants, loath to discard anything that could be salvaged. Still, he confessed, he had to throw out an appalling number of rubber plants and philodendrons and other tropical species that had gotten too cold and wet after the roof had fallen in.

As Gerald had reported, most of the flowers had survived in a less damaged section, enough to keep Gail's and Charlie's shops supplied through the upcoming holiday season. They'd been lucky in that respect. And electricity had been restored to the greenhouse two hours ago, so Peter no longer had to keep the generators fueled.

The phone rang, a distant repeated buzz from the back room. Elisa cocked an eyebrow at Peter. "Will Beth get that?"

Peter shook his head and started to reply, but then the cell phone attached to his belt bleated. He shook it open, said, "Peter here," and listened for a moment. "Four dozen Stargazers, two dozen Callas—pink or white? Okay, got it. I'll have them for your driver at two o'clock, Charlie."

He snapped the phone closed. "Your sister's having a run on lilies today. And Gail called earlier wanting roses and carnations."

"I'm glad something's selling." She nodded at the cell phone on his belt. "When did you get that?"

"Gerald set up this system a couple days ago, so we could manage with fewer people."

She wondered what other innovations Gerald had come up with in her absence. "Have there been any messages for me?"

"Gerald's been listening to your voicemail, taking care of things for you."

What was Gerald was saying to callers—that she was out of the game, that Langston Green was a total loss, that it was being sold to a developer? "I'll take my own messages from now on," she told Peter. "But why isn't Beth answering the phone?" During the day, the thirty-year-old woman usually handled calls and rang up sales to drop-in customers at the check-out desk in the front room of the greenhouse. Beth was a Nguyen, too, niece or cousin or some relation to Peter.

"Gerald told her to stay home for now. I guess he figured that with the business closed, there wasn't enough for her to do."

"Where *is* Gerald, anyway?"

Peter shrugged. "I listen to the voicemail a couple times a day, and so does he. Between us, we've been taking care of the things we can handle, putting off the rest."

Elisa shuddered at the image Langston Green was projecting to the public. Her father had always taken pride in Langston Green's personal touch.

"Come," Peter pulled her through the double swinging doors to the back room.

There, across from his own scratched desk, was another desk and chair, crowded into the small space. He'd laid out a legal pad and a jar full of pens. In one corner was a vase of peach-colored carnations.

"For you," he beamed. "Or Gerald. Or whoever."

She gave him a quick squeeze on the arm. "Thanks, Peter. I couldn't get along without you."

He smiled shyly, suddenly seeming more like a teenager than a sixty-year-old man.

"I'll get Beth back," she told him. "Even if we aren't open yet, she can answer phones from nine until five. And I'm sure you can find work for her between calls, right?"

He exhaled heavily. "I could sure use somebody. Well, I'd better go sort out those lilies. Thanks, boss."

Boss. The word weighed a ton. Everyone was counting on her to pick up the pieces. She sighed. Might as well go see just how many pieces she had left. Leaning heavily on her crutches, she exited the greenhouse.

Three vehicles were now parked in the lot next to her own pickup. She knew Gerald's Pontiac Firebird, but didn't recognize the gray Land Rover next to it. Beyond that was a white van with a Woodinville Fire Department emblem.

Gerald stood within the fire debris, talking to two men. One was dressed in the navy uniform of the Fire Department. The other man wore a black jacket. A camera dangled from his neck. The clipboard he held and his auburn hair gave away his identity. Damn it! Jake Street said two o'clock. Why was he here an hour early?

Chapter 6

Elisa hobbled across the parking lot. As she ducked under the yellow tape, she noticed its black lettering: "Crime Scene—Do Not Enter."

"Hey!" the Fire Department uniform barked at her.

"I'm the owner," she told him.

The uniform stepped forward. In one hand he clutched a pocket-sized notepad and an old Polaroid camera. He extended the other hand toward her. "Fire investigator David Wasserman."

"Elisa Langston." She wiped the sweat from her palm on her pants leg before placing her hand in his.

Wasserman gestured to Jake Street. "And you two know already each other."

"We've met." Her eyes met Street's. What had he told Wasserman about her?

"Please don't move beyond this area." Wasserman's gestures demarcated the small space in which the four of them stood, clustered around the blackened trunk of the fallen Douglas fir. He turned his attention back to her business partner.

"Anyway, like I was saying, I'm sure it was that kid," Gerald told him.

"What kid?" Wasserman asked.

"That Mexican kid, Timo." Gerald rubbed his head. "Elisa, what's his last name?"

All three men swiveled toward her.

She looked at Gerald. "What about Timo?"

"I was telling Street and Wasserman that it had to be him that cleaned out the petty cash."

"What?" How could there be even *more* bad news?

Gerald gestured toward the charred area that had been the main office. He pointed at the safe, which had been hidden in a cabinet but now sat forlornly on the ground, its door open to reveal a vacant cavity.

"We had twelve hundred dollars in there." Gerald tapped Street's clipboard, insisting he make a note of it.

"Minus three hundred and seventy, which I took," Elisa reminded him.

"And gave to Timo," Gerald added.

Street made a sound in his throat and wrote something on his clipboard.

"Did this Timo see you open the safe?" Wasserman asked.

"Timo Martinez wouldn't steal from us," Elisa protested. "We were out by the back fence when I handed him the cash." That sounded suspicious, like she was paying him off or something. She hastened to add, "It was the day of the earthquake. We were planning a big tree-planting project. I told him to hire some men he knew and buy some tools."

Street cocked an eyebrow. "Who were these men?"

"I don't know." Was he intentionally making her feel incompetent? "That's why Timo was doing it; he knew some guys who were looking for temporary work."

"I see." Street made another note on his pad.

Turning now to Gerald, Wasserman asked, "Why do you suspect this Timo?"

"He's been in the office. He knows where we keep the cash. He saw Elisa take out money to pay him, several times." Oblivious to a hiss of disapproval from Wasserman, Gerald strode toward what remained of the staircase. "And look." He thrust his right index finger toward the ruins of the bottom step.

There, amid blobby smudges that might have been left in

the muck by Elisa's own buttocks, was the triangular toe imprint of a shoe.

"Looks like the kid's cowboy boots," Gerald said.

Street bent, snapped a photo, checked it in the window of his digital camera while Wasserman took a Polaroid. They turned to Elisa for confirmation.

She shrugged. "Timo does wear cowboy boots. He's been in the office several times, and he even came up to my apartment for a sandwich a couple of times. But what does a shoe print prove, even if it is his? There are dozens of prints in here." She gestured at the filthy area around them. The sludge held myriad imprints, of shoes, of dragged fire hoses, of objects that had fallen or been moved.

Wasserman's Polaroid chimed and rolled out the photo, which he waved in the air to dry.

"This print is in slimy muck." Street pointed at the offending mark on the step. "But it's overlaid with ashes. So whoever left it was here between the time that the tree opened up the roof and the time the fire broke out. The safe, too, was emptied before the fire, because its exterior is evenly coated with smut from the fire. There are no fingerprints or tool marks on top."

"Timo's an honest young man," she told the two investigators.

Gerald injected, "He barely speaks English."

Elisa frowned fiercely at him. Street watched their interaction with interest. Wasserman was studying debris a couple of feet away, but she was sure he was listening.

Street made another note on his clipboard. "Can I have a copy of Timo's work records?"

Wasserman straightened. "Ditto for me."

Gerald looked toward the charred metal cabinets in the corner. "Well, maybe. The file cabinets are supposedly fireproof. May I?" He gestured at the cabinets.

Wasserman nodded. Gerald waded through the muck

toward the blackened metal.

While Gerald rummaged, Street and Wasserman walked carefully amid the wreckage. Elisa maneuvered around the remains of a joist. Her crutch smacked a black object, which spun across the floor before coming to rest against a piece of charred wood. Both investigators turned to glower at her.

"Stay put," Street told her.

"Please," Wasserman added.

"This is *my* building, gentlemen." Balancing on her crutches, she leaned over to grab the object. Rubbing the sooty ceramic across her pant leg, she uncovered an image of a wolf howling at the moon. "And this is my favorite coffee cup."

Street straightened, holding a piece of debris by the tips of his fingers, which she now noticed were covered by clear latex gloves. He glanced at her. "Put that cup down where you found it, and don't touch anything else," he said.

She frowned at his mandatory tone.

He noticed her expression and switched to a softer voice. "Should you be on your feet? You're just out of the hospital. You could rest in the greenhouse, or sit in my car if you like."

She wasn't going to fall for his act. "I'm touched by your concern, Mr. Street. But I'm fine. I'm staying put. And I'm keeping my coffee cup. Haven't I lost enough to satisfy you?"

Street retrieved a small black scrap from the ground. "Aha!"

"What?" Elisa demanded.

Stepping close, Street held the objects out on the palm of his hand. He stood so near that she felt the warmth of his body in the cool afternoon air. She bent over his hand. Charred paper with metal staples and little blackened stubs of cardboard alternating directions like bristles on a hairbrush. The remains of a cheap matchbook. And a scorched stub of cigarette filter.

"So we have smokers that come in here. Came in here."

Wasserman explained, "It could be a timer. You interweave the filter end of a cigarette through a matchbook, light the cigarette, place the whole shebang next to something flammable. When the cigarette burns down to the match heads, presto—ignition. Gives the arsonist time to get away."

"Arsonist?" She raised a hand to her mouth, suddenly realizing that the lamp oil in her apartment had been dumped only a few moments before her arrival. She'd seen a shining stream of liquid. If the bottle's contents had spilled when the fir fell on the building, the kerosene would have soaked into the woodwork. Then there was the swirling smoke. "I did have this feeling that someone was in the building with me last night," she told Wasserman.

She could feel Street staring at her. He was no doubt thinking that the arsonist hadn't gotten away, but was standing in front of him with the blisters on her face to prove it. It was her business and her apartment. Worse, it was her lamp oil, and she'd been seen leaving the premises while the fire was still burning.

Jake watched Elisa. Since this morning, she'd traded her pink pajama bottoms for too-big sweats and the paper clips for a green twist-tie that bound half her hair at the crown of her head. She was thinking hard, one hand raised to her mouth. Suspects often unconsciously covered part of their faces when they were getting ready to lie. She stared into space, her dark eyes darting back and forth, dancing to inner thoughts. Was she reviewing her own guilt, pondering a cover-up for someone else, or what? Wasserman asked her if *she* thought it was arson, but she didn't respond.

"Ms. Langston?" Wasserman prompted, jarring her back from wherever she'd been.

"I don't know." She sounded scared. For herself, or for someone else? Jake felt an insane urge to put an arm around her.

"Could it be your vandal?" he asked.

Wasserman perked up. "Vandal?"

"Or a disgruntled employee?" Jake asked.

Her knuckles whitened on the crutch grips. "None of my employees would do this. And the vandal has never done anything this dangerous."

"Until now." He watched for her reaction.

She stared at him for a minute, then swallowed. "I don't want to think ..." She shook her head. "You don't even know if it's arson yet. These could just be left over from a cigarette break. The fire *could* have been the result of earthquake damage, right? A pocket of gas, friction, spontaneous combustion from spilled liquids?"

"That last one sounds interesting," Wasserman said. He glanced at Jake, who dipped his chin to show he'd noted Elisa Langston's suspicious behavior, too.

"Who smokes around here?" Jake asked.

Donaldson, with several sheets of paper in hand, joined them just in time to say, "That kid—Timo—does."

Elisa threw him a dirty look. "Many of our customers and suppliers smoke. I've seen Tiffany light up in here, too."

"She quit," Donaldson retorted.

"She was holding a pack of cigarettes in the hospital two days ago," Elisa said.

Jake looked from Elisa to Gerald Donaldson. "Who is Tiffany?"

"My fiancée," Donaldson told him.

"I'll take those," Wasserman said, holding out an evidence bag to Jake for the matches and filter. "I've got a friend in the Seattle lab who will run them quickly."

Elisa interrupted them. "'Run' them?"

"Test them for fingerprints, DNA," Wasserman told her. "You do want whoever's responsible for this to be caught, don't you?"

"Of course. But even if you can prove who the smoker is,

how can you prove that he's an arsonist?"

Smart, Jake thought. Maybe too smart?

Wasserman shrugged. "There might be something in this smoker's background."

Donaldson thrust a page toward Jake. "Here's the paperwork on Timoteo Martinez."

Elisa intercepted the paper before he could grab it. His fingers brushed hers in the process. Such small, cool fingers. But the expression on her face was anything but cool.

"Why should we hand you a copy of our workers' documentation?" She glared first at him and then at Wasserman. "You're not law enforcement."

"No, ma'am," Wasserman said. "But I do have authority. And we could bring the police in if you like."

Why didn't Elisa want them to check out this Timo character? Jake reached into the pocket of his jacket. "Do you prefer to have law enforcement involved?" he asked her. "It will make the investigation longer, but it's your choice, Ms. Langston. I can arrange it right now." He pulled out his cell phone and flipped it open.

Their gaze locked for a beat before she gave in. Turning her back on him, she handed Wasserman the page. "Timo's not guilty of anything," she said.

Elisa's head ached nearly as much as her broken leg. Why was Gerald so determined to finger Timo for this? And why were Street and Wasserman so eager to believe him? She turned to Gerald. "Think back to the day of the quake. You're sure the money was there when you left?"

Gerald looked surprised. "Of course I'm sure."

"And the next day, after you found out that the tree had crushed the building?"

His face took on a sheepish look. "The building was unstable. I made sure the gas and electricity were turned off, but I never thought about the money until this morning."

"So the money could have been stolen any time between the earthquake and the fire," she summarized. "That's three days."

Wasserman chimed in, "The safe was not forced open. Who knows the combination?"

Elisa felt the color drain from her face. Another finger of blame pointing in her direction. "Gerald and I," she responded in a soft voice.

"Do you keep the numbers written down anywhere?"

Elisa shook her head. Gerald looked more embarrassed. "I have the combination in my daytimer." He pulled a slim black volume from his trouser pocket. "But it's disguised to look like an alternate phone number for the office."

He opened it and showed them. The digits appeared under Langston Green and he'd added a zero and punctuated them to look like a phone number. Wasserman and Street nodded.

"So," Wasserman said, "The thief could have been either of you, or someone who has access to Gerald's book *and* would know this number is not an office phone number. Or someone who has observed you opening the safe."

Street asked, "You last saw this Timo on the day of the quake?"

She'd had enough of this line of questioning. "That's right. He rode away on his bike around six." She turned to face him.

Street tilted his head back. "The earthquake hit at six-thirty, just after it was fully dark." He turned to Elisa. "What were you doing out in the field after dark?"

How did the man make everything she did sound so incriminating? "Well, you mentioned our vandalism problem. I had decided to keep watch a couple of hours after dark, to see if I could catch whoever was doing it. Normally I'd be in my apartment then, fixing dinner."

"You believe your vandal knows your schedule?" Street asked.

"I thought it was possible," she answered. "All the incidents have happened at night."

"Martinez—" Gerald started.

"Shut up about Timo!" she hissed, cutting him off.

"Sometimes teenagers set fires just for excitement." Wasserman's soft voice came over her shoulder.

"Timo's not a thief *or* an arsonist," she protested.

Jake Street shrugged. "Maybe not. The money could have been stolen and the fire could have been started by a lot of people," he acknowledged. "Timo Martinez, another worker, Mr. Donaldson."

Gerald squawked, "Hey!"

Street continued. "It could have been a stranger, just passing by; a bum coming in out of the rain. It could even have been *you*, Miss Langston."

Her chin came up. "Why would I want to destroy my own business?"

Street clutched his clipboard to his chest. "Yesterday afternoon, I told you the building was salvageable and the insurance claim was too high. Then, last night, that salvageable building burned to the ground. Anyone can buy cigarettes." He raised a sleek brown eyebrow into a question mark.

Gerald addressed Street. "As for the claim sounding too high, of course I made it for the maximum I thought it could possibly add up to." He surveyed the blackened wreckage surrounding them. "And now I'll have to up it even more. But that's the way the insurance game's played, isn't it?"

Street ignored that and turned to fire investigator. "Are we done here?"

Wasserman nodded. "I'll take the safe and file cabinets." He held up a hand to head off Gerald's objection. "You'll get them back as soon as we've dusted for prints and made copies of anything we need. I'll send a tech to dust for prints in here, too. Not much left, but we'll get what we can. We'll do the inside of the electrical panel. An arsonist might have tried to turn on lights."

It was Street's turn to look uncomfortable. "You're likely to find my prints in several places," he said. "And prints from these shoes. I was here the night of the quake."

Wasserman and Gerald looked to Elisa for confirmation. "He's the guy that found me," she told them. And she'd thought him so nice then. Now she didn't know what to think.

Wasserman turned to Elisa. "We'll need fingerprints from you and all your employees, from everyone who's in and out of here regularly." He tucked Timo's paperwork into his notebook. "I should get back the lab results in a week or so. Until then, nobody goes back inside these yellow tapes except for the fire department. "

"I'll fax those PD records to you," Street told Wasserman just before the arson investigator turned away.

"PD records?" Elisa asked.

"Your vandalism reports." Street peeled off his latex gloves.

Elisa didn't want to think about vandalism and arson any longer. She was exhausted. She couldn't wait to go to her new office, put her leg up, and start planning how to pull Langston Green out of this nosedive.

Street's hand landed on her shoulder. "Ready for that inventory evaluation?"

She felt like whimpering in self-pity.

"We could put it off for awhile if you like."

And put off the insurance check, too? "No way," she said. "I'm ready."

Chapter 7

Street insisted on starting at the far border of the property. Halfway there, Elisa began to wonder how she would ever make it back. Crutches didn't work very well in bark chips and slippery mud.

"So," she said between gasping breaths, "You made an appointment to meet Gerald and Wasserman before meeting me."

Street slowed his pace a little. "That was a coincidence. I got here early. I was going over papers in the car when Wasserman arrived, and then your partner. It seemed only natural that we look over the fire scene together."

"How did Gerald react when he saw the ruins?"

Street stopped. "Donaldson stood and stared with his hands on his hips," he told her. "Why?"

She shrugged and swung forward again. She didn't want to believe that the Gremlin was someone she knew, but Gerald had recovered from hearing about the fire awfully quickly. He was ready to pin everything on Timo. And he wanted to sell out to Baker. Gerald could easily buy a pack of cigarettes, or borrow one from Tiffany. But Elisa couldn't picture Gerald plotting arson. They'd worked closely in the last two years since her father had died. Gerald had never shown any animosity toward her or Langston Green. Being averse to physical labor didn't really count, did it?

The lost cash was troubling, she had to admit. She remembered the light in Timo's eyes when she pressed three hundred and seventy dollars into his palm. Missing cash, missing employee: she could see why the men suspected him. But they didn't know Timo. She shook her head.

This time, Street's hand was surprisingly tentative, his fingers gently touching her shoulder. "Are you all right? We don't have to do this today if you're not up to it."

The concern in his voice undammed the tears that suddenly pooled in Elisa's eyes. Of course she wasn't all right. Her leg was broken, her throat hurt, and her business was in ruins. But she'd never let Jake Street believe she wasn't 'up to it.' She jerked her right crutch out of a soft patch for the umpteenth time and shook a glob of mud from the crutch tip. "I'm not fond of being treated like a criminal."

His eyes widened. "I'm sorry if I gave you that impression. But you understand that Atlas Security cannot simply hand over money for every claim we receive. It's my job to investigate claims, to make sure they're val—" he stopped himself and ended with "...accurately documented."

"How precise of you," she said sarcastically.

How was she supposed to feel about Jake Street? He had been her rescuer. She owed the man her life. And something about him felt familiar, like he was a long-lost friend. She stopped at the fence and turned to face him.

Sunlight brought out the cobalt tint of his eyes, highlighted the mahogany in his thick hair, shadowed the strong planes of his face. He straightened, briefly flexing muscles in his arms and shoulders that were defined even through his shirt and jacket. Charlie was right. 'Our Jake' was one striking man.

And an insurance *investigator*, she reminded herself. Atlas would not have sent an investigator if they simply intended to pay the claims as submitted. While she might admire the man like a piece of art, he was not someone she should trust. Why, then, did she keep longing for him to touch her again?

Street fidgeted under her scrutiny. "Shall we get started?"

She continued to stare at him, savoring the fact that she

could make *him* uneasy for a change. The man didn't quite add up. He seemed much more comfortable sifting through ashes with the arson investigator than sorting through inventory and paperwork.

"You don't seem like an insurance man," she said.

"I always dreamed of being a tax accountant," he joked, folding back a page. "Now, on to the inventory list."

"You don't seem like the tax accountant type, either."

He smiled and crossed his arms. "What type do I seem like?"

She let her gaze travel down his lean figure. The type that women want in their beds at the end of a long day? She winced inwardly. Where had her mind suddenly dredged *that* thought from? She was definitely spending too much time with Charlie.

Swallowing to regain her composure, she considered Jake Street. The confident bearing. The interrogator's manner. The well-muscled physique. The way he'd treated Wasserman like they were comrades. "I'd say you were a cop."

His eyes instantly sobered and his jaw tightened. Well, well, well. The first time she'd fired a volley at him, and she'd scored a direct hit. It felt good to have Investigator Jake Street on the defensive for a change. "So, why aren't you a cop now?"

He lowered the clipboard to his side. "For one thing, I make almost three times what I did as a detective. For another, police work's not all it's cracked up to be."

"What does that mean?"

He jerked his gaze away from hers. "It means that now I focus on inventory lists. We're burning daylight, Ms. Langston. Let's get on with this." He pointed to the fallen trees. "What are these?"

"American sweet gums."

He consulted the inventory list Gerald had given him. "Four hundred and ninety nine dollars? Each?"

She bristled. "They're eight years old. Not many nurseries

put that much time into trees. It's hard to find mature ones like these."

"It must be, if you can charge prices like that." He marched down the row, counting, stepping over trunks and branches.

She followed more slowly, estimating whether each tree could be salvaged and, if so, how much it might now be worth.

The white snowy cone of Mount Rainier loomed against the blue skies to the south. The sweet gums had previously blocked this view. Maybe she'd move the tall trees off to the east side of the property so she could enjoy the vista from her bedroom window this winter. Then the loss hit her again. She had no bedroom.

"I'm sure you can buy trees this big for under a hundred." Street nudged a sweet gum with his shoe.

"You might get some tall *thuja pyramidalis*. But not American sweet gums. They're much more valuable. Before the earthquake, I had a contract to plant fifty of these for seven hundred dollars apiece. I can show you the written agreement." Hopefully it had been in the fireproof cabinet, not on her desk.

When they reached the spot where she'd lain, Street picked up a penlight from the mud. "Yours, I presume." He handed it to her, then spotted something else. He retrieved the cylinder of pepper spray from the ground and held it up, a question on his face.

"That's mine, too." She held out her hand for it. "I dropped it when the tree nailed me."

"So you *are* afraid of this vandal."

"Gremlin. I call him the Gremlin. But I'm not afraid of him. He's probably just a kid. Or maybe multiple kids."

"Why do you say that?"

"For one thing, that's what the police keep saying; you've read the reports. For another, all the vandalism incidents have been little things: gunking up the irrigation system, tools disappearing. Stuff like kids might do."

"The arson was no 'little thing.'"

"But I'm responsible for that."

Taken by surprise, he gaped at her.

She quirked an eyebrow. "Isn't that what you think, that I burned the place down?"

He quickly recovered his poise. "I'm considering all possibilities." His brow creased. "You were lucky to escape alive from that fire."

Didn't she know it. She shuddered as she relived the flash of ignition from last night.

Street moved beyond the sweet gums. "What are these things with the purple berries?"

"Beautyberries. People buy them to add color to their gardens in late fall."

He checked his list. "They're listed at $17.95. That can't be right."

A huff of annoyance escaped her lips. "Do you even have a garden?"

"I have a plant." He frowned, trying to remember. "No, I have two, actually."

"What are they?"

"Hmmmm. A tall spiky dangerous thing by the patio door and a dangly one that hangs over the stair railing."

She snorted. "Judging by the amount of care you lavish on them, I'm guessing a sanseveria and a philodendron. Common house plants that can survive nearly anything. Depending on size and subspecies, you've got twenty to forty dollars worth of plants there. So take another look around and start adding it up."

He moved further down the row. "What are these?"

She hastened to catch up with him. The rubber tip of the right crutch skidded on a leaf and went out from under her. She dropped it and hopped sideways, reaching out for the closest support, which turned out to be Street himself. He wrapped his arms around her.

"So," he said in a soft voice, "I may have to carry you after all." His breath smelled of spearmint. Was that a smirk on his face?

She would have ended up on her backside if he hadn't been there. "Thanks," she said. "I mean, for grabbing me."

"I believe it was the other way around." He was definitely grinning. She hadn't realized until now that his eyes had little gold flecks in them. She could feel the clipboard in his hand digging into her back, but in front, the heat of his body, the rock-solid muscles of his arms and chest were all too palpable though their clothes.

"You can let go of me now," she said, just because she thought she should.

"Yes, ma'am." He steadied her carefully on the ground, retrieved the fallen crutch and handed it to her. As he stepped back, his hand briefly brushed his forehead in a two-fingered Boy Scout salute.

There was something unsettling about that gesture. She fumbled with the crutches. "Don't call me ma'am. I can't possibly be much older than you are." Could she? Timo had looked at her like his mother, and now Street was calling her ma'am and giving her Boy Scout salutes? His arms had felt like heaven. She would love to rest there for a while. But she was the client—or suspect—and he was the investigator. Flustered, she muttered, "Let's get on with the inventory."

Two hours later they'd made their way through most of ten acres and stood in front of the largest tool shed, which, Street noted in his accountant tone, was undamaged. The backhoe was parked under the carport next to the shed. He patted one of the backhoe's giant wheels. "This piece of equipment looks fine."

"It darn well better be: I just had the engine rebuilt. The

Gremlin dumped sand into the gas tank. Three, maybe four months ago." She was exhausted and covered with mud from the knees and crutch grips down. Jake Street, on the other hand, was exasperatingly clean. He seemed to be enjoying this expedition.

"I remember the claim. Does Donaldson drive the backhoe? Or maybe Timo Martinez?"

Elisa rolled her eyes. "Gerald can barely drive his automatic Firebird. I don't know if Timo has ever driven anything. *I* drive the backhoe. You think that just because a piece of machinery is big, it takes a man to handle it?"

He smiled then, and she realized that in her aggravation she'd cornered him with her crutches up against the backhoe. He held up two fingers in a peace sign.

"I believe that women can handle all kinds of things," he murmured, his voice suddenly husky.

His eyes were suddenly so soft, so welcoming, and his face so near... and then his gaze shot to a spot over her shoulder and he let go of her.

He cleared his throat. Elisa squelched an urge to fan her flaming face. They both turned to watch a man approaching. The newcomer wore the unlikely garb of a Texas cowboy.

"Know him?" Street asked.

"Unfortunately," she groaned.

Not waiting for Elisa to introduce him, the man thrust out a hand toward Street, a business card neatly in place between two fingers. Did he keep them up the sleeve of his cowboy shirt?

"Walt Baker," he said. "Baker Development."

Baker's southern drawl seemed thicker than ever today. He was probably laying it on extra heavy for Street's benefit. From Tiffany, Elisa had learned that Walt Baker and his wife Cissie actually hailed from Ellensburg, a small town in the foothills east of the Cascades. And while cowboy garb was not out of place in Ellensburg, Southern accents most certainly were. The pretense was one reason she disliked the man. The other was that his condo developments were burying the rich farming soil of her valley under high-rises and putting greens.

She'd never seen Baker without a cowboy hat, and now, up close, she realized why. His gaze was at most a few inches above hers. Sans high-heeled boots and high-crowned hat, the developer was a Bantam rooster. "You didn't have to come all the way out here, Mister Baker."

He rocked back on his heels, slipped a little in the muck, recovered his footing, then smoothed his dignity by adjusting his hat. "Of course I did, Miss Louisa."

"Elisa."

"And you'll call me Walt." He smiled, displaying perfect teeth that were a shade too white to be natural.

"I doubt that," she said. Out of the corner of her eye, she noticed the hint of a smile flash across Jake Street's features.

The brightness of Baker's own smile flickered only briefly. "You're laid up and all." He gestured at her cast."And it appears you didn't hear about my offer."

"Offer?" Street was instantly all ears.

"I heard," she told Baker. "I'm not interested."

Walter Baker turned to Jake Street. "Three million dollars," he told him. "That's what I'm offering for this prime piece of real estate."

Street whistled a low note.

Baker nodded. "Well, it's not so prime, now, of course." He looked pointedly in the direction of the charred building. "Especially after last night." He nodded toward the group of buildings just beyond the wooden fence. "But as you can see, this is condo country. That's Baker's Acres right over there. We'll start framing building number ten tomorrow, right in that gap there. We lucked out in the quake; only one chimney down and half a dozen cracks to plaster over. That's quality building for you. We'll be opening in a couple of weeks."

Elisa pressed her lips together to keep from blurting out something she'd regret. Before Baker's Acres—a stupid name if she'd ever heard one—had spread like a fungus, the property had been a small organic farm. They'd sold the best herbs and salad greens. In the springtime, asparagus that would melt in your mouth. In late summer, the sweetest, firmest tomatoes. And now the place would produce only yuppies and golf balls.

The two men chatted for a while, Street seemingly enraptured by the idea of a condo complex complete with golf course, and Baker more than happy to carry on about it. Elisa sagged between her crutches. Would this day never end? Had she only imagined that magnetic moment between her and Street a few minutes ago? Now it didn't seem even remotely possible. Must be the Charlie factor; all her sister's suggestions about the investigator's attractions.

The developer finally wound down and thought to inquire about his audience. "You're in the nursery business, too, then?"

"Insurance," Street said. "I'm here checking earthquake damage."

"Aha!" Baker winked at her. "Louisa, this is your big chance to score twice. Collect on the insurance, and then sell the whole shebang for a whopping profit."

Before she could respond to that outrageous suggestion, Baker said, "My offer stands for thirty days. That should give you plenty of time to think about it. Considering the state of things around here, I'm being more than generous." He tipped his hat and strode away.

Street watched him go. "Collect on the insurance, and then sell for a whopping profit," he echoed. The twinkle was definitely gone from his eyes now, replaced by cool suspicion.

She sighed dramatically. "You got me. That was my plan all along. And I orchestrated the earthquake, too. Not only am I amazingly brilliant, but I also have godlike powers."

He shot her a look of exasperation. "Why is your property is the only one in the area that is experiencing vandalism? And why now?"

"Don't you think I've asked myself that a million times?" Her voice cracked on the word million. Embarrassing. But she kept her gaze locked with his even while she felt her face flush.

He looked away first. "Okay, let's assume for now that you're not the Gremlin."

"Thank you." Her words dripped with sarcasm.

"I need to talk to Timo Martinez. Can you get him here tomorrow?"

Now she'd have to admit it. "I told you I last saw him on the day of the quake. I haven't been able to locate him since then. His phone's not working."

"Really?"

Was she misinterpreting or did Street suddenly sound hopeful? "It's not like Timo to simply disappear. He's a workaholic. I'm worried that something's happened to him."

"I'll find him." He tucked his clipboard under his arm and took a step closer. "Same time tomorrow, shall we say? Would you like some help back to your car?"

"It's a truck. And what are you going to do, carry me?"

He put his face so close to hers that she could see the tiny gold flecks in his blue eyes again. "Would you like me to?"

Oh jeez, would she ever. There must be something seriously wrong with her, some logic connection the earthquake had jarred loose. "No, Mr. Street, I wouldn't like you to carry me. I'm fine on my own."

"Okay." He strode off through the broken vegetation, following the trail made by Walt Baker.

Elisa was grateful that Street's inquisition was over, but she was a bit sorry to see the man go. With so many plants fallen, the fields seemed vast and empty; and with the sun setting, the breeze was cold. It blew right through her sweatpants and jacket, whipped her hair around her face. She surveyed the acres of broken trees, the shrubs and smaller plants, half uprooted, some leafless. The still-smoking ruins of her office and apartment.

What would she do if Atlas Security didn't pay the claims? She'd have to take out a huge loan to restock; rebuild. She'd have to use the land as collateral. If Baker was right, her property was worth millions.

Her thoughts paused on Baker. A better suspect than Gerald. The man wore cowboy boots. He was overseeing the work on Baker's Acres, he cruised by Langston Green regularly. He'd know when the place was occupied and when it was not.

Timo pressed one eye to the crack of light next to the tool shed door. Elisa Langston was so close, he could almost reach out and touch her. She looked sad, and in pain. Her leg must hurt, but he was glad to see that she seemed otherwise all right. The nursery was a mess: there was plenty of work to be done here, but he didn't dare approach her now.

Trouble was following him. The six friends he was going to hire for Elisa had disappeared, just like his mother. And now there was this man Street, who acted like a cop even if he didn't wear a uniform.

Elisa's partner Gerald was not on his side, either. The guy looked at him like he was a mangy dog that wandered in from the alley. The Chinese guy that ran the greenhouse seemed nice enough, but Timo doubted that he could keep secrets.

Worst of all, he couldn't go to Elisa. She didn't even realize how much danger she herself was in. Timo had a fleeting vision of his father's body dropping into the dust of their garden, of the pool of blood that leaked out all around him. He swallowed hard. Was burning Elisa's house the worst thing? Or would there be even worse things to come?

A chill ran down his spine at the memory of his name coming out of Street's mouth, the way the tall man promised, "I'll find him."

Jake drove back to his condo in the Ballard area of Seattle, his mind barely registering the bumper-to-bumper traffic on the streets and the floating bridge. Why, in heaven's name, had he grabbed Elisa Langston? She'd reached out for him first, but what was his rationale for holding her in his arms? If she complained to his boss, he'd be fired for sexual harassment. He'd never done anything like that before. He'd never *wanted* to do anything like that before. And then there was the second time. He'd have had his lips on hers if that cowboy developer hadn't shown up.

He'd wanted to embrace that woman since he'd first seen her fifteen years ago. Although she stood only a fraction over five feet tall, Elisa was no child. She was curvaceous, sturdy, without an ounce of fat on her compact frame. A Latina wildcat. He shouldn't have held her like that. But he also had the notion that she hadn't exactly hated his touch.

He shifted uncomfortably in the car seat. Why was he getting aroused at the mere memory of how Elisa Langston had felt in his arms? He'd lusted after her before, wanted to prove to her that he could be her hero. Instead, she'd shown him up, along with all his friends. Humiliating.

Was he never going to get over that silly escapade? He'd been a kid then. Now he was a man. He straightened and loosened his grip on the wheel, tried to relax his tense shoulder muscles. If he'd crossed the line in the way he'd touched her, he knew he'd also crossed it a couple of times during his questioning of her. *These are clients*, he could hear his boss telling him: *until you're sure they're criminals, treat them with respect.* Instead, he'd accused Elisa of being an arsonist. He kept falling into his old detective habits of trying to provoke confessions from people.

He didn't really want to believe that Elisa was a vandal and an arsonist. There was a lot of evidence pointing to this Timo Martinez. As a former cop, he was well aware of just how much trouble teenagers could get up to. He'd be a rich man today if he had a hundred bucks for every time parents swore that their little Johnny or Raul or Leroy simply *couldn't* have committed a crime. As for motive, there was the missing money. A teenager was definitely capable of torching a building to cover up a theft of twelve hundred dollars. If Martinez had stolen the cash, it was no wonder the kid had disconnected the phone and vanished. While Elisa was still on the suspect list, Timo Martinez was currently suspect number 1.

And there were other candidates as well. Gerald Donaldson seemed an odd duck. And Baker had been very definite about wanting to get his hands on Langston Green. He made a mental list. Get his old partner Valetti to run some names through the department computer system for him. Check for other incidents of vandalism or arson within ten miles. Keep up with the results of the Fire Department investigation. The odds of retrieving any usable fingerprints from the match-book or cigarette remains were slim, but there was the ghost of a chance that they might nail the arsonist that way. Ask around the neighborhood, find out if anyone had seen anything that might lead to identifying Elisa's Gremlin. Interview all the Langston Green staff.

Most important, tomorrow he'd stick to the job, keep his hands on the clipboard and off Elisa Langston. "Maintain your professionalism, Detective Street," he cautioned himself aloud.

But no, that was wrong as well. He could no longer call himself Detective. He was just a Mister, like every other man on the street. He gripped the wheel hard. The good old days seemed so long ago. But he had hope that he'd get them back soon.

~

After a messy shower with the shower curtain wrapped around her cast, Elisa pulled on one of Charlie's sweaters, rolling up the sleeves. Her own jeans and turtlenecks might be old and worn, but at least they fit. All of her clothes, except for her boots and filthy canvas jacket, were ashes now. As were all her books. The Guatemalan pottery her mother had left behind. Her thoughts echoed Street's: Why me? Why now? Quelling a pang of self-pity, she splashed her face with cold water.

Charlie and Gail were preparing supper in the kitchen and wanted to know all about the fire. "Oh, that beautiful old house where Terry was born," Gail whimpered. Elisa couldn't look at her stepmother's sad face for fear that they'd both burst into tears.

"The arson specialist was out there for a couple of hours," she told them.

"Arson?" Gail's voice rose nervously.

"I'm sure the investigation's just a formality," Elisa reassured her. "It was more likely an unlucky combination of friction and spilled lamp oil."

Gail put her hand over Elisa's on the table top. "The insurance will pay for the damage, won't it?"

"Assuming that Investigator Street signs off on our claim," Elisa said. "He's being—" she started to say *a horse's ass*, then changed for her stepmother's benefit—"exceptionally thorough."

"You were alone all afternoon with Jake Street?" Charlie's eyebrows wiggled suggestively.

The last thing Elisa wanted to talk about was the insurance investigator. What could she possibly say? One minute she wanted to punch him and the next she wanted to kiss him. "He's making me account for every single plant. So many are too badly damaged to sell, at least this year. I don't know if we'll be able to carry them over until next summer." She swallowed against the growing lump in her throat.

"You'll put it back together, Elisa." Gail patted her shoulder. Charlie chimed in, "You can handle it."

Elisa bit her tongue to keep from screaming. When she didn't respond to their assurances, Charlie quietly asked, "You *can* keep the shops supplied, can't you?"

Her father had been a rock. She'd never seen him break down. *Langstons never give up.*

"No problem," she told them. Weary of pretending to be upbeat, she carried the remainder of her dinner to her father's old recliner in the den, where the footrest supported her cast. Using the remote, she switched on the television to catch up on the news. In her drugged state in the hospital, she'd slept through most of the earthquake stories over the last four days.

"The biggest news story today is one that didn't happen," The reporter intoned, staring earnestly at the camera lens. "We'll be back in just a moment to tell you all about it."

Elisa leaned back in the chair to wait for the story of the news that didn't happen. Within minutes, she was out.

Chapter 8

At six-thirty, the kitchen coffeemaker clicked on. Charlie or Gail had covered her with a blanket, and Simon was sharing it. He leapt from her lap and stalked to the back door, yowling, reminding her that dawn was prime rodent-hunting time. "We'll go out in a few minutes, when it's light," she promised him. "I can't run the risk of losing you in the dark."

The cat beseeched her with his glass-green eyes. She shook her head. He turned, stretched, and raked the back door with his claws.

"Oh, great. Thanks a bunch." She pulled herself out of the chair and lumbered into the kitchen to inspect the damage. Having made his point, Simon returned and took her place in the recliner, curling up in the nest of comforter. "I know you want to go back to the nursery. I want to go home, too." But all that now waited for her at Langston Green were problems. And a handsome but intimidating insurance investigator.

Charlie padded in, wearing rose-colored slippers and a matching quilted robe, her blond hair somehow elegantly tousled by sleep. Yawning, she stretched extravagantly, raising her slim arms above her head.

"Coffee?" Elisa retrieved two mugs from the cupboard. She filled them, added milk, and handed the rose-colored mug to her sister.

"Did I hear that cat in here?"

Elisa kept her gaze away from the back door. "Did you?"

"Where is he?"

"In my bedroom?"

"He'd better stay there." With coffee in hand, Charlie sleepily wandered back toward her bedroom without spying the scratches on the door. Elisa examined them. Nothing that some fine sandpaper and some touch-up stain wouldn't cure; she'd bring some back with her from the nursery. She spent a few minutes with Simon outside in the cold morning air before capturing him again. He reluctantly followed her back to her old bedroom.

"Litter box." She pointed toward the plastic basin filled with clay pellets. "Why can't you use one like other cats?"

Simon's green-eyed stare was as uncomprehending as if she were speaking Croatian.

"I promise," she told him. "I will get you back to Langston Green." She could get Peter Nguyen to feed Simon. But would the cat miss her so much that he'd wander away? She couldn't bear it if he disappeared again.

Elisa parked herself at Charlie's computer. This game she was playing with Jake Street had been, so far, all to his advantage. He knew all about her; she had nothing on him. Except for that lucky guess about the cop background. Now it was time to level the playing field.

She pulled up her favorite search engine, typed in "Jacob Street." At first she got a list of worthless leads: she had no idea there were so many streets named Jacob and Jacobson. She added "+police" and finally scored a list of newspaper articles from the *Seattle Times*. She decided to go through them in chronological order, first opening the one titled "Youth Killed in Police Shootout."

The incident had happened a little over two years ago. After a drive-by shooting, several police cars had chased the suspects' car until it plowed into a parked vehicle. The occupants wore the insignias of a well-known gang. One of the gang members leapt from the car as Detectives Street and Valetti closed in. The boy emptied two rounds from a stolen pistol into Valetti before Detective Street, although wounded himself, stopped the boy with a bullet to the chest.

The shooter had been only fourteen years old, and there was a follow-up article that highlighted the kid's youth and his unfortunate death at the hands of a police officer. And then another. And a study of teenagers killed by police across the nation. Jake Street had been tried in the newspapers.

Finally, an article stated that Detective Jake Street's actions that night had been deemed by an investigatory board to be justified, and he'd returned to active duty. His partner, Paul Valetti, was still convalescing at this point, five months after the shooting.

After a couple of angry letters to the editor, there was nothing more for two months. Then a police-support organization had named Detective Benjamin Jacob Street "Officer of the Year" due to his heroic actions in defending his partner. The furor had started all over again, but then seemed to peter out after a few months.

Now she understood how a police detective might end up as an insurance investigator. Elisa shut down the computer and dressed for work. On her way to the nursery, she drove the Langston Green van down the street where she'd last seen Timo, past the Valley Café. Men looking for work often stood outside, hoping that someone would stop and offer them a temporary job. She'd assumed that this was where Timo would meet his six men. But today the sidewalk and outdoor tables were empty.

Had all the usual job seekers found employment in the after-quake cleanup? Was Timo with them? Who would know? She racked her brains. Only one place occurred to her, sort of a local hangout for Spanish-speakers, where information was shared and friends from other countries kept the memories alive. She'd check it tonight.

She worked through the lunch hour at the desk in the greenhouse, coming up with a plan of action to get the nursery back into business. Langston Green would have to remain closed for at least a week, cleaning up and salvaging what they could. That would push them to late September. Then there'd be a long dry stretch until Thanksgiving, and then the Christmas season, selling potted chrysanthemums, poinsettias, forced paperwhites and amaryllis, and, oddly enough, orchids: for some reason people got an itch to try growing tropical flowers during the short winter days in the Pacific Northwest.

After spring sales, Christmas was Langston Green's biggest money-maker. And the money was more important than ever this year. As usual, they'd set up display tables at the front of the greenhouse, string tiny lights along the metal ribs of the building. Elisa frowned. Christmas lights and flapping plastic: that would never do. The glass panels had to be repaired as soon as possible. She needed that insurance settlement *now*. Could she press Street for an advance payment? Fat chance.

She stared at the photo on the wall above Peter's desk. In the picture, taken three years ago, her gray-suited father held center stage, a glass raised in his right hand. His merry gaze was on Peter Nguyen, who clinked his own champagne flute against Terry Langston's. And Gerald and Beth and Elisa were there, too, in party clothes, laughing, joining in the toast. All the permanent staff of Langston Green. Everybody looked happy. She was glad her father couldn't see his business now.

The office seemed way too quiet. Beth Nguyen was back, helping Peter with the greenhouse plants. But where the heck was Gerald? She dialed his home phone number.

He answered on the third ring. "What?" He sounded as grumpy as she felt.

"It's Elisa. I'm just checking in. I'm working in the office of the greenhouse." Hint, hint. She imagined him sipping a cup of coffee and perusing the newspaper, maybe doing research for the investment seminars he and Tiffany attended in the evenings. "Having a nice day at home?"

"I'm having a *stupendous* day. Wasserman deigned to release a few files, and I'm sitting at my kitchen table trying to piece together an inventory list for the office contents. My condo smells like a trash incinerator."

Elisa tightened her fingers around the phone cord. Why did she always assume the worst about Gerald?

"I don't suppose you kept a list of the contents of your apartment?" he asked.

"Uh, no. Just assume basic furniture and contents for a one-bedroom apartment. Thanks, Gerald." She hung up quickly, feeling guilty now.

Jake Street was fifteen minutes late today. The sympathy she'd felt for him that morning evaporated. So what if he'd had a hard time as a cop? Now he was an insurance investigator. How nice it must be to have everyone cowering before him, to keep schedules as he saw fit, to have everything happen for *his* convenience.

She could use a little convenience right now. How on earth was she going to whip this nursery into shape again? In her present condition, she could take half an hour to re-pot a single plant. She had to find field help. The summer employees had agreed to put in a few hours on Saturday and Sunday, but the short autumn days didn't allow time for outdoor work after school on weekdays. According to the agencies, all the other casual labor had been swallowed up for earthquake repair work elsewhere. If only Timo and his six *hombres fuertes* would magically show up. She thought about where he might have gone, doodled a few notes on her calendar.

She hobbled to the bathroom. When she emerged, she stopped just outside the door. Jake Street was thumbing through her desk calendar. "What do you think you're doing?"

He straightened, but his expression remained impassive.

"Waiting for you."

They spent the afternoon as they had the previous one, taking inventory in the fields, arguing about value and whether or not plants could be saved. The difference was that, even though she slipped a few times, Jake Street made no move to touch her. In fact, he rarely even looked at her. Today, he'd clearly made up his mind to be all business. At one point, he said, "I think you're more optimistic than you're letting on."

The man was exasperating. "What makes you say that?" she asked.

He pointed to the blueberries they'd inventoried yesterday. "You said half those bushes would probably not live."

Today all the blueberries were neatly repotted, broken branches trimmed, standing in soldierly rows. Damp soil showed evidence of watering. The beautyberries too were restored to a semblance of order.

How in the world had that happened since yesterday? Peter? She doubted it: he had his hands full putting the greenhouse back in order. Beth? No, as far as she knew, Beth never left the greenhouse, either. Gerald? Even less likely. Could he have hired someone? Doubtful. She frowned. She was supposed to be running this place, and she didn't have a clue what was going on out here. She glanced at the nearest surveillance camera. She'd have to check the tape later.

Street was staring at her. There was no way she'd admit her confusion to him. "Just because the plants have been repotted doesn't mean that they'll live," she said. "We won't know for a week or so."

"No problem," he replied smoothly. "I'll just delay submitting my report for a week, then."

Was he deliberately trying to drive her crazy? She needed the money as soon as possible. She grabbed a fistful of fabric at the front of his windbreaker. "Now look here, Street—"

"You obviously can't keep your hands off me." His fingers

closed over hers, and he smiled. "You're not going to threaten me, are you, Elisa?" he asked in a quiet voice. It sounded like a dare.

She caught her breath and pulled her hand out from beneath his. She stepped back. "Of course not, Mr. Street. I think we both know who has the power here."

She meant that he was in control, of course. But as he studied her smoldering eyes and felt the voltage ricocheting through his body from her touch, Jake was not so sure. He was in dangerous territory again. Good thing it was nearly dark, time to put the next step in his plan into effect. "We're done for today," he said.

The food court at Crossroads Mall was lively, as usual. Tonight was Open Mike Night: anyone could sign up for a half-hour of time before the audience. When Elisa walked in, a guitarist occupied the small stage.

Other musicians jammed at tables near the other end of the court. And in between, the place was filled with a buzz of multiple languages. Thai, Greek, East Indian, Vietnamese, Russian, Japanese, and Korean restaurants attracted customers, along with stands offering hamburgers and pizza. Families and groups of friends clustered around white plastic tables while aproned staff cleared away abandoned dishes. At one end of the mall, a group of men moved pieces of a giant chess set across the floor.

The Pacífico del Sur Mexican restaurant was strategically centered. Those who sat inside its low walls could order beer, but even those outside could watch the big screen television, which usually featured one of the Spanish-language talk shows or a *fútbol* game from south of the border. This was the informal center of the Spanish-speaking community on the east side of Lake Washington. Odds were good that someone here might know Timo.

Elisa ordered a plate of hummus and pita bread from the Middle Eastern restaurant and then took a seat near the pickup counter. As she waited for her order, she studied the crowd at Pacífico del Sur, trying to determine who might be best to approach.

Three young men laughed together at one table. Two Latinas in jeans and tight sweaters sat outside the beer boundary, sipping Cokes and glancing shyly over the low wall at the men. A knot of older men alternately cheered and booed at the soccer game on television. The camaraderie of the scene made Elisa feel a little lonely. She was Latina, but not part of this crowd. And she was only half Latina. Half Langston. What did the whole add up to? She'd never been sure.

A trio of tough teen boys strutted through the crowd. Their extra-large jeans barely clung to their hips, exposing white jockey shorts between their waistbands and red tee shirts. Two of the boys wore blue bandanas rolled and tied around their foreheads; the other had one knotted around his bicep. The crowd watched them with disapproval.

The youth who worked in the Middle Eastern booth yelled her order number. She waved a crutch in the air and he brought over her tray. Using a wedge of fresh pita bread, she scooped up a dollop of creamy hummus.

Then she saw him. Sitting off to one side, close to the stand that sold pizza by the slice. He wore a grimy baseball cap and his usual denim jacket. In front of him was only a red plastic glass, the type in which all beverages were served here. When one of the young toughs raised a hand in a split-fingered greeting, Timo quickly glanced away.

The boy looked physically okay, at least what she could see of him. But his eyes were sad, and his shoulders hunched defensively. His clothes looked as if he'd slept in them. His gaze wandered the room. When it reached her table, his dark eyes fixed on her with a sudden jolt. He stiffened in his chair.

She gestured for him to come over. After a long moment, he rose from his chair, studied the room around him, and then maneuvered his way through the crowd, narrowly avoiding a collision with a couple of Vietnamese kids playing tag among the plastic furniture.

Elisa patted the chair next to her. Timo cautiously perched on the edge. His eyes brimmed with tears. She wanted to hug him, but knew that he'd flee at her touch. Now was not the time to question him about the disconnected phone and fake address.

"*Qué pasó*, Timo? I've been worried about you."

A tear escaped from his right eye. He quickly smeared it over his cheek as if scratching an itch. "Señorita Langston—" That was as far as he got before his voice broke.

"Elisa, remember? I need you to come work for me again," she said, filling in the gap. "And I could sure use those six *hombres fuertes* now." When he didn't respond, she put her hand over his. "Are you okay? Is your mother okay?"

He struggled for control. "I ... my mother ..." He stopped, gulped, pulled his hand from beneath hers, and started again. "Señorita Langston, the money—"

Suddenly his eyes grew round with alarm. He scooted his chair back. She followed his gaze to a familiar tall figure standing near the back mall entrance, the door closing behind him. Jake Street. His eyes quickly zeroed in on her and Timo.

"Timo, it's okay, I'll—"

But she was talking to the boy's back. Timo disappeared toward the front exit before she could push herself up from her chair. Dodging a worker with a cartload of dirty dishes, Street ran after the youth, rushing through the door into the parking lot. Elisa knew there was no way she could make it to the door in time to watch the action. She chewed a mouthful of pita and hummus while she wondered what was happening out there.

After a couple of minutes, she had her answer. Street entered through a side door and strode toward her, his expression dark. The crowd parted before him as though they didn't want to be touched. He threw himself into the chair Timo had vacated. "So," he said, unzipping his jacket, "We meet again."

"What a coincidence," she said wryly. "Are you tailing me?"

He managed to summon a surprised expression. "I came to hear the music, get a bite to eat."

"All the way from Ballard?" She'd looked up his home address in the phone book. She briefly enjoyed the startled expression on his face before it faded to wariness.

"Why not?" he said coolly. "I'm sorry I didn't get to meet your friend."

"You scared him away."

He splayed his fingers on the table top. "Timoteo Martinez, I presume. Why did he run?"

She wiped her fingers on a paper napkin. "Let's see ... maybe he's afraid you're going to try to pin some crime on him, like stealing money. Or setting a fire or trashing a nursery."

"But if he's innocent—"

"He's only a boy, Street." She'd been so close to finding out what was going on. "If a big thug started chasing me, I'd run, too."

"So you think I'm a thug?" He ran his fingers through his hair. "I shaved and everything."

"So you're a tidy thug," she said.

"You say he's a boy. I thought he was nineteen. That's what his papers say, right?"

"Nineteen is a boy," she told him.

He was quiet for a minute, his eyes sober. Was he thinking about the dead fourteen-year-old? "I checked the address Martinez listed on his employment application," he finally said. "It's a tennis court."

She widened her eyes. "Really?"

He leaned so close that she could smell his aftershave. "Elisa, I'm trying to help you. What's up with you and this kid?"

So they were using first names now. He sounded sympathetic. But it was probably an act. Would he have chased Timo if he believed her when she'd told him Timo was innocent?

"I try to look out for all my employees, Jake." She ate another bite of hummus and pita.

He watched her in stony silence. Was he hoping she'd reveal some guilty secret under his scrutiny? She was overly conscious of his hands on the table a foot away; she could feel the heat of his leg close to hers under the table. Why couldn't she be sitting here enjoying the music with this attractive man instead of having this—whatever it was? Battle of wits?

She waited him out, matching his silence with hers. On the television set, the team in blue jerseys scored a goal, and the residents of the Mexican restaurant cheered. The music stage had been taken over by a folk group performing a children's song with a lot of animal noises.

Had Timo ever gotten the chance to be a child? She doubted it. He seemed to have the weight of the world on his shoulders. Clearly, Timo had secrets. Had he stolen the petty cash? Was that what he was going to say? Still, even if he'd taken the money, her heart felt lighter knowing that he was alive and healthy. Maybe Gerald was right: maybe she did have an affinity for 'strays.' She cast a sideways look at Jake. There was no way she could share these thoughts with him.

He shifted in his chair, making the legs squeak against the tile floor. "Well," he finally said, "I can see that I'll get nowhere with you tonight."

"And here I thought you came for the music and the food." She smiled sweetly. "See you tomorrow?"

He stood. "We should be able to wrap up the inventory in one more afternoon, don't you think? Then I'll be able to figure a total for the fields and greenhouse, present it to my management for payment."

So he had been bluffing about waiting a week? "Good. Then maybe I can finally get my business back on track. But what about the replacement money for the main building?"

"That," he said, "Will take more time. We have to wait for the Fire Department report."

Elisa and Timo Martinez were in cahoots. The way their dark heads had bent close to each other, the meaningful looks exchanged by their brown eyes. Partners? In the crime or the cover-up? The kid had to be the key to the mystery. Jake pressed a button on his home speed dial to connect with a direct number within the Seattle Police Department.

"Valetti."

"It's Jake."

"If you're calling to get my opinion on the yacht or the BMW, I say go with the car. Nobody likes to sail in the rain."

"I'll keep that in mind," Jake said. When his former partner wasn't razzing him about Jake's new salary, he was carrying on about how nice it must be to forego required annual fitness and shooting tests. "How goes the battle in Seattle?" he asked.

"Like wrestling an octopus, man. And it keeps growing new arms." A female voice in the background said something about an interrogation. "In a minute," Valetti answered.

"Is that Lakotis?"

"Yep. My new teammate."

Sherry Lakotis. A leggy woman with honey-blonde hair. And no shortage of brains. Jake had invited her out for drinks a couple of times, but she'd slipped away each time before any real heat had built up between them. He supposed that was smart of her, too, given his toxic position in the department at the time. She'd been promoted to detective to fill his spot.

How he missed the dance of investigating a criminal case,

the banter of the squad room. "You and Sherry will make a good team," he told Valetti. "Not to mention that she's a lot better looking than I am. You're moving up in the world."

"Yeah, she's magical. She walks in a room—presto, I'm invisible," Valetti chuckled.

Maybe he should ask Sherry out again, Jake thought. They could swap police stories. She could take his mind off the Latina client he should be investigating, not lusting after.

Valetti interrupted his thoughts. "How's the insurance game?"

"It sucks." Jake tried to think of something amusing to add, but drew a blank. Should he tell his old partner that he'd applied to the FBI? No, he decided, imagining the humiliation if it didn't work out. "Say, Paul, can you run a name for me? It's a juvenile, I doubt if you'll score, but you never know." He pulled the information from his pocket and read it off. "Martinez, Timoteo." He spelled it. "Yeah, no kidding: Tim Smith. No clue on middle initial. According to the info I have, he's nineteen, from Margarita, New Mexico, now living in the Woodinville area. But none of that may be accurate. He looks younger than nineteen to me. He might be illegal."

"That should make it *much* easier," his old partner groaned.

"And I'd like you to run Gerald Robert Donaldson and Walter Francis Baker, too." Jake gave Valetti the specifics on Elisa's partner and on the developer.

"This'll take awhile," Valetti warned. "I'll get back to you as soon as I have something."

"I owe you."

"Never." Valetti's voice slid down the scale a notch. "It'll be the other way around, for the rest of my life."

Jake's throat tightened. He missed spending days with his partner, sharing experiences, fears, and the occasional victories of detective work. "You're not going to get all touchy-feely on me, are you, Valetti?"

"Gotta go, wise-ass. There's a ... um ... citizen waiting for me in the interview room."

"You wouldn't want to keep a citizen waiting," Jake said.

There was an uncomfortable pause, then Valetti said, "You know, you didn't have to leave."

Jake switched the phone to his other ear. "Yeah, I did." They'd had this conversation a dozen times. The Chief of Police had made it clear that Jake took their deal to quit or they'd find a way to force him out. Not your fault, the Chief acknowledged, shaking his hand; but you're a liability the department can no longer afford.

Valetti cleared his throat. "Let's share a couple brews sometime soon, partner."

"The sooner the better." Jake hung up. On his way to his kitchen to scrounge the meal he hadn't eaten at Crossroads Mall, he passed by the dangly plant—a philodendron, he now knew. The heart-shaped green-and-white leaves were dusty and curling at the edges. At the tap, he filled a glass with water for it. As he watched the liquid rise to the top, he reflected that he was getting awfully soft when a pot full of wilted greenery could make him feel guilty.

Chapter 9

After three hours of work the next afternoon, Elisa and Jake finished the inventory of Langston Green's fields, ending up in the far southwest corner by the new road that passed the nursery to enter Baker's Acres. While a couple of buildings on the outskirts were still in the framing stage, the center of the condo complex was nearing completion, just as Baker had bragged. Today, under the developer's supervision, workmen were hanging an "Opening Soon" banner across the building nearest the street.

The real estate cowboy caught sight of the two of them. He touched his hat and waved enthusiastically. Street held up a hand in acknowledgement. Elisa turned her back and surveyed her domain instead.

The restored area had grown larger overnight, now encompassing a patch of fruit trees that had been staked upright and heeled into the soft earth. Yesterday, after Jake had left, she'd checked the tape from the video camera out in the field. It had shown nothing, but there was a time gap in which the camera had not been operating: someone had shut the power off while working in the field. She had arrived just after dawn this morning, hoping to encounter her Good Samaritan, but he'd already come and gone, and she hadn't been able to distinguish any footprints aside from hers and Timo's and Jake's in the aisles between plants.

"I'll work up the total and get back to you." Street tapped his pen on his stack of inventory sheets. "That's a lot of plants."

"And you thought it was just a hobby," she chided him.

They began the long trek back to the greenhouse and parking lot.

Jake walked behind her, noticing that today Elisa had used a piece of brown twine to tie her hair back. While she had grown more agile on the crutches in the past couple of days, she was still slowed by the soft earth and the plant debris everywhere. He followed her closely, trying not to reach out every time her crutches slipped.

At one point she sidestepped and jerked her head over her shoulder toward him. "Look out."

A few inches in front of his left boot lay a slender snake, dark gray with light blue horizontal stripes. Startled, Jake stepped backward and nearly fell over a potted plant. His sudden movement frightened the snake as well, which slithered toward a pile of flagstones.

Elisa's brown eyes glinted with amusement. "It's only a garter snake."

He watched the tail end of the reptile disappear into a gap in the stacked stones. How did he always manage to embarrass himself in front of her? He felt like he was in high school again.

She grinned. "I didn't want you to step on him. They're slow this time of year. I need all the garter snakes I can get. They're one of the few critters around here that eat slugs."

"Most people just use slug bait."

Her chin came up. "I don't use poisons. It amazes me how blithely people spread them around. Do they honestly think that only slugs eat that stuff?"

"I thought they made non-toxic slug bait now."

After a brief pause, she blew out a breath and then said, "I'm sorry. Garden chemicals are a big gripe of mine. We do use non-toxic slug bait in the greenhouse. But not out here." She pushed a tendril of hair out of her face, adding a smudge of dirt to her cheek in the process. "I wouldn't want the snakes to go hungry."

As they walked on, Jake watched the ground carefully. Would a sane man find it sexy that a woman worried about snakes going hungry? What excuse could he use to see her tomorrow?

She stopped near the back of the greenhouse, in the middle of a particularly sad section of vines. Most had toppled, breaking their fragile trellis supports as well as their slender stems. Elisa picked up a section of broken vine covered with creamy white flowers. "Autumn clematis. Normally one of my best sellers this time of year."

He took the greenery from her, sniffed the blossoms. "Smells like honey." It was news to him that some plants bloomed when most were shedding their leaves. The notion seemed improbably romantic, that even as the days grew cooler and the nights grew longer, flowers opened to perfume the autumn air. He had a wild urge to tuck an ivory blossom into the thick black hair that spilled over Elisa's shoulders. Instead, he handed the plant back to her.

"What am I going to do with all this?" Her gesture took in the acres of mangled plants.

"How about a class on composting?" he suggested.

"Composting? Very funny." Was she imagining it, or was Street stalling, delaying his departure? Somehow, after the showdown at Crossroads Mall, they'd crossed an invisible line and become less formal with each other. Or maybe it was all the hours they'd spent together.

"You could do something for Thanksgiving," he suggested. "Let's see ... pumpkins, Indian corn ..."

"We don't sell pumpkins or Indian corn."

"I'm brainstorming, cut me some slack." He continued, "Turkey, dressing, cornucopia..."

"This is a nursery, remember? Besides, Thanksgiving is

nearly two months away. I need to come up with an idea right now."

"Halloween?" he suggested.

"Not usually a big day for plants, only for pumpkins." She shrugged. "I suppose I could get in a load of pumpkins. Maybe that'd bring people in. But Halloween's nearly a month away, too."

"I have it! Plant First Aid," he said.

She raised an eyebrow.

"You could teach people what's salvageable and what's not, how to cut back, prop up, re-pot, whatever. There are thousands of damaged trees and house plants out there right now."

He had a point. A class wasn't a bad idea at all. Maybe even a series of seminars. On crutches, she was next to useless in the field, but she could teach. But where? "I don't have a room for classes. It's too cold outside."

He pointed. "How about the barn? People love the rustic touch."

The barn had been built around 1900. It was definitely rustic, huge and solid, built of rough-hewn beams and thick cedar siding. The earthquake had knocked its walls only a couple of inches out of plumb. It had water and electricity. Part of it was used for storage, but most of the building was just a huge dusty cavern. With a few days of work, the unused space could be converted into a classroom. Maybe into offices, too, until she could replace the main building. It was a little annoying how Street had spotted this opportunity before she had.

"It might work," she said.

His idea of classes set her mind working at light speed. First, Plant Rescue, and yes, maybe even Composting. Several of Langston Green's competitors drew in customers with free seminars. Her mind raced ahead into the next few months.

"Beyond Cornucopia!" she blurted.

He looked at her as if she'd lost her mind.

"For Thanksgiving, I could do a class on creating living centerpieces. Beyond Cornucopia, that's what I could call it. And in December, a seminar on making Christmas gift containers." She could see it now, mixes of native ornamentals and seasonal flowers: when the blossoms died back, the other plants would still look decorative. And by packing a variety of plants into bright pots, she could move a lot of not-quite-perfect inventory. Plus, it might even be fun.

She felt like kissing him. Instead she gave his forearm a gentle squeeze. "Thank you."

Her whole face lit up. Her cheeks were accentuated by a blush and sparks flitted through her clear brown irises. At that moment, Jake knew Elisa was not the one damaging her business. Clearly, this petite dynamo loved Langston Green and her place in running it.

Inspired, he cupped his hands around her shoulders, bent down and pressed his lips to hers.

She kissed him back, but when he pulled her tighter, she drew back, her expression confused. "You always kiss clients you suspect of insurance fraud, Jake?"

"It's my way of determining their guilt or innocence, Elisa." This time he wrapped his arms around her and kissed her slowly, deeply, thoroughly. She dropped her crutches to clutch his arms and it was he who pulled back first.

"Innocent," he said decisively. "In matters of criminal behavior. In other matters, well, maybe not quite so innocent."

While still clutching his arm with one hand, Elisa bent to retrieve her crutches. If this was a new tactic to catch her off guard, it was working. When she stood erect again, she took one look at his smile and said, "Get a grip on yourself, Street."

"Yes, ma'am." He gave her that sappy two-fingered salute.

Then she was sure. "Oh, God, it *is* you, isn't it? Benjamin

Jacob Street. Little Benjie from the Adventurers Club."

He grinned wholeheartedly, showing the dimple in his right cheek. "I think you mean Boy Scouts."

She shook her head. "I was never a Boy Scout. The bureaucracy may have called us Explorer Scouts, but we called ourselves Adventurers, remember?"

Of course he remembered. Explorer Scouts, Search and Rescue Unit. Sixteen-year-old Elisa Langston, not wanting to acknowledge any division of the Boy Scouts, even one that admitted girls, had insisted on calling them the Adventurers Club and had promptly taken over as the student leader of their unit. She was the one who sent everyone else down when snow began to fly during a search mission on Tiger Mountain. When the Scouts regrouped at base camp, they'd discovered that Elisa was still somewhere up on the mountain.

Jake remembered well that night from his adolescence. The adults at base camp had insisted that none of the Scouts venture from their tents. Elisa was his idol, and he'd been sure that she was a dead idol, frozen forever in death like Juliet in the classic romance. But in the morning, instead of having to dig out her body, the Explorers met Elisa on the trail, stuttering from the cold but stumbling toward camp. In her arms, she held the missing three-year-old boy. Although they'd been glad to see her alive, many in the troop were secretly aggravated to be bested so overtly by a small sprout of a girl.

"You were always a bossy little thing," he told her now.

"You probably thought that because I was in charge." One of her sleek ebony brows rose slightly. "Don't you find it odd how that adjective—bossy—is never applied to male leaders?"

He quickly searched his memory for an account of a bossy male CEO or politician. There had to be one somewhere. Didn't there? The only so-called bossy celebrities that came to mind were Hillary Clinton and Martha Stewart, and that certainly didn't help his case. "Don't change the subject," he said.

"I thought that *was* the subject." Her full lips softened into a smile. "You were the one that brought it up."

How was it possible for such a tiny female to be simultaneously so attractive and so annoying? Not to mention so charmingly disheveled. He found himself staring at a strand of hair that had escaped from the right side of her center part, crossed over, and now dangled enticingly down her left cheek.

She tucked the strand behind her ear. "You were a grade behind me, weren't you? A year younger?"

Finally, an easy shot. "I still am a year younger," he happily reminded her.

It was unnerving to realize that this impressive example of manhood had known her during her awkward teenage years. But then, he'd been awkward, too. Underdeveloped, a regular little geek. When had he grown into this stunning specimen? She couldn't remember Benjie after the Tiger Mountain incident. "You dropped out of the club."

"The Scout *troop*," he corrected. "My family moved to Puyallup." He cocked his head. "So now you remember who I am."

She reached up to stroked one finger along the scar on his left temple. "I even know how you got this, Mr. Officer of the Year."

His face clouded over and he brushed her hand away. "How'd you learn about that?"

"I researched you on the 'net."

He rolled his eyes. "I'm on the *internet*?"

She shrugged. "*Seattle Times* archives. You clearly deserved the award."

He huffed out a breath and focused his gaze on the far horizon. "No one should get an award for killing."

He looked suddenly so morose that Elisa wanted to take him in her arms again. But he didn't really look as if he wanted to be comforted. He looked more like he wanted to break something. Or someone.

She leaned forward on her crutches and touched his hand. "We've come a long way since high school," she said. "I remember little Benjie Street—"

"It's Jake now. And I'm not so little anymore."

So true. Everything about him, from his broad muscular shoulders to his flat stomach to the sharp planes of his jaw, spoke of prime adult male. She was sure now that on the night of the earthquake, he *had* told her that she'd always been strong. But had he really called her *sweetheart*?

He pulled a small white cardboard box out of his jacket pocket. "Here."

She stared at it. What in the world?

He impatiently waved a hand in the air. "Open it, for heaven's sake."

She did. Inside was a beautiful silver and copper piece, delicate swirls of filigree surrounding a stylized bird. An exquisite barrette. "It's beautiful. But why—?"

"Because I can't stand it anymore." He thrust his clipboard at her. "Hold this."

Taking the barrette from her, he stepped around her. "I've seen you wearing paper clips, twist-ties, and a piece of baling wire in your hair. And this morning, it's some kind of string."

He deftly pulled the bow of twine from the crown of her head, spilling her long hair down her cheeks. Then his fingers gently stroked her scalp as he gathered up her tresses with both hands and clipped them at the crown with the new barrette. "There. Much better."

He stepped back into her line of vision, took the clipboard from her. "Nobody with such gorgeous hair should tie it back with string."

"Jake," she started, then realized she didn't have a clue what she intended to say next. *Gorgeous hair?*

She was thoroughly befuddled by this sudden twist in their relationship. A kiss and a gift? Out of the corner of her eye, she caught a flash of movement, and saw Gerald watching from behind a moisture-streaked greenhouse pane. Jake turned to look, too, and the three of them stared at each other for an uncomfortable moment before Gerald withdrew into the depths of the building.

She turned toward Jake, feeling like a teenager caught necking in the bushes. "Well," she said, but didn't get any further.

"There's no need to make a big deal out of it." He took the box out of her hands, stuck it back into his pocket, then turned halfway from her. "I'll be back in a couple of days, when the Fire Department report is in. Then I can give you a better idea of where you stand. In the meantime, I'll look for Martinez."

She stepped away from him, back into familiar territory. "Let me look for him, Jake. Why are you so determined that Timo's involved in this?"

"Why are you so adamant that he's not? What do you really know about him?"

She couldn't tell him about the Mayan accent, about the way Timo's smooth brown skin and sculptured face tugged at her heart. "I know that he's a hard worker. He's used to doing jobs outdoors. He knows plants."

"Did he come with references?"

She shook her head. "To be honest, I didn't ask. He showed up in May, said he wanted to work here. I always need good field hands." She looked at the mess around her. "I sure could use some now."

"If he's such a great employee, where is he?"

She sagged on her crutches. "That's why I think he's in trouble. Timo would never voluntarily miss work. You saw him yourself last night. He looked worried, didn't he?"

Jake snorted. "He was running too fast for me to tell."

"Look," she said. "Even if Timo did take the petty cash—and I'm not saying he did—he wouldn't burn me out."

His expression was skeptical.

"There's only one person I know who wants me out of business," she told him. "Walt Baker. Check him out."

"I'm looking into his background, too. I'm also checking all your employees." He put his hand on her shoulder. "I've got to go now. Watch your back, Elisa."

She bristled at his tone. "I can protect myself."

"Not against a true criminal, you can't," he said. "Vandalism, petty theft, monkeywrenching, major theft, arson." He ticked them off on his fingers. "You need to start taking this seriously. I worry about you. You think you're so tough, so smart. Has it even occurred to you that these crimes are escalating? That these attacks could be personal? What's next, murder?"

A sudden chill prickled through her scalp. "Who would want to murder me?"

His eyes were blazing now. "You need to think about that, long and hard. And like I said, watch your back."

An hour later, Jake pulled up to a hotel in the university district. He let the valet take his car, then straightened his jacket and tie before walking into the lobby.

A tingle of guilt crawled over him. Elisa Langston was a client. Even if she were innocent of any crime, even if he'd known her in the past, he shouldn't be leaping on her like a buck jumping a doe in mating season. Until the case was wrapped up, he needed to be dispassionate. He ran a finger across his lower lip, remembering the feel of her mouth on his. Then, mindful of hotel security cameras, he forced his features into a solemn façade. The last thing he needed was for the Feds to think he was a fool.

The desk clerk directed him to Conference Room B, where he was told to take a seat. Eight chairs lined the walls, but he was the only person waiting. A nearly empty carafe of coffee and multiple stained cups littered the table. He drained the dregs from the pot. Lukewarm. Abandoning the vile brew, he sat down, crossed his legs. He was clearly the last contestant of the day. Was that bad or good? He struggled to keep from drumming his fingers on the chair arm.

After ten minutes, a young African-American woman came to get him. He followed her to a door labeled Conference Room D, furnished with a small round table and comfortable leather chairs. Two of the seats were occupied by a gray-haired man and a younger Asian-looking fellow. The woman took the third, and indicated that Jake should sit in the fourth.

After introductions and offers of fresh coffee, the woman folded her arms and summarized the situation. "Mr. Street, we've reviewed your history. You were a detective with the Seattle Police Department, but then you chose to quit the force. Now you've got a good job, with much better pay than we could offer. Why do you want to be an FBI agent?"

This was it. This was his opportunity to get his self-respect back. He shoved the seductive image of Elisa Langston out of his thoughts, clasped his hands together on top of the table, and focused on the challenge at hand.

"I was forced out of the SPD; it was a back door agreement with the brass there to put out a political fire." He leaned forward. "I did nothing wrong, and I regret now that I did not stand my ground."

"Our records indicate that you retired a hero."

"Funny how you can be a hero and persona non grata at the same time. No municipal police department wants to touch me; they're afraid of attracting media attention. But I'm a damn good detective, and I want back in the game."

Chapter 10

Jake stuck his foot in the door before the grandmotherly woman could close it in his face. "Mrs. Renaldo, I'm sorry to bother you. I'm looking for Timo Martinez."

"Seemo!" the toddler on her hip squeaked.

"Shhh!" the woman hissed to the child. She looked back at him. "I don't know any Martinez."

"That's odd." He waved Timo's work application in the air. "He listed your phone as his contact number."

She glanced at it. "Not my number."

"It's your old number."

She put on an enlightened look. "Oh, Timo. I take messages for him once in a while. But he's gone now. All Martinez are gone."

"Where'd they go?"

Her shoulders quickly lifted and lowered. "No idea."

He tried a little misdirection. "Back to California? To where they're from?"

"Yes! Back to where they're from." She pursed her lips for a moment. "But I think they said *Nuevo Mexico*, not California."

"And all five of them went back?"

"The whole family," she said warily. "I don't have number or address."

"I'd like to speak to the building manager."

She pulled herself erect. "I *am* the manager. And I say no Martinez are here."

Clearly, he wouldn't get anything more out of her. Jake

thanked her and left. If Timo Martinez was as trustworthy as Elisa claimed, why was he hiding out?

After spending the better part of three days with Jake Street, Elisa felt like half her team was missing when he didn't show up for the rest of the week. He'd embraced her and then he'd just disappeared? She fingered the barrette he'd given her. *Gorgeous hair.* He'd told her to watch her back; that murder might be next on the Gremlin's calendar of events. Think about it, he said. How could she think about anything else? She found herself eyeing everyone with suspicion now: the mail carrier, the estimator who came to bid on greenhouse repairs, the driver of Gail's delivery van, even Beth and Peter Nguyen.

Jake was making her crazy. In every way. She smoothed a finger over her pursed lips. He'd accused her of arson and fraud, and then he'd kissed her? Just a 'Glad You Finally Recognized Me' kiss from little old Benjie? Or an 'I'll Show You the Difference' kiss from Jake? In any other context, it didn't make sense. Grilling her one minute, kissing her the next. Promising her the settlement for the greenhouse and plant stock, then telling her that the claim for the old home-stead building might never be settled. How was she supposed to act around him now? But then, he wasn't around at all, was he?

She straightened in her desk chair, aggravated with herself. Jake was out somewhere going about his business; she should be doing the same. Banishing thoughts of him, she made a few calls, then busied herself with plans for a class on salvaging damaged plants, along with ideas for holiday centerpieces, gift containers of mixed plants. It was time to stop wallowing and get back to work.

To her surprise, Gerald answered her call right away. By ten-thirty A.M., he sat across the desk from her in a folding chair, his steaming coffee cup opposite hers, a yellow tablet in front of him. Behind his glasses, his gray eyes were questioning.

"Classes?" he echoed. "But there's nowhere to hold them."

She clasped her hands together on top of the desk. "I'm remodeling the barn."

He blinked in surprise. "You'll never find anyone to work on it now."

"I already have." She tried not to gloat. "Remember the group of retired craftsmen we used a couple years ago to build displays? Since they're not listed in the yellow pages, it seems that they've been largely overlooked in the rush to repair earthquake damage."

Gerald's forehead creased. "Really?"

"Five of them will be here tomorrow morning to start the job."

He shook his head. "I don't know, Elisa. I understand you wanting to rebuild, but our cash flow ... well, that's the problem, partner. There is no cash flow." He sat back in his chair. "Did you even consider Walt Baker's offer?"

How could Gerald call her 'partner' in one breath and urge her to sell in the next? When he married Tiffany, he'd be Walt Baker's brother-in-law. Was it possible the two of them were conspiring against her?

"We're rebuilding." She stated it in a flat, purely informational tone. "We're starting classes. We're having a little get-together for the business community in two weeks."

"Get-together?" Gerald groaned.

"We need to let people know we're back in business." She tapped his blank notepad. "And if you no longer want do your job, Gerald, I'll find someone who will."

He raised his head. "You can't fire me. I'm a partner."

"Minor partner," she reminded him. "With a quarter vote."

His eyes narrowed. Elisa read resentment there, its jagged edges softened by another emotion. Regret? Envy? Guilt? She couldn't decipher it. "Are you in or are you out?"

The old folding chair squeaked as Gerald shifted position. He pushed his glasses up on his nose and took pen in hand. "Your little 'get-together.' What do you want? And how do you propose to pay for it?"

"With the company credit card. I'm charging everything." She swallowed the lump of uncertainty in her throat. "We'll keep it a small gathering, just the people who are likely to do business with us in the near future. By the time the bills come due, the insurance money will be here."

The look he gave her said that he doubted that, but he dutifully wrote down a few notes, then flipped through the desk calendar for the date. "So, a get-together for our most consistent customers. I think we should invite the other business owners on the block, too. That way the word will get around faster that we're back in business."

"Good idea," she said. "Add them to the list."

He sat thinking for a moment, his pen doodling a geometric shape in the margin of the notepad. "Didn't I suggest the idea of classes to you a couple of years ago?"

Had he? "I don't remember. If you did, I'm sorry I didn't go for it. Sometimes I can be a little hard-headed."

"A little?"

She smiled ruefully, spread her hands in a what-can-I-say gesture.

He leaned forward. "Classes are a great way to move additional products. Pots, baskets, ribbons, tuteurs, artsy stuff."

Gerald had warmed to the idea surprisingly quickly. "Artsy stuff?" she asked warily.

"Brass dragonflies and grasshoppers, blown-glass hummingbirds, silk flowers, ceramic elves."

She flinched. "Ceramic elves?"

Gerald's laugh startled her. "Okay, maybe not elves," he said. "Squirrels? Birds?"

"Don't order any of this er, artsy, stuff without my approval, okay, Ger?" But even as she said it, she knew that all the doodads Gerald had suggested were a brilliant idea. This was the reason her father had hired him, given him a share of the business.

He lowered his gaze to his notepad and began stabbing dots across the page with the pen.

"Oh, what the hell," she told him. "Order anything you think will sell."

He stilled the pen, lifted his chin, and studied her for an uncomfortably long time. They'd worked together for nearly five years now, but did she really know this guy? He'd been her father's pick, not hers. "I need your help, Gerald," she said, softening her tone. "Together, we can get Langston Green back on its feet."

Finally, his lips parted in a tentative smile. "You know," he told her, "I really thought the place was a total loss. But I took a look around before coming in here and saw how you're getting it all put back in order. You're amazing, Elisa."

She felt a twinge of guilt. She hadn't really done much, other than get the summer kids to come in on the weekend and start to pick the place up. The real work was taking place in the northeast corner. Thanks to the Good Samaritan. It was disconcerting how events, good or bad, just seemed to happen on her property. Whoever had been sneaking onto the property knew how to unplug the surveillance cameras. She'd thought about hardwiring them or hiding new ones, but hated to discourage her anonymous helper. Was it possible that the Gremlin had reformed and was making amends?

"And now you've come up with all these ideas," Gerald continued. "I can see how Langston Green could be reborn. A phoenix rising from the ashes. I can see how it could be like the good old days."

The good old days? She blinked at him, perplexed. His eyes

briefly flicked to the photo on the wall—Terry Langston clinking champagne glasses with the staff—before he turned his attention to his notebook.

Ah, yes, the good old days. She swallowed painfully, brushed a strand of hair back from her forehead. "Gerald," she said, "What made you increase our insurance coverage when you did?"

He looked up. "You don't think that I—" He stopped in midsentence, his mouth still open.

"I just wondered how you thought of it. I never would have."

"That's why I'm here, isn't it?" He clicked his pen, leaned back in his chair. "I was going through the bills, especially the invoices for the irrigation system and backhoe repairs. It suddenly hit me how much things cost to fix around here, and I wondered if we had sufficient insurance to cover the place in the event of real disaster. Maybe it was a premonition?"

"Whatever it was, thank heavens you had it when you did. You saved our butts." She raised her coffee cup in salute to him.

They wrote class descriptions together, Elisa describing her ideas and Gerald translating them into advertising lingo, using a new laptop computer he'd leased. As they were finalizing the schedule, the distinctive tap of high heels on the concrete floor announced Tiffany's arrival.

She wore a slinky dark green dress that set off her chestnut hair. Above her left breast was pinned the tasteful gold badge of Riley's, where she served as hostess. Her eyes widened when she spotted Gerald and Elisa sitting across from each other.

"Well, isn't this cozy?" Then, focusing on Elisa, she asked, "Doesn't Gerald rate his own office anymore?"

Gerald rose hastily. "It burned, honey, you know that." He held out his hand, and Tiffany intertwined her fingers with his, pulling him close.

Turning her back to Elisa, she brushed an invisible piece of lint from his shoulder. "I'm on my lunch break," she said softly. "I thought we could share a nice seafood salad at Orizio's. We might see Cissie and Walt there."

"I'll sit with you for a half hour," he offered. "But then I've got to be off. I have a million things to do. You won't believe all the fantastic plans Elisa and I have cooked up."

"Really?" Looking over her fiancé's shoulder, Tiffany cocked an eyebrow at Elisa. "I thought you were going to close the business."

"Turns out I was wrong there, Tiff," he told her. "We're going to remodel the barn, try out a few new things. If Langston Green goes down, at least we'll go down fighting."

Dropping Tiffany's hand, Gerald swiveled to face Elisa. "Hey, Elle, I just had a flash. That little get-together? Let's make it an earthquake survival party. And we'll have it next week, on the day of your first class."

Elisa had an instant panic attack. He wanted to move everything up a week? How in the heck could she manage that?

Gerald recognized the look on her face. "Don't worry. I'll handle the party. Tiffany can help, can't you, hon, with the catering?"

His fiancée gave a reluctant nod. "If Mr. Riley wants to."

He turned back to Elisa. "It's good if the place is still sort of tumble-down. Adds to the earthquake aftermath atmosphere. We can announce a big sale on slightly damaged plants."

Only a marketing man could have thought of an earthquake theme party. But she'd have to sort and mark down plants, get the barn in order...

"We'll make it a short party, just a couple of hours. Say, an hour of nice hors d'oeuvres for our best customers; then we'll get out the cheap snacks and open it up to the public."

The public? This plan was rapidly getting out of hand.

Again, Gerald read her mind. "It's a reopening, remember?

And a sale. We can move a truckload of mums alone, especially the autumn colors. We'll serve hot cider, have a contest for the best earthquake story. It'll be fun."

He did make it sound promising. Not to mention more immediately profitable than her little 'get-together' with only the biggest clients.

"I'll bet we can even get a TV news crew out here. They're happy to milk any natural disaster for as long as possible."

A news crew? She blanched at the notion, imagining the rebirth of Langston Green billed as the next 'big story that didn't happen.'

"Elisa?" Gerald was waiting for her agreement.

Get a grip, she told herself. She and Gerald and Peter would make sure Langston Green's reopening *would* happen. And a television story would be better advertising than she could ever afford any other way.

"Let's do it, partner," she told him. "Make it so."

He smiled. "I'll get an announcement in the paper."

"Gerald!" Tiffany tapped her foot impatiently. "I only have sixty minutes."

He took Tiffany's arm and walked a few steps with her, then whirled around again. "Oh, Elisa—the paper will want a photo of you."

Ghastly thought. "Whatever for?"

"You have the best earthquake story of all. They'll want to tell it."

Elisa groaned. Did she really want the world to know her own tree had nearly done her in?

"She doesn't want to be in the papers, Gerald," Tiffany told him. "I mean, with the broken leg and her face and the fire and all, things are really hard for her right now. A woman wants to look her best in a photo."

"Please," Gerald begged. "It'll bring in the customers in droves."

"Oh, jeez." Customers in droves? The sympathy vote?

He grinned. "I'll tell them they can come out the day after tomorrow." Then he vanished, pulling Tiffany out the door with him.

She sat for a minute, her eyes focused on the vase of wilting peach carnations. A party, a sale, newspaper coverage. Classes. Repairing. Remodeling. Rebuilding. What had she gotten herself into? She hobbled into the company bathroom and regarded herself in the mirror.

A woman wants to look her best in a photo. Tiffany Verlitz always made Elisa feel like a ragamuffin. And today her physical image definitely matched her mental one. The scratches and bruises on her face had nearly faded away, but Charlie's old cable-knit sweater was at least three sizes too big and its pale yellow color made her look like she was coming down with the flu. No way could she stand up in front of strangers dressed like this, and she was certainly not letting any camera near her.

There was no getting around it: she had to face one of the tasks she dreaded most. Shopping.

An hour later she was perusing the sale racks at Naturally Yours, a store that carried petite clothing, a rarity these days. Shaking her head, she bypassed the dresses and silk blouses, trying to remember the last time she'd worn anything fancier than gabardine slacks and a clean T-shirt. She zeroed in on a heavy flannel shirt in a bronzy plaid, cotton turtlenecks in cream and gold, a turquoise pullover, and an exquisite red-orange cable-knit sweater. She added some underwear and a couple of pairs of rather odd blousy-legged, multi-pocketed pants that looked as if they'd fit over her cast. Done.

She drove back to her childhood home, feeling more in control than she had since the earthquake. Since she could not use the clutch in her old pickup, she'd swapped it for the Langston Green van normally driven by Peter. It was one of the larger and more ungainly vehicles on the road, and she was amazed at the lengths to which other drivers went to avoid driving behind her. A BMW shot out in front of her from a side street and she had to brake hard to avoid plowing into it as the light ahead changed to red. Her gaze leapt to the rear-view mirror, worried that the tailgater behind her would hit her. No, the lady in the green SUV reacted just fine. The black Acura behind the SUV screeched and swerved, but also managed, barely, to avoid collision.

The light changed and Elisa turned right at the next corner. The black Acura turned as well, right behind her. The driver wore a baseball cap, pulled so low she couldn't see his eyes. Which was a little weird, because the sun was already behind the bluff to the west. She turned right at the next light. When the black Acura followed, Elisa's stomach tightened. The hairs on the back of her neck prickled.

She tried to get a better look at the driver, but between the van's bad sight areas and the dearth of street lights on the road, it was next to impossible. He'd dropped back a little, but was definitely taking the same route. Jake, tailing her? No, Jake drove a Land Rover. A cold chill descended on her. The Gremlin?

No way was she going to lead the Gremlin to Gail and Charlie's house. Instead of making her usual left at the stop sign, she went straight, then made a quick right into a driveway. The black Acura drove past and turned at the next four-way stop. Elisa let out a long breath. Baseball Cap probably lived in the neighborhood. Watching for the black car, she backed out, turned around, and sped home. Drat Jake Street! His dramatic warnings were making her jumpy. The fire department report wasn't even in yet; she didn't even know if the fire had been arson and here she was, behaving like a self-obsessed lunatic. But just in case, she parked the van across the street and two doors down instead of in front of the family home.

~

"About time!" Charlie regarded Elisa's purchases. "Cool pants," she crooned, holding the black slacks up to her own waist. "Harem meets grunge. Would this style look good on me?"

"I don't know," Elisa said hesitantly. "They might make you look fat." The last thing she needed was Charlie dressing like her more elegant twin.

Her sister dropped the slacks back onto the pile. "You're probably right."

Elisa felt mean. The pants might very well look better on Charlie than they did on her. But the short dark sister had to get the upper hand over the tall blond one once in a while, didn't she?

"I love the barrette," Charlie said, touching a fingertip to the filigree bird clip Jake had given her, "But what are you going to do about your hair?" She fingered a strand of Elisa's raven tresses.

"What's wrong with my hair?"

"I guess it's fine, if you want to go your whole life looking like ..." Charlie hesitated. Elisa was sure she was going to say "an Indian." She was preparing her retort about *being* half Indian, when her sister surprised her by finishing with "...a hippie."

Charlie pulled a pair of small sharp scissors from a kitchen drawer.

"Peace, Sis." Elisa held up her right hand in the traditional two-fingered sign.

Charlie advanced. "Just a few inches. I promise, nothing drastic."

"Charlie, I'll look like a hippie the rest of my life if I choose to. Just imagine what *you'd* look like with a broken nose."

"Why would I have a broken nose?"

Elisa waved a crutch in her direction.

"Oh." Charlie returned the scissors to the drawer and sat down. "Party pooper."

Gail entered the kitchen. "What *are* you girls up to?"

Elisa and Charlie looked at each other. "Nothing, Mom," they chorused.

The doorbell rang. Charlie hopped up to admit Leon Maxwell and Jonathan Park. They'd already been here twice in the last week, and seemed on their way to becoming permanent fixtures.

"Don't you guys ever work?" Elisa asked.

Leon laughed. "Even us all-American heroes get days off now and then."

"*We* all-American heroes," Gail corrected.

"So now you're one, too?" Leon grabbed a kitchen towel and snapped it at Gail's behind.

Elisa couldn't remember ever hearing her stepmother squeal like that. Gail made a grab for the towel, chased Leon into the foyer, with Charlie and Jonathan following close behind.

Elisa tried to ignore the giggles and muffled murmurings from the hall. It was so unfair. Gail and Charlie had simply reached out and snagged two great guys with no effort. Elisa's accident had actually been the catalyst that had brought them together. And what did she have to show for it? A cast on her leg, and now she'd been interrogated, kissed, and discarded.

Suddenly she felt like flattening something; she couldn't wait until she could drive the backhoe again. Another two weeks, the orthopedist promised, and they'd saw her out of the heavy plaster, remove the metal pins, and give her a lightweight removable cast.

Gail and Leon trooped back into the kitchen, now wearing jackets as well as smiles. A pang of further resentment struck Elisa at the sight of her stepmother beside a man other than her father. But Leon and Gail looked natural together. Comfortable. Her stepmother had found warm relationships with Charlie's father, with Elisa's father, and now with Leon Maxwell. Elisa wondered if she would ever find comfort with even one man.

"We're going to see the new movie at the mall," Gail told her. "Want to join us? You'd have time to change if you hurry."

"Yeah, Elle, c'mon," Charlie cooed from the doorway.

Coming up behind Charlie, Jonathan wrapped his arms around her waist, rested his chin on her shoulder. He and Charlie were exactly the same height. "Yeah, Elle, c'mon," he echoed.

If this wasn't pitiful. She wasn't up to being a fifth wheel. She felt more like a flat tire. "No thanks," she told them.

Was that a look of relief she saw on her stepmother's face? "You sure?" Gail asked.

"I'm done in." Elisa stretched and yawned for effect. "You have a good time."

After the cozy foursome left, Simon ventured into the kitchen, which was now so quiet that she could hear the battery-powered wall clock ticking. The cat leapt to the table top.

"You're not allowed on the table," she admonished.

Purring loudly and slobbering a little, he rubbed against her forearm, turned his back on her and brushed her nose with his tail.

"This is not your best side," she told his rear end.

He whirled, came back for another pass. She grabbed him and forced him to sit. She stared into his sea-green eyes. "Simon, have I always been such a drip?"

He butted his furry head against her cheek. "Rowrr." His hot breath smelled like something dead.

"Well," she sniffed. "I don't think the opinion of a guy who eats mice really counts for much."

Timo knocked on the scarred door of the apartment across from where he used to live. The door opened. The gray-haired Hispanic woman blinked at him from behind thick glasses.

"Ah, Timo," she said, "Come in."

"*Buenas tardes, Señora Renaldo.*" He pulled off his baseball cap as he stepped into her ancient spotless kitchen.

The curly-haired toddler playing with measuring cups and wooden spoons on the linoleum looked up at him. "Seemo!" she lisped, displaying the tiny baby teeth in her upper gums. She raised her chubby arms toward him.

The woman picked up the baby and held her out. Timo took her reluctantly, balanced her on his hip as he'd seen his mother do.

"I'll get her jacket." Señora Renaldo returned with a tiny pink parka, and pulled the child's arms through it. Leaning forward, she planted a kiss on the little girl's plump cheek. The child's hand rubbed at the area as if she'd been bitten.

"*Adiós, Rosita,*" the woman said, her voice wavering a little.

"Señora Renaldo, I have money," Timo began, "I can pay you every week. Every day if you want."

"It's not the money. It's the neighbors. They know that Rosa's not mine. I stop taking messages for you on the phone, tell them that I don't know any Martinez, but they don't stop calling. So I change the phone. But—" she looked toward the toddler—"many people know Rosita. This morning a Señor Street comes looking for you. I can't have trouble." She thrust the duffel bag full of Rosa's clothes and toys into his arms, and pushed him toward the door.

"But what am I supposed to do?" Timo whined as he stepped over the threshold. The toddler caught his mood and began to whimper uncertainly, squirming in his arms.

"Why don't you go to that lady you work for? You told me Señorita Langston is very nice. God bless you, Timo. *Buena suerte.*" She closed the door before he had a chance to tell her that Elisa Langston was the last person he could turn to for help.

Buena suerte. "In English, we say 'good luck'," he translated for Rosa. Her round face was scrunched up into a worried grimace.

"Lugg!" she chirped, brightening a little.

He hefted her a few inches higher. "I'll teach you another English expression, Rosa. Can you say 'Fat chance?'"

She liked this game. "Faa chaz!" she burbled loudly into his left ear.

Timo pushed the outside door open with his backside. "That's what we have, Rosa. We have a fat chance of good luck."

He carried her out into the cold night air. Judging by the clouds scuttling across the moon, it was going to rain tonight.

Chapter 11

Jake couldn't stop wondering what Elisa was doing. But while waiting for Wasserman's call about the arson report, Jake forced himself to stay away from Langston Green and catch up with the other claims on his case list. It was tedious work, mostly cut-and-dried cases of earthquake damage: trees falling on cars or buildings, buildings falling on cars, or trees and buildings just falling down. By the end of the second day, he was ready to pick a fight with someone to alleviate the boredom. A hefty paycheck couldn't make up for forty hours a week of filling in forms, of listening to people whine about money.

He went to the gym, worked out on the machines for a while, then swam a mile in the Olympic-size pool, getting into the rhythm, trying to shift his mood in a positive direction. He wasn't at all sure that the FBI interview had gone well: the interview committee had seemed suspicious about his reasons for quitting the Seattle police department. Maybe mentioning departmental politics hadn't been a smart thing to do: the FBI was certainly sensitive to political currents. Maybe he wasn't Fed material, after all.

He pushed off the wall at the end of his lap and stroked back toward the other side of the pool. Maybe he'd move to a different state, take a job with the state patrol. Work someplace rural, without gangs. Oregon, Idaho, somewhere close enough that he could come back often. *Come back for what?* his conscience asked. His parents lived in California now. He wasn't even dating Elisa Langston.

She'd left him a voicemail wanting to know about the

schedule for this case, about how the process could be expedited. Just straight to the point, cool and businesslike. Show me the money. She hadn't given him a hint that she was interested in him personally. Or had she? He thought about the kiss, about how she'd dropped her crutches to embrace him. He sucked in a mouthful of chlorine-flavored water instead of air and came up choking. Darn that woman! Even when she wasn't present, she had the ability to transform him into a klutz.

The phone was ringing when Jake let himself into his condo. He dumped the mail he carried onto the kitchen table. One envelope bore an FBI seal. He picked up that envelope, along with the portable telephone receiver. "Street here."

"I think I have the wrong number. I was looking for Avenue."

"That joke was lame the first time you told it, Valetti." Cradling the phone between his shoulder and his ear, Jake ripped open the FBI envelope. It would contain a rejection, he was sure. He was a damaged former cop, even if a decorated one. He braced himself for the inevitable polite negatives.

His old partner chuckled at the other end of the line. "I got the results on those names from NCIC and AFIS for you, bud."

"And?" Jake fought to keep his mind on Valetti's conversation as he read the letter. Did it say what he thought it did?

"Nada on Walter Baker except a couple of speeding tickets, absolutely nada for Gerald Donaldson. Timoteo Martinez came up once, picked up six months ago with a whole carload of Tibs."

"Tibs," Jake echoed. "You mean Tiburones?" Los Tiburones—the Sharks—were a Latino gang, Jake knew, but more of a wannabe gang than a group really into crime. They seemed to be held together by a common language and a lack of anything constructive to do.

"What were they picked up for? The Tibs were never very ambitious."

"That was true in the beginning," Valetti told him. "But they've gotten more active in the last year. They're expanding: they've got branches in Auburn and Bellevue now.

"Bellevue?" Bellevue had long been considered upscale, but it was also home to Crossroads Mall, where he'd spotted Timo.

"Your Martinez and friends were picked up right after a couple of Molotov cocktails were lobbed into a house nearby. Remember that meth lab that burned outside of Redmond six months ago? The place belonged to the Island Boys," Valetti said, naming a Samoan gang. "Although of course now that the evidence is toast, nobody can prove it. Just like nobody can prove that the Tibs torched it. But they were bragging that they forced the Boys out of their territory."

"Interesting," Jake said. If the Tiburones considered Bellevue and Redmond to be their territory, then maybe they'd progressed to Woodinville as well. And Langston Green was in the heart of Woodinville. Timo Martinez, a Tiburones member, worked there, and had a knowledge of arson techniques. It was more important than ever that he get his hands on this kid. For Elisa's sake.

"Do you have Martinez's age down there?" Jake asked.

There was a shuffling of paper at the other end of the phone. "The report says sixteen, but there's a question mark after it. It also says New Mexico, with another question mark."

"Got an address?"

Valetti started to read off an address south of downtown Seattle, then stopped midway. "I happen to know that's the address of a warehouse store, because Lakotis and I just hauled in their manager for selling goods off the loading dock."

So that address was fake, too. "There's nothing else?" Jake asked.

"That's it."

"Thanks, partner."

"Hey, you sound almost upbeat," Valetti remarked. "Either you found some real crime to investigate, or you finally met a willing woman."

Jake chuckled. "A little of both, although I'm not yet sure how willing she is. Plus, I've just been accepted to the FBI."

"No shit! Jake Street, a G-man? I've got to hear about this. Meet me at The Ballard Pub in half an hour."

"I'll be in the corner booth." Jake put the receiver back into the cradle, and perused the letter again. Providing he passed the physical next week, he was to report for training at Quantico in six weeks.

Most of him was elated. Sure, the salary was less than what he was bringing home now, but he'd be doing something real again, something important, not just putting in time every day.

But a small part of him was disappointed. Joining the FBI was a little like joining the military. They decided where to station their agents. Quantico was in Virginia. While Elisa Langston was firmly rooted in Washington State.

The reporter and photographer were scheduled to show up at ten thirty, so Elisa dressed carefully in the new paprika sweater and olive paratrooper pants. Studying herself in the mirror, she had to admit that the new clothes were a big improvement over her usual dress. Maybe they would be accompanied by an upswing in her fortune.

Those hopes were dashed when David Wasserman from the Fire Department called to set up an appointment. He sounded grim. When he appeared at nine-thirty, his fire department uniform was crisply pressed, and his expression was all business. She'd barely had time to offer him a cup of coffee when Jake strode in.

Her heart skipped a beat. He wore a suit and a tense expression. Today there'd be no embraces, she could tell. Why had he shown up so suddenly, without even a phone call? Were there cops outside? Was she about to be taken away in handcuffs?

They sat down at her desk table, she on one side and the two of them on the other.

"Fast work," Jake said to the Wasserman.

"I put a rush on the lab work, and then I put in overtime writing it up." Wasserman pulled three sets of pages from a manila folder, handed one set to Elisa and another to Jake. "The gist of the report is this: the fire that destroyed your main building was definitely arson."

Both men watched for her reaction. She looked at Jake. He looked down at the table. She'd been dreading this. Now what?

Wasserman turned to Jake. "The fire started on the second floor." His gaze then flitted to Elisa. "Your apartment. Looks like the accelerant was kerosene."

The bottle of lamp oil she'd found. She opened her mouth to say so, then in the next second decided that it might not be wise to admit to that knowledge. It was suspicious enough that she'd been in the building when the fire broke out.

"The ignition source was the cigarette and book of matches you found, Street."

Jake looked up from his notes. "Prints?"

"None on the matchbook." To Elisa, Wasserman said, "Everyone on the employee list reported to give us their prints. Everyone but Timoteo Martinez."

"He's still AWOL," Jake said. "I spotted him with Ms. Langston last week, but he cleared out before I could question him."

Now she was 'Ms. Langston' again. Hopefully that was only in front of Wasserman. "You scared him," Elisa told Jake. "I'm trying to find him. Give me a chance."

Wasserman turned to Elisa. "The address and phone number on Martinez's job application are invalid."

She squirmed. "That phone number used to work. I never

had any reason to check out the address before; Timo always showed up on time and he collected his checks here." She didn't like the way Wasserman studied her, and she liked even less the fact that Jake was doing nothing to defend her.

Finally, the fire investigator glanced back at his notes. "We dusted everything we could salvage. We came up with matches for Ms. Langston, Ms. Nguyen, Mr. Nguyen, Mr. Donaldson, and Ms. Verlitz on drawer handles and kitchen appliances downstairs. "

Jake's brow creased. "Verlitz? "

"Tiffany Verlitz," Elisa supplied, "Gerald's fiancée. She comes around fairly often to meet Gerald for lunch or after work. She's a hostess next door at Riley's."

Wasserman continued. "In the debris from the upstairs apartment, we found several prints we haven't matched. At least not yet. But on the bottom of the toilet seat, we found a print that matches Martinez."

Elisa was confused. "But you said you didn't get Timo's prints."

Jake and Wasserman exchanged a glance. "He's already in the system," Wasserman told her.

"The system?"

"The crime computer. He's been picked up and finger-printed before."

"Really?"

Wasserman nodded. "Suspected of setting a fire, along with a carload of known gang members."

"What?" She leaned forward. "Gang members? Setting a fire where?"

Wasserman flipped a page and read an address from it. "Abandoned house, later discovered to be a meth lab."

Elisa studied Jake's face. She could tell that this wasn't news to him. Why hadn't he told her? Had his embraces, his kisses, his present, been designed to lure her into a confession or to get her to lead him to Timo? On TV, police detectives sometimes romanced their suspects to get the information they needed. Had Jake played her for a fool?

It didn't look good that Timo's fingerprints had been found in her apartment. Wasserman, and even Jake, might be thinking that she and Timo were partners in crime. But she knew that Timo was not an arsonist.

Both men were watching her. She leaned toward them and said, "Look guys, this is my business. And it used to be my home, too. Timo is one of my best employees. I've let him come upstairs several times, given him a sandwich, a soda, let him use my bathroom. There's nothing odd about finding his prints anywhere at Langston Green." She paused. "Maybe the fire in your records was a teenage prank that got out of hand. You said the house was unoccupied."

"So was yours on the night it burned," Jake pointed out.

She could almost hear the gears turning inside his head. Teenage pranks. Like monkeywrenching a backhoe, like sabotaging a sprinkler system, like pilfering tools. Like all the things the Gremlin had been up to over the last year. She herself said that the vandal was probably a kid. Her defense of Timo was only serving to make *her* look guilty, too.

A memory of the three Latino toughs in Crossroads Mall flashed into her mind. They'd signaled to Timo. *Could* he be involved? Had he been playing her for a fool, too? She took a long breath, forced herself to keep her hands away from her burning cheeks. "Let's cut to the chase, gentlemen. What does this all mean?"

Wasserman closed the manila folder in front of him. "It means, Ms. Langston, that we know it was arson, but we can't prove who set the fire. Timoteo Martinez is still a person of interest as far as the Fire Department is concerned. Woodinville PD and King County Sheriff's Department are looking for him."

She fought to keep the dismay from her face. She'd have to work hard to find Timo before the authorities scared him into disappearing for good.

Jake rose from his chair. "Atlas Security won't close this claim until Martinez has been cleared." He looked at his watch. "I'm sorry, but I've got to run." He turned without looking at her.

The office doors swung open and Beth stuck her head in. "Elisa, there are two men here from the Valley News."

Damn. The photographer and the reporter. The investigators slipped through the door Beth held, out into the greenhouse. Elisa hustled to follow them on her crutches.

"I need to talk to you, Street," she shouted at Jake.

"I'll get back to you later," he shouted back. "Wait up, Wasserman." He disappeared through the exit, following the fire investigator to the parking lot.

Elisa scowled at Jake's retreating figure. Damn the man. Even if he didn't want to admit to knowing her, to kissing her; he was still her insurance rep. She needed a time estimate from him if she was going to get this business back on its feet. And then there was their embrace. Was she just supposed to forget about that?

"Andy Fisher." The Valley News reporter shook her hand almost absentmindedly as he, too, watched the departure of Jake and Wasserman. "Trouble?" he asked eagerly.

"Routine," she told him. "Insurance stuff. You know we had a fire."

Fisher scribbled something down in his notebook. She had a flash of anxiety about what might appear in the paper the next day, and was thankful for Gerald's timely appearance.

"What do you want to hear about first, the earthquake or our plans for the grand reopening?" he asked.

He filled Fisher in on the earthquake damage and Elisa's accident, making it sound much more dramatic and less humiliating than it actually had been. The reporter mentioned the fire, and Elisa had to bite her tongue when she heard Gerald telling about Elisa's 'heroic rescue of her cat.' Gerald, bless him, did not mention the word 'arson.'

The photographer checked out several locations in the greenhouse before settling on the tropical section. She tried to stand up straight between her crutches and erase the worry crease from her brow as she pretended to examine a tall shelf full of orchids. Look like a successful business owner, she told herself. Look like a Langston. She stretched to add another inch to her stature.

Gerald examined the photographer's digital results and agreed with the fellow's choice. After handing each of them a press release about the earthquake party event and upcoming classes, he escorted Andy Fisher and the photographer to the parking lot.

Elisa watched her business partner in action. Gerald was smooth, somehow acting like the media's best friend while telling them exactly what they should print. Elisa could see why Tiffany was ambitious for him: he'd do well as a stock broker or investment counselor. In fact, today he looked like a well-to-do corporate exec, in a white shirt and red tie and dark gray sports jacket that she couldn't remember seeing before.

"Nice jacket," she commented when he returned.

Grabbing her hand, he pressed her fingers to his lapel. "Feel. It's cashmere."

"Wow," she said softly, slipping her hand out from beneath his. "I didn't know sports coats came in cashmere."

"Me, neither. Tiffany bought it for me."

"Riley's must be paying her well." It was a nice restaurant, but how much did hostesses make?

"She got a big bonus and went on a shopping spree. Most women would spend it all on themselves, but Tiff bought new clothes for both of us. She's always looking out for me and my future." He looked chagrined as he amended, "*Our* future."

Suddenly, Elisa wondered how far away Gerald was from his investment degree or certificate or whatever it was. Was he about to leave the company? And when he did, would she have to buy him out? What would she do without him?

She bit her lip, refusing to take on another worry right now. "Gerald, got a few minutes? We need to have staff meeting. Could you ask Peter and Beth to step into the office?"

When her entire permanent staff of three was assembled in the narrow space between the two desks, she gave them the results of the fire department report.

"Arson?" Beth's eyebrows joined in a frown to form a straight line across her forehead. "But that means it was on purpose."

"Exactly."

Beth and Peter looked around nervously, as if expecting terrorists to burst in through the greenhouse doors.

"Can you think of anyone who might be angry enough at us to do this?" She looked at each of them in turn.

Silence reigned for several minutes.

"Anyone who was angry at all?" she prompted.

"I remember that George Luhann was a little pissed off," Peter murmured.

"George Luhann?" Elisa didn't know the name.

"He owns GL Supply Company. We used to buy all our pots and fertilizer from him."

"And why don't we now?"

Beth gave Elisa a significant look. "Because you said that you wanted only pots from recycled materials, and organic fertilizer. So we switched to Earthwork Supplies."

"Ah." Elisa rubbed the knot at the back of her neck. How many other decisions had she made that might have earned her enemies?

Peter crossed his arms over the plastic apron he wore for

potting plants. "George came around a couple of times, trying to get us to reconsider."

"He doesn't really seem like a violent type," Gerald added.

Was arson an act of violence? It seemed a rather cowardly crime to Elisa. "Anyone else come to mind?"

"Trent Noonan?" Beth offered.

It took Elisa a beat to match the name to a face. "That kid was only here a week, wasn't he? In fact, he was barely here at all. That's why I canned him."

Beth shrugged. "He called me a nasty name when I gave him his dismissal check."

"How about the rest of the summer crew?" Elisa asked. "Were they okay about their jobs ending?"

Beth's shoulders lifted again. "They expected it."

A bell rang in the greenhouse, signaling the entry of a customer.

"Peter, you and Beth go see about that." Elisa turned to her business partner. "Gerald, stay for just one more minute, okay?"

After the door closed behind both Nguyens, Gerald sat down on the edge of Peter's desk. "Yes?"

"I know you spend time with Walt Baker," Elisa told him. "Do you think he's capable of stealing money and burning down our building?"

"Walt?" Gerald was incredulous. "He's made out of money. I hardly think he would resort to stealing a few hundred dollars. And why would he go in for arson?"

"He wants this property."

"Yes, but he's made an incredible offer that I still think you should—"

"I'm *not* going to sell. But maybe he thought that if I lost the main building I would."

Gerald's jaw clenched. "I don't think Walt would be so underhanded."

"You really know him that well?"

"No, probably not," he admitted. "But Tiffany's over at her sister's a lot. She's a good judge of character, and she adores Walt." Gerald used his index finger to slide his glasses up his nose a fraction of an inch. "The man may be frustrated about not getting Langston Green, but he's got plenty of fish to fry. He's already talking about a new complex up north." He stood up. "Are we done here? I've got a ton of phone calls to make if this shindig's going to happen on time."

"The office is all yours." Pulling on a smock to protect her good clothes, she left the desk and computer to Gerald and gimped out to the barn.

After only a few hours of work, the crew of retired carpenters and electricians had added insulation to the old walls, bright overhead lights, and heaters so her students wouldn't freeze in the newly constructed classroom. It was a bit of a slapdash job, but all that time and budget would allow right now. The packed earth floors would remain, not only for economy's sake but because they were in keeping with the rusticity of the place. Maybe she'd even stack some hay bales here and there, with some strategically placed mums and foliage plants for color.

An electric saw whined from the rear of the building. The new bathroom back there would involve some digging for the plumbing, but should be ready in a few days. After making sure the contractors were working efficiently, she took a stroll through the fields. Actually, a galump through the fields: that, she had decided, was the verb for using crutches. Galump.

Everyone was looking for Timo. She missed the boy. The nursery felt incomplete without him. Oh, she wasn't so naïve as to think he was an angel. She could imagine him spray-painting graffiti on walls. But a gang-banger? He seemed too shy. At Crossroads, when the big-trousered toughs had flashed a sign at Timo, he'd looked away. Why would Timo set fire to her building? He valued her friendship and his job at Langston Green. It just didn't make sense.

But what was the explanation behind the tears in the boy's eyes? And why had he said, "The money—"? He couldn't mean the money from the safe, could he? He'd been about to tell her something, something important. Drat Jake Street! Her fists clenched. If he hadn't been so hell bent on pursuing the kid, she'd know what it was that kept Timo away. And now the police were looking for him, too. She had to find him first.

She also had to find out what was going on in her fields. The renewed section next to the fence that bordered Baker's Acres had expanded. Had anyone else noticed that plants were crawling back into their pots, that broken branches had trimmed themselves and that the pots were lining up in neat rows? The irrigation system had miraculously been repaired, too, and plants had been watered.

Had her Gremlin changed into a Good Samaritan? Instead of destroying inventory and equipment, someone was now fixing things. Maybe one of the summer workers? It didn't seem in character; she'd always had to supervise them closely, and they'd always wanted to be paid for every minute they worked.

Gerald? He'd been cooperative in the last few days, but she'd never known him to volunteer for field work. Peter spent all his time in the greenhouse. Certainly not Charlie, nor Gail. Jake? She scoffed at the thought of him straightening a nursery. Still, the mental image was nice. She could picture his strong arms setting a sapling to rights, imagine him shirtless, muscles rippling in the sun as he hefted a bag of cedar bark.

Muscles rippling in the sun? What was *wrong* with her? Just because he'd saved her from falling, because he'd kissed her on impulse, just because they shared some ancient history when they were silly teenagers, that was no reason to think he was romantically interested. He'd made it clear today that he was an investigator out to prove that a Langston Green employee was perpetrating insurance fraud.

In high school, she'd been the leader of the Adventurers Club. In those days, *she'd* been the strong one. And now... She stared angrily at her mud-stained cast. In her experience, the more helpless a woman was, the more attractive men found her. And she must seem pretty helpless now, limping around on crutches, with her business in ruins. Hence the kisses. But still men fled from her; Jake fled from her. Was she really that unlovable?

Had her father had these same sort of thoughts? Her mother had been a malleable young girl from a Mayan village. Terrence Langston showed her the wonders of the United States, taught her how to be a modern American. It must have come as a shock to her father that his wife was not impressed enough with him or her new life to stay. Elisa scuffed the heel of her cast in the soft dirt. Her mother hadn't been impressed with her daughter, either.

No, her father had told her, you're wrong about that. Your mother loved her country so much that she had to go back, but she left you here because she loved you even more. She knew you'd have a better life here. She knew that being a Langston means something important.

But her father's words couldn't make up for the pain of her mother leaving. And now her father was gone as well. And once the insurance business was settled, Jake Street would be out of the picture, too.

Others were depending on her; she had to stop feeling sorry for herself. She focused on the straight rows before her, the trimmed, repotted plants. Why had the corner next to Baker's Acres been restored first? Maybe, she thought, Walt Baker was trying to get on her good side, helping her out. After he torched her home? It didn't make sense.

A board in the fence, near the corner, was uneven, its edge standing out a little from the others. She checked it, found it hanging from only one nail, easily swung out of the way. Was the gap it left big enough for a person? She eyed it. Maybe a slender person. A barely noticeable path led away from the gap toward the condo complex. It could have been made by raccoons, possums, even by Simon and his feline competitors. She bent to study a small print in the damp earth next to the fence. A rounded print, probably a cat's, and next to it, a bit of blue cloth, ground into the mud. She tugged at it and was surprised to see its size when it came free. A bandana.

The blue cloth was stamped with fish shapes. White zigzags lined the edges. She'd seen the bandana before, or at least one like it. Where? Her mind just wouldn't provide the answer. Feeling wiped out, she decided to call it a day.

Before going to bed that evening, Elisa studied herself in the privacy of her bedroom. Well, in what used to be her bedroom. It didn't much resemble the room in which she'd spent her formative years. But then, neither did the face that looked back at her in the dresser mirror.

Today, for the photographer, on Charlie's advice, she'd worn red lipstick, highlighter, and bronze eye shadow. The makeup was attractive, there was no denying it. She couldn't help wondering what Jake had thought.

Simon leapt to the top of the dresser and massaged his lean flank against her cheek, smudging her lipstick. Now she looked like a floozy. Nudging her compact to the edge of the dresser with his paw, Simon watched with satisfaction as it fell to the floor, spattering powder across the silver carpet. He returned to the collection before the mirror. An eyeliner pencil caught his attention. He rolled it expertly to the edge, gave her a crafty slant-eyed glance, then scooted it off. Turning to a dish of dried lavender, he dug in a white paw.

"Stop that!" She gently pulled his tail.

He stretched and did his best to dig his claws into the polished wood of the dresser top.

"Stop that, too." She scooped him up. "I know. Makeup, lavender, silver carpet. Makes me feel ornery, too. Although we should be grateful, Simon. When your house burns down, it's good to have someplace as nice as this to come to." She restlessly glanced around the pretty room. "But it's just not home, is it? It's too neat. Too tame. You and I, we need a little dirt, don't we?"

He mewed his agreement, reaching a paw toward her dangling earring. She caught his outstretched claws before he could connect. To distract him, she grabbed the bandana she'd found that afternoon. As she dragged it across the dresser, he batted at it with his paws. Now washed and dried, the design was clearer. The fish were sharks. And the zigzags around the border, shark teeth.

"*Tiburones*," she translated for Simon. Then she remembered where she'd seen the bandana. Timo had worn it, sometimes around his neck, or if it was hot, around his forehead to stop the sweat from running down into his eyes. When she'd asked about the unusual design, he'd explained, a little embarrassed, that it was a symbol of Los Tiburones, a Latino club. The three toughs who'd tried to signal Timo at Crossroads had worn blue bandanas.

Wasserman had said something about Timo being involved with gang members. But maybe what the police thought of as a gang was only a club for Latino boys. She'd ask around. With a little luck, she'd be able to track down Timo before the police got to him.

Simon snagged the bandana with a claw, ripped it from her fingers, threw himself down on the dresser and tried to eviscerate the fabric by raking it with his hind feet.

She stood up. The cat momentarily abandoned his shredding efforts to stare at her. "Simon, we're moving back to Langston Green. We'll both be wild things again."

Chapter 12

Two weeks after the earthquake, the doors of the remodeled barn swung open for Langston Green's earthquake celebration and re-opening get-together. It was an early afternoon event on a Saturday. The first hour, devoted to wine and hors d'oeuvres with their best clients, mostly professional landscapers, was cordial but quiet. The atmosphere changed sixty minutes later, when Gerald and Tiffany brought out the doughnuts and hot cider and opened the doors to the public. The crowd that poured in was much larger than Elisa expected. Half the town of Woodinville seemed to be here.

Elisa scrutinized the men in the crowd. Two dark-haired men in the center were tall enough, as was the ragged, square-jawed blond fellow leaning against the far wall between racks of potted plants. The blond's eyes met hers as her gaze swept over him, and his head dipped in acknowledgement.

But none of the men had reddish hair. Jake Street was not here.

And why should he be? He was her insurance rep, for heaven's sake, nothing more. Actually, he was not really even that. He had been sent by her insurance company to investigate her.

Elisa's enthusiasm dimmed further when Walter Baker and his wife Cissie joined the crowd. At best, Baker was a greedy developer who wanted her land. At worst, he was an enemy who had torched her home.

Feeling several pairs of eyes on her, she straightened and pasted a smile on her face. Gerald had not succeeded in attracting a television crew, but a female reporter and a photographer from the Valley News were in attendance. She approached the serving table, where Gail and Leon Maxwell handed out doughnuts while Charlie and Jonathan Park filled cups with cider, laughing at their own sloppiness.

"This reminds me a little of the good old days," a middle-aged woman told Gail. Her husband nodded in mute agreement. "Every year, we looked forward to Harvest Fest at Langston Green. We really missed it the last two years. It was like a family tradition."

The good old days. The exact expression that Gerald had used for the time when her father was in charge, when Langston Green was a community gathering spot. When life was easy.

Eight people had signed up for Gerald's earthquake story event: each had five minutes before the microphone. After two similar tales of trees falling on houses, Walt Baker approached the podium.

Whatever Baker was underneath, he was all charm on top, and of course she couldn't turn him away; she had agreed that Gerald should invite the local business community. Today the cowboy developer was dressed in black leather pants, boots, vest, and hat. The only spot of color was his fancy western shirt whose turquoise hue uncannily matched that of Elisa's sweater. From beneath heavily lacquered lashes, Baker's wife Cissie glared at her as if this fashion coincidence was Elisa's fault.

"It was pitch black in that basement. I couldn't see a thing," Walt Baker spoke so quietly that the audience all leaned toward him. "But I could hear heavy breathing. Huhhh, huhhh, huhh," he huffed into the microphone. "And whatever it was, it was coming toward me at a fearsome pace. Huhhhh, huhhhh, huhhhh. I was shaking so hard that I could barely flick my Bic."

The audience chuckled uncertainly. Baker pushed his cowboy hat back on his head. "But when I finally got a flame to rise up, what did I see in the circle of light? Three black masks!"

"Ooh!" a little girl gasped. "Robbers!"

"No, young lady," Baker crooned, "Although that was my fear at the time. On that fateful day I was trapped in the rubble not with a trio of burglars, but with three very excited raccoons!"

Everyone laughed. Only one of the following five stories, a tale of a geysering broken pipe, came close to Walt Baker's in entertainment value. As Elisa listened to the woman's description of the unexpected waterfall down her stairs, she felt a prickle at the back of her neck. Without turning her head, she slid her gaze sideways to the far wall. The rough-looking blond hadn't moved from his position between the shelves. He hadn't shifted his attention, either. His pale eyes were fastened intently on her.

She didn't know the man. She'd remember a man like that, a square man, solid and angular from his work-booted feet to his straw-colored crew cut. He looked like an extra from a World War II movie, an S.S. officer out of uniform. A thug. Elisa moved her gaze back to the speaker, her stomach fluttering.

Why was he staring at her like that? Maybe he'd seen her photo in the paper? That didn't explain the malice in his eyes. As the last contestant finished her story and the crowd clapped, she chanced another quick glance at him. When she again connected with the stranger's cold stare, he winked at her.

A chill ran down her spine like a drop of cold sweat. Could this guy be her Gremlin? Jake Street's words came back to her: *Monkeywrenching, theft, arson. What's next? Murder?*

"It's your turn," said a soft voice at her shoulder.

Elisa jumped.

"I finished counting the votes," Beth told her. "Everyone's waiting for you to announce the winner."

Elisa gulped, aware that many faces in the audience were

now focused on her. "And the winner?" she asked in a whisper.

"Walt Baker." Beth's voice was equally soft.

Damn. Elisa thumped her way to the podium and awkwardly bent the microphone down to her level. How had her father done all this so naturally?

"I'm Elisa Langston," she said. "Thank you all for coming to Langston Green's reopening. I'm pleased to announce that we're beginning a series of seminars, starting with Plant Rescue in a half hour in our new classroom. You'll find information about all our upcoming seminars on the blue flyers next to the exits. Please tell all your friends." When she paused for a breath, the microphone whined loudly as if to fill the empty air space. Yanking it toward her, she said, "The winner of the earthquake story contest is Walt Baker." She slid the microphone back into its holder and stepped away from the electronic equipment before it could embarrass her again.

Baker made a big display out of adjusting the microphone stand upwards, although he was only a few inches taller. "Our hostess is a game little lady, isn't she?"

Elisa hoped her smile remained intact as she nodded. *Little lady*. She felt like braining the developer with the trophy, a brass replica of Atlas holding up a cracked Earth. She forced herself to hand it to him instead, and then stepped down from the stage and stood close to Gerald and Tiffany.

Baker thanked everyone like he'd received an Oscar, then leaned toward the microphone. "I expect to see all of you at our grand opening at Baker's Acres next Sunday. C'mon out for a down-home barbeque and a free tour of our new luxury townhomes!"

How dare he use her event to advertise his own! Elisa shot a glance toward Gerald, who gave her a chagrined expression and lifted his shoulders slightly as if to say *What else can you expect?*

Someone behind her whispered, "This isn't as good as it was

before, but it's better than nothing, isn't it?"

And instantly, she knew who was responsible for giving them nothing. Elisa Langston, the new owner. Terry Langston had held a big party every year for the whole community: Harvest Fest. But, after his death, after the nursery had passed to his daughter, Elisa Langston had not followed up on the tradition. She'd given the community *nothing*. It was no wonder that her father had been adored as if he were the captain of the Love Boat, and she felt as if she were in charge of the Titanic. It was no wonder that business was falling off. *Langstons make their own luck.* Peter and Gerald and Beth had all been waiting for her to lead the way. What had *she* been waiting for?

Elisa took a step toward the stage, determined to throw Baker off, and then the developer redeemed himself. Plucking a potted orchid from a nearby shelf, he held the delicate pink blossoms high. "I'm purchasing this beautiful orchid for my own rare flower, my wife Cissie."

All eyes turned to Cissie Baker, a shapely redhead with big hair. She blew Walt a kiss. Her earrings glittered under the lights.

Tiffany nudged Gerald. "In a little while, that'll be *us*," she purred. She tapped an index finger on her earlobe. "He bought Sis those earrings for their anniversary. Real diamonds."

"Before leaving Langston Green," Baker continued, "Buy someone you love something beautiful. If there's one thing we've all learned from our natural disaster, it's to enjoy every minute of every beautiful day, right?"

Gerald murmured, "God bless you, Master Baker." He sounded like Tiny Tim in the Christmas tale. Had Baker's speech had been prearranged between them?

Elisa hopped up to the podium. "Thank you, Walt." She nudged him aside. "And thank all of you for coming today." Then she took a deep breath and said, "But the real celebration is yet to come. As most of you know, my father, Terry Langston, always sponsored a big Harvest Fest party at the end of October. And I'm pleased to announce that this year we will be continuing that tradition. So please come back one month from today, and bring all your friends."

A huge cheer went up from the audience, followed by a roar of chatter as Elisa stepped down. Several people patted her shoulder as she approached Gerald, who now wore a deer-in-the-headlights expression.

"Surprise," she said.

He leaned close. "Elisa, can we afford this?"

She shrugged. "Can we afford not to?"

He closed his mouth, but still looked stunned. Tiffany jabbed him from the other side with an elbow. "You didn't tell me about this!" she hissed. When Gerald didn't respond, she turned to Elisa. "What's Harvest Fest?"

"It's a Langston tradition," Elisa told her. As newcomers to the community, the Bakers and Tiffany had probably never heard of the big annual party. "You'll love it." At least she hoped it would turn out well. She'd never actually been involved in preparing for it before.

"Well, *there's* something to look forward to," Tiffany drawled, sounding rather put out by the whole notion of another party.

Clutching Gerald's arm, she steered him toward another couple. Elisa turned to study the blond thug between the shelves in back. Walt Baker now stood in front of the man, one hand braced on the wall next to the stranger's head. Whatever Baker said to the man made him push off from his resting place and stride out the exit. After watching him go, Baker took a place in the line at the serving table.

As soon as Baker turned his back to the door, a short, dark, slender man, also dressed in dirty jeans, sweatshirt, and scuffed work boots, slunk out behind the blond. Now where had *he* come from?

Elisa had no time to reflect on the two men. Peter Nguyen was at her shoulder, asking if she would approve a ten percent discount for a customer who wanted to buy a dozen potted orchids. She agreed, happy to see Langston Green's merchandise moving again.

A mug of hot cider appeared under her nose. The enticing odor of cinnamon and cloves drifted up on a plume of steam. Unfortunately, the hand holding it out to her belonged to Walt Baker. She carefully balanced on her crutches and took the mug from him. "Thank you."

"My pleasure, neighbor."

"That was an amusing raccoon story," she told him. "Did it really happen?"

His grin was wide. "I'd bet Bill Clinton's reputation on it."

"I saw you talking to a blond guy over there." She gestured at the wall. "He looked like a tough customer."

"Sorry about that. He's one of my laborers." Baker shrugged. "You have to keep your eyes on these guys on work release."

A prisoner on work release? The thuggish aura wasn't just her imagination, then.

Baker was astute at reading facial expressions. "Oh, I'm sure Quentin's not really dangerous," he backpedaled. "I meant that you have to keep track of them because they're slackers. I told him to get back to work."

"And the dark guy? Kind of short, thin?"

A frown darkened Baker's face. "Dang it! Wingate was here too?"

"He tip-toed out right behind the other one."

"Sorry," Baker apologized again. "They probably came for the free eats."

Elisa sipped her cider, none too thrilled at the idea of crews of prisoners working just beyond her fence. And a few of them obviously knew their way around Langston Green. "Do any of your work-release types do night work?"

He shrugged again. "Once in awhile. I have to arrange it in advance, so it's sort of a pain, but I like to do my part, hire the guys that really need the jobs. I've noticed that you do a lot of that in your business too." He flashed his perfect teeth.

What the heck did he mean by that? Was he referring to Timo, because he was Latino? Or Peter and Beth, because they were Asians? Or the summer crew of high school kids? She took another gulp of cider, searching for an appropriate response.

Baker nudged her shoulder with his. "Well?"

"Well what?"

"The offer. You've had plenty of time to think about it."

Elisa gestured at the crowd. "I would have thought this speaks for itself."

"What, this little ol' party?" Another sip of cider. "It's a good idea. The get-together, the classes. The Harvest Fest might be going a little overboard, but that's none of my concern."

"Langston Green is revived," she said. "Back in business."

His thick fingers clutched at her arm. "Oh, honey," he drawled, "I never for a minute intended to put you out of business. Haven't I made that clear?"

He'd made it about as clear as the winter fog on Puget Sound. Elisa was perplexed by Walt Baker, who employed needy convicts, offered her millions, and was simultaneously charming and insulting. Could he be behind the Good Samaritan act taking place next to their mutual property line? "Was that you," she said, "Helping out?"

Baker's face went blank for a second, then morphed into a little half smile. "I always help out whenever I can. Like I said, you can keep the greenhouse. The barn. The parking lot. A couple acres surrounding them. I've got plans to make it all blend together, golf course and gardens. It'll be great for both of us." He gave her bicep a little squeeze.

She resisted the impulse to lean down and bite the fingers gripping her upper arm. "That's not going to happen, Walt. I've got plans of my own."

He frowned and let his hand drop.

"Check 'em out." Lifting a crutch, she pointed toward the far wall, where sketches and blueprints for a remodeled Langston Green were tacked to the rough paneling.

As Baker approached the display, she couldn't help smiling. The new office/private-apartment building was smack-dab in the middle of the sixty acres he wanted. The inside wasn't all laid out yet, but the architect had sketched the outside to look similar to the old Langston homestead. A larger, updated Victorian, with expanded office space and a lounge as well as a kitchen, and this time with a separate entrance to a larger two-bedroom apartment upstairs. The separate entrance/exit building with checkout stands was something they'd needed for a long time. But she particularly liked the new pond and water garden in back of the barn. Water plants would make a nice addition to the business. She'd also added a small organic section where she'd grow salad greens and tomatoes for her own use and to sell to customers. Maybe she'd add an organic gardening class to the schedule.

She followed Baker to the drawings. "You can see, Walt, that the shenanigans going on around here did not pay off after all."

One bushy eyebrow rose. "Shenanigans?"

"Most of the little tricks were merely annoying, but I've got to admit that the fire was a real zinger."

He glared at her from beneath the brim of his hat. "I'm befuddled, ma'am, about why you're talking to me like this."

He did look confused, and maybe a little angry behind that. But then, the guy was a master con artist. "I want you to know, Walt," she told him, "that no matter what anyone pulls to try and put me out of business, it won't work. Langston Green is going to continue. In its present size. Better than ever."

Baker's eyes darkened. "You'll regret that decision later. Call me when you do." He turned on his heel and melted back into the crowd.

Gerald let the cider and doughnuts run out, signaling the end of the party. As the crowd dwindled, Elisa nervously prepared for her first class, Plant Rescue. Peter and Gerald had already helped her assemble various wounded plants, including a couple of small trees. These sad victims lined the walls of her new classroom. She took her position at the front of the room and watched as the twenty attendees trickled in to sit at the long tables, leaving one seat open in the back.

She introduced herself and welcomed them. The door opened. Jake, dressed in casual Irish fisherman's sweater and blue jeans, slid into the empty seat. Her heart lifted at the sight of him before she remembered to squelch that feeling. How could he just slide into and out of her life like that?

She stared at him, open-mouthed. "What are you doing here?"

The class eyed them warily, no doubt wondering if violence was about to erupt.

"I signed up, just like my fine fellow students," he said, making the others smile.

"But you don't even like plants. You told me you have a spiky thing and a dangly thing."

The class laughed, and blood rushed to her cheeks. Would she never cease to have these attacks of foot-in-mouth disease?

"And you promised not to tell my personal secrets in public." There was a twinkle in Jake's eyes. She dared to hope that it would stay there.

More hoots. When the noise died down, he said, "I signed up because if Sally and Phyllis ever need me, I want to be there for them."

"Sally the sanseveria? Phyllis the philodendron?" This time

she laughed along with the class, but inside she was wondering if Jake was going to be there for *her* in the future.

Everyone was watching. She looked away from him and began with a discussion of the importance of root systems, pointing out an ornamental pepper that could be saved even though it had been dumped out of its pot and broken many of its leaves, and a miniature fir that could not, because its main root had snapped.

"Oh, no," the chubby woman next to Jake moaned. "I have a Norfolk Island Pine that looks *exactly* like that. You mean it's not going to live?"

Jake patted her hand. "You'll feel better after you get a replacement. And as for the Norfolk pine, have you signed up for the composting class?"

Jake quickly became the class favorite. He charmed the older ladies, lifted pots and held plants for the handicapped instructor whenever Elisa needed assistance. The class spent two hours examining plants, pruning and repotting and even splinting and bandaging split branches with special tape. At the end of the class, Elisa donated the plant 'patients' to the students who wanted them, and Jake offered to help carry them to the parking lot.

Elisa noted with satisfaction that several students stopped at the greenhouse register to buy horticultural tape, rooting hormone, or potting soil. Fourteen of the twenty signed up for next week's class on making autumn centerpieces. It wasn't a lot of money or a crowd of new customers, but it was a start.

Jake never returned from the parking lot and Elisa steeled her heart against the disappointment. Had he really come to learn about plants? Or maybe he was checking up on her, ensuring that she made good her plans for the classes? Her feelings bruised again, she headed out the back door of the barn. The sun was setting, and her mood was sinking to the horizon as well. A cup of coffee couldn't hurt.

The aluminum steps of her newly-rented camper sank slightly as she mounted them and turned the key in the lock. The camper was a temporary measure, leased from a local rental outfit happy to give her a good deal during their slow winter months. It was what they called a fifth wheel, a fairly big rig designed to be towed with a large pickup. But it was still small for a woman on crutches. She'd learned to leave her crutches outside and carefully negotiate the narrow spaces within.

The camper was nowhere near as comfortable as the house she'd shared with Gail and Charlie. But with a quilt that her Nana Langston had made for her (preserved, thank God, in a cedar chest at Gail's house) on the bed, her photos and *huipil* on the wall, and a couple of pieces of her mother's Guatemalan pottery (likewise preserved by Gail) in the kitchen, it felt like home. Simon had taken to it right away, bringing her a slightly chewed field mouse as a housewarming gift.

She stepped into the compact kitchen. After dumping the stale dregs from the coffeepot, she rinsed the glass container. Then she heard a small noise behind her. Simon.

"If you had any consideration, you would have already made the coffee," she told him.

"And just what would I get in return?"

Startled, Elisa whirled, backed up against the counter. On the far side of the table, Jake sat in the shadows. After groping for the switches and mistakenly starting up the garbage disposal, Elisa finally flipped on the light over the dining table, illuminating his wolfish grin.

"That door was *locked*," she hissed.

"True. I even locked it again after I came in." He pointed to the window beside the door. It was screenless, pushed halfway open. "Is that your idea of security?"

"That's for Simon. He jumps up on that picnic table outside—"

"And if his paws were longer, he could reach through the

window and unlock the door, too. Just like I did."

"You've got a lot of nerve, Street."

"Jake." He leaned forward, his blue eyes serious. "I'm worried that you don't seem to be taking this situation seriously, Elisa. You shouldn't be living alone here. The vandalism incidents, the fire—"

"Now you're my protector?"

"Someone needs to be."

She was used to being told that she was hard-headed, to hearing other people call her tough, stubborn. No man had ever wanted to protect her. "Why are you really here, Jake?"

He waved a slip of paper in the air. "I brought the check."

"Yahoo! " She lowered herself onto the bench opposite him and held out her hand.

He handed her the check. "It's only a partial payment, for the greenhouse repairs. Another for damaged inventory will show up in about two weeks."

"Does the 'damaged inventory' include the main building?"

He grimaced. "Atlas Security is holding up the payment for the building for awhile."

She frowned. "How long is 'awhile'?"

He moved his shoulders in a non-committal gesture. "It was arson. So Atlas Security, naturally, would like to identify the arsonist. And make *him* pay if possible."

"They *have* to pay off eventually. Don't they?"

He smoothed his hair back from his brow. "Unless they come up with evidence that you or one of your employees burned down the place."

"You mean unless *you* come up with the evidence."

"Have you located Timo?" he asked.

"No. You haven't chased him down and beaten a confession out of him?"

"Not yet," he told her. "But I'm on it."

She shook her head. "You're looking in the wrong direction,

Jake. Are you checking on Walt Baker? He has some shady-looking employees. They're on work release."

That stopped him. "Work release?" After a moment of considering, he said, "You bet I'll keep an eye on Baker and check out his crew. But I'm not dropping Timo from my list."

A light knock on the door was followed by a shout. "Hey, Elisa, you in there?"

She got up to let Gerald in. He hesitated when he saw Jake at the table behind her. "If this is a bad time—"

"It's fine, Gerald. Mr. Street just dropped by to bring us a check for partial payment."

Jake showed no signs of getting up. Instead, he reached for the paper folded up onto the seat beside him and shook it out as if he intended to read it right there. He looked disturbingly comfortable in her camper. Exasperated, she turned back to her business partner. "I'm surprised you're still here. Did you need me?"

"I just wanted to say that I thought everything went really well. Everyone said your class was great, and we moved more inventory than we have since last summer. The party was—"

"A fantastic idea," she finished for him. "You deserve all the credit for coming up with it."

He beamed. "The photographer got a couple of really good photos of the crowd. The paper's doing a follow-up article. And announcing Harvest Fest, too. One month from today, right?"

Elisa felt as if a bucket of cold water had been dumped over her head. "That *is* what I said, isn't it?"

Gerald locked eyes with her. "Whatever possessed you?"

She gulped. "Temporary insanity?"

"That's what I thought."

"I want to get the good old days back, Ger. The Langston tradition. You'll help, right?"

He gave her a nod. "You can count on me. Tiffany, too." Gerald peered at Jake uncertainly before he turned back to her. "Well, if you don't need me, I'm taking off now. Tiff's waiting for me at the restaurant with her sister and Walt."

"Have a nice evening."

He shut the door behind him. The camper rocked slightly as he moved off the bottom step.

Jake lowered the paper and stared at her over the newsprint. "Your business partner's in love with you."

Where did he come up with *that*? "Don't be ridiculous! Gerald and I couldn't be less alike if we were raised on different planets. And he's engaged to Tiffany."

"None of which changes the fact that he lusts after *you*."

This talk of love and lust felt extremely personal. Elisa felt a blush rising from her neck to her cheeks. When Jake slid out from the table and stood up, his head only inches away from the low ceiling, the tiny room seemed barely large enough to contain his strong male presence.

To her dismay, he shrugged on his coat. He was leaving so soon? "Hell hath no fury like a man scorned," he misquoted. "I'd keep a close eye on him."

She looked away, afraid that he'd notice the disappointment in her eyes. "Seems like you want to keep a close eye on everyone I know."

He pointed a finger at her. "Elisa, someone wants your business to fail. They want you, personally, to fail. And the key word there is personal. Whoever's behind this is someone who knows you. Remember that." His voice softened as he added, "I don't want anything to happen to you."

"Nothing's happened since the fire."

"Which was only two weeks ago," he reminded her.

"Fifteen days," she corrected. She wanted to tell him that her Gremlin had changed to a good Samaritan. But then she'd have to admit that there were more unexplained events on her property.

He zipped up his windbreaker. "I don't like the idea of you living here right now."

Yet you're leaving, she wanted to say. But there were no promises between them. She told him, "Gerald and I installed new security cameras and motion-sensor lights yesterday."

"That's good." He looked around the interior of the camper.

"The monitors are in the greenhouse. There's no space in here."

"I guess that's better than nothing." He took a step toward the door.

Earlier today she'd been feeling upbeat for the first time since the quake. The earthquake party had felt like a celebration. Langston Green was off and, if not exactly running yet, at least back in the race. Gail and Charlie had left with their firemen, Gerald with Tiffany. And now Jake was leaving, probably off to some date with a former prom queen. She held the door open for him, barely leaving him enough space to squeeze past. "Thanks for the lecture," she said coolly.

Without warning, his arms were around her and his lips were pressed against hers, hot and eager. Startled into breathlessness, she put her hands to his shoulders, then stretched her fingers up the back of his neck, into his hair. She could feel him, hard against her, insistent, and she knew that he wanted her as much as she wanted him.

Then, suddenly, he broke off contact. Stepping back from her, nearly falling down the steps outside, he said, "Did I tell you that you did great today?"

Before she could gather her wits, the door banged shut behind him and he was gone. She raised her hand to her mouth as she stared, dazed, into the growing darkness. Her lips still burned from his embrace, as did other parts of her body that she didn't want to dwell on.

"Damn it, Jake Street," she muttered to the still evening air. "What the heck do you want?"

Chapter 13

Now he was kissing her again. What the hell was the matter with him? He had already mailed his acceptance of the FBI offer. This was his chance to get his honor back. He was leaving in a little more than five weeks. A new career was waiting for him. Providing he passed the physical and did well in the training. He wasn't concerned about the medical exam, but the classes were a different story. He'd be a lowly student to start out with, and probably one of the oldest ones, too. He hadn't studied since the police academy, and that was nearly nine years ago. He'd have to exercise self-discipline, get back in shape both mentally and physically. He didn't need distractions. Especially not ones as all-consuming as Elisa Langston.

This was stupid, it really was. He was a grown man, for God's sake, not some horny teenager. His mind was flooded with images: the hand-stitched Tree of Life quilt on her bed, the pottery bright with flowers and birds and butterflies, the wonderfully ornate *huipil* she'd shown him. Everything so rich with color. So daring, so lively. So Elisa. Then there was the turquoise sweater, how it had hugged her luscious figure, how it complemented her smooth olive skin. And she'd worn the antique hair barrette he'd given her from his grandmother's collection. It looked perfect in her shining raven hair.

He hadn't seen her fixed up before. Not that she didn't look good dressed in Charlie's castoffs with smudges of dirt on her cheeks and twist-ties in her hair. Elisa Langston would be enticing no matter what she wore. And she'd be just as hardheaded, just as determined that she was always right, that she could manage everything without anyone else's input.

He gripped the steering wheel hard as he stared at the inky waters of Lake Washington. Finally under control again, he steered the Land Rover from the tiny park in which he'd taken refuge, and started for home. It was completely dark now. The constant stream of lights on the 520 floating bridge told him that rush hour was in full swing. He headed for the freeway intersection to join the slow ooze of cars across the lake. The snail-like pace would give him time to get his head straight.

He had to sniff out the Langston Green arsonist and get the insurance file squared away, so that he could leave the Seattle area, his job, and Elisa Langston with a clear conscience. He'd told his bosses that Elisa was definitely not capable of setting the fire. Still, they didn't want to pay off until he'd checked out all the Langston Green employees, and he hadn't yet located Timoteo Martinez.

Elisa's office calendar hadn't provided any clues as to the kid's whereabouts this afternoon, but a sketchpad in her camper had yielded some interesting notes. Among drawings of Victorian farmhouses and maps of fish ponds, there had been the mysterious scrawl *T—CM, PS? T* was probably Timoteo. And *CM* could only be Crossroads Mall. *PS...* Hadn't the Mexican restaurant there been called Pacífico Sur? Something like that. His tired brain couldn't summon up the specifics. It was late, and he really should stop back in at the Seattle office. He'd check out the Mexican restaurant in the mall tomorrow.

He also needed to dig deeper into Walt Baker and his work-release laborers. Although the developer had no criminal record, he certainly had a motive for harassing Elisa. And he had a connection to Gerald Donaldson through the fiancée, Tiffany. As Elisa's business partner, Donaldson would know everything about the property and about Elisa's schedule. Working together, Baker and Donaldson had motive and opportunity to commit vandalism and arson.

Elisa was right, the cops were pretty useless in this situation. With limited manpower, police departments really weren't set up to prevent crimes, especially hit-and-run crimes against property like the ones that plagued Langston Green.

Jake raised a hand and wearily rubbed it across his forehead, catching the faint scent of the woman he'd just left. He moved his fingers to his nose, inhaled. Not perfume. Soap, and something vaguely herbal, aloe vera or cucumber, or maybe both. Probably lotion of some kind. It would be green. Elisa Langston would use green lotion.

He pictured her drinking coffee at the tiny table of her rented camper, the light spilling out the windows into the dark fields. Why had she moved back onto the property? She was all alone out there.

The floating bridge loomed ahead. The heck with the routine, with the office. He was sick of the routine, and he'd be done with Atlas Security Insurance soon anyway. Jerking the wheel, he gunned the engine and whipped across the carpool lane to the exit.

The woman's dark eyes were deep, dark brown, so close to black that it was hard to distinguish pupil from iris. Romance novels described green eyes as emeralds, blue eyes as sapphires. Why were there no wonderful words for brown eyes? Chocolate was about as attractive a description as she'd ever heard.

Elisa laid the old photograph on the bedspread and touched a fingertip gently to the glass over her mother's face. Brown eyes. Dark, straight hair. Petite stature. Those things she shared with Maria Elena. Although Elisa's own eye color could not even be described as chocolate. More like tea. Weak coffee. At best, brandy. And her skin: olive. Sounded more like a cocktail than a woman.

In the picture, Terrence Langston towered over Maria Elena

by a good twelve inches. His arms, around her, were pale in comparison to her skin. Her parents had been so different in looks, not to mention language and nationality. And temperament? Elisa remembered doing things with her mother that others considered wild. Picnics on rocks in the middle of streams, the water rushing loudly around them. Feeding the wild jays up at the pass. Dancing at concerts, even when everyone else stayed in their seats. Chasing butterflies, not to capture them but just to follow their beauty wherever it floated.

She'd always thought of her mother as a butterfly. Like a monarch that had to fly south to its homeland. Only her mother had never returned. Had never written.

What had happened between her mother and father? A flame of passion that had flared up during Terry Langston's Peace Corps years, and then been quickly snuffed out on his return to 'real life'?

"I loved your mother so much," her father had explained. "But she missed the mountains and jungles of her native country. The food. The Maya people, all her relatives. Guatemala called to her, and she had to go back."

As a child, Elisa had imagined Guatemala as a forest spirit, singing in the trees, luring unwary wanderers deeper and deeper into the woods until they simply vanished.

She set the photo back into its new pedestal on the bedside table. Her mother and father had fallen in love, produced a child. But their love hadn't lasted. They were just too different.

She turned out her light and lay in the dark, listening to the breeze outside, not really sleepy. It was not quite ten o'clock, even if it had been a long day. A good day, though: things had worked out nicely. But here she was at the end of it, alone again. She sighed and stretched out her hand to stroke Simon.

The cat bolted upright, growling. He leapt from the bed and stalked toward the kitchen. Elisa sat up. She sucked in a breath and crept down the hallway after Simon. Staring out the window in the door, she scanned the blackness, focusing on the far corner where the tidying up had been occurring. The Gremlin? The Good Samaritan? She could discern no movement other than a gentle swaying of vegetation in the light breeze.

"I can't see anybody out there, Simon." She stroked the stiff fur at the back of his neck. "Is it a feline intruder, peeing on your property?"

He growled in response, trying to convince her of his seriousness. His green-eyed gaze never wavered from the square of glass set into the camper door. Normally, Simon eagerly confronted other tomcats in his territory. But the window beside the door was still half-open, and the cat made no movement toward it. Her stomach clenched. Whatever was out there, Simon was afraid of it.

She let her gaze roam over the nursery property closer in, searching for the slinking trot of coyotes, the lumber of a raccoon. It was dark tonight, with only a sliver of moon peeking between jetting clouds. Beyond the pool of brightness shed by the new security light at the back of the barn, Elisa couldn't see much. She recognized the spiky silhouettes of a stack of bareroot fruit trees, waiting to be tagged and displayed. A couple of two-wheeled carts upended next to the trees. The angular hulk of the storage shed.

There. In front of the upended carts. Her breath caught in her throat. A tall black figure, barely visible among all the other shapes. A man. The Gremlin.

A chill shot through her body, raising pimples on her bare arms. The window by the door was half open. The door was locked, but as Jake had demonstrated, anyone could easily enter by reaching in through the window and unlocking the door. If she shut the window now, the Gremlin would see her for sure. If she didn't shut it, would he try to come in?

She dropped out of sight from the windows, and crawled to the kitchen. Reaching up, she felt for the cast-iron griddle she'd left on the stovetop. She sat on the floor, trying to catch her breath, anticipating the ominous tap of footsteps. After a long moment of listening to Simon's growls and hisses and to her own heartbeat thudding in her head, she began to feel like some comic-book woman, dashing for a frying pan to use as a weapon. Moving to the window, she raised her head just enough to peer out.

The Gremlin hadn't moved. She ducked her head, sat down next to the door with her back against the wall. Simon had slunk into the dining area. He perched on top of the table, hissing like an outraged mongoose. The noise was not helping her nerves.

She chanced another quick peek. If the intruder had changed position, it hadn't been more than a few inches. He was big. The sinister image of Baker's blond work-release laborer rose up in her imagination. What was that he held in his hand? Looked like a short club of some kind: what did they call it, a sap? That's what she was starting to feel like, a sap of a different sort.

Maybe he was waiting to make sure she was asleep before ... before what? Up to now, the Gremlin had focused on property damage. Jake had suggested he might be escalating, and might even attempt murder. Elisa's stomach somersaulted as a thought suddenly occurred to her, a crime that would combine property damage and murder. Maybe he didn't need to come in to get to her. Maybe the Gremlin had attached a bomb to the camper and was waiting for it to blow.

Whatever he had in mind for her, she wasn't going to wait for it. Elisa wormed her way across the floor back to the bedroom, tucking Simon under her arm. He growled and struggled. She held on. She verified that the Gremlin had no accomplice in back of the camper. Then she silently inched open the window over the bed. After dropping Simon out, she followed, thrusting out her cast first and then hanging onto the window casing as she lowered herself to the ground. With her feet on the ground, she released the window casing slowly, hoping the shifting of the camper wouldn't be noticeable in the dark. Then she limped through the shadows toward the new storage shed.

Jake moved the bottle of wine to his other hand, debating what to do. All lights were out in the camper. Elisa must have gone to bed, even though it was not quite ten o'clock. He was reasonably sure she was still here; the company van and her pickup were in the parking lot. Was she asleep? Did he dare knock on the door? This was a stupid, whimsical thing to do. He really ought to take the wine home and drink it himself.

Was that a flicker of movement inside? The camper rocked slightly. He straightened, his muscles taut now. Was someone inside with Elisa?

Out of the corner of his eye, he caught a glimpse of movement. A lithe black-and-white form streaked through the shadows. Her cat, Simon. Then he heard a muffled noise behind him. Then another. Footsteps, deadened by the soft dirt underfoot. He was not alone out here in the dark. He tensed, feeling for his pistol before he remembered it was locked in the glove box of his Rover.

It had to be Elisa's Gremlin. Whatever he was up to, this would be the end of his escapades. Jake quickly searched the surrounding area for something that would serve as a better weapon than a bottle of pinot gris.

Keeping to the shadows, Elisa grabbed a shovel from the tools grouped by the shed's back door. It was cold out here. All she had on was an extra-large T-shirt that only reached her thighs. Why didn't she sleep in something more sensible, like long johns or sweats? Hadn't she of all people learned by now, that at any moment one could be surprised by an earthquake or a fire? She really should be more prepared for disasters: they seemed to happen to her regularly these days.

She couldn't yet see the man, but she feel him waiting. There. The darker spot among the shadows, over by the bareroot fruit trees. She was in luck; he still had his back to her. She swung the shovel over her shoulder like a baseball bat and limped toward the Gremlin.

The best weapon Jake had been able to come up with was some sort of bush. There was a whole pile of them nearby. At least this one had a sturdy trunk and its roots were bound in a solid ball of dirt and burlap. He could hear the intruder approaching from behind, but decided to let the Gremlin believe he had the element of surprise.

At the last minute, when he sensed that the shadowy presence was just behind him, Jake hefted the bush and swiveled around to face his attacker, swinging the heavy root ball like a medieval mace.

Elisa aimed for the back of the Gremlin's head. The shovel had nearly connected when the intruder pivoted, now clutching something more stout than a sap. The shaft of his weapon blocked the shovel, which flew from her fingers and bounced off his shoulder before clattering to the ground. In the next second, the end of his weapon whizzed by her face. Instinctively she ducked and it grazed the side of her head just above her left ear before it cracked in half, the heavy end flying over her shoulder to impact the shed behind her.

The figure, suddenly unbalanced, staggered back and collided with an upended cart. He grappled with the unfamiliar object for a second before he picked up another weapon. She recognized the object in his hands now: one of her bareroot fruit trees.

"Drop that goddamn tree," she yelled. "Or I'll shoot you right where you stand!"

The figure stopped in mid-stride. "Since when do you have a gun?"

She straightened. "Jake?"

"If you were ready to shoot me, why did you hit me with a shovel first?" He rubbed his shoulder gingerly.

"You smacked me with a root ball!" she retorted. "What the heck are you doing out here, sneaking around, destroying my inventory?"

He came a few steps closer. "I thought you were the Gremlin."

She rubbed her head where the burlap had connected, raking out a few pieces of dirt. "And I thought *you* were the Gremlin. But that still doesn't explain what you're doing out here."

Simon came forward from the shadows, his patches of white fur glowing in the dim light. He made a quick pass, rubbing across Jake's shins, then stood on his hind legs and dug his claws into Jake's khaki-covered thighs.

"Yow!" Jake bent over and batted at the cat's paws.

"Kill, Simon," Elisa said.

Jake unhooked Simon's claws from his pant legs, but then, taking advantage of Jake's bent position, the cat jumped onto his shoulder. Jake straightened, but Simon crouched next to his neck, digging his claws in. The tomcat rubbed his cheek against the man's chin.

"Call off your cat," Jake muttered, while gently stroking Simon's tail.

"Not until you tell me what you're doing here skulking around in the middle of the night."

"It's not even ten thirty." Man and cat took a step forward. "I ... uh ... thought I may have left a little ... hastily. I brought you a bottle of wine." He thrust it toward her. "Oregon pinot gris."

"My favorite." But what did his return mean? "Is the wine

cold?" The words sounded inane, but she couldn't think of anything else to say.

He touched the bottle against her bare arm, and she flinched back from the cold glass. Jake reached for her, wrapped warm fingers around her biceps. "I believe this wine is about the same temperature as you are," he remarked.

"Got that right," she said. Whatever it meant, Jake was here now. She took Simon from his shoulder and snuggled the cat's warm body into her arms. "Let's continue this inside."

"I thought you'd never ask."

He followed her to the camper door. Which was, of course, locked. After shooting an exasperated look at her, Jake climbed to the top of the picnic table, reached through the open window, and unlocked the door.

As soon as they were inside, he set the wine on the table, pulled off his jacket, and wrapped his arms around her. Elisa nestled against Jake's chest. So warm, so broad. Lean muscles under the sweater. It had been a long time since she'd let herself get lost in a man's embrace. He pulled her closer, his hands on her hips now, pressing her tightly against him. The hardness she felt through his clothes left no doubt about what he had in mind.

"You came back," she said breathily.

His mouth pressed urgently against hers, then released just long enough for him to say, "Of course."

His lips moved across her brow, gently nibbling at her hairline, at her left ear, leaving a trail of fire in their wake. He paused to rub a clot of something from his lower lip. Dirt. He smiled and pressed her close again. "My earth goddess."

"Now I'm a goddess, not an arsonist?"

He picked her up, set her on the cool Formica tabletop, pressed himself between her legs. "I have a new theory about the fire." He tugged the sleeve of her loose tee shirt over her shoulder and applied his lips to her bare skin.

"Mmmmm?" It was the most coherent response she could manage under the circumstances.

"Spontaneous combustion." These words were whispered into her right ear during a pause from nibbling her neck. "You could melt anything." His fingertips grazed her breast now, teasing.

Her nipples hardened in response. She groaned.

"Do you want to?" he whispered hoarsely.

"Melt?" she asked mischievously. "Oh, yes, Jake. Yes. But—"

"I've got protection." His lips tickled her earlobe now.

She blushed. Of course a man like Jake would be carrying. And it was a good thing, since she hadn't purchased condoms for longer than she could remember. "That's good, Jake, but I actually meant, well, my cast—"

"Trust me," he murmured in her ear, "I can work around it."

He swept her up from the table and staggered clumsily through the narrow hallway into the bedroom. Somehow he managed to pull her tee shirt over her head as he tossed her onto the bed. Her fingers fumbled at his fly while he ripped off his shirt. And then they were gloriously unclothed, marveling in each other's bodies. Elisa was grateful for the cool breeze from the open window. It did seem that their heat could ignite a conflagration.

Timo watched the camper for a few minutes to be sure no further violence erupted. Elisa had ended up going with the man willingly, although they'd fought each other to begin with. She obviously had no idea that the man was the enemy. Americans could be so clueless.

Yawning, he returned to his labors. Another hour, then he could sleep. A wail from beyond the fence made him stiffen. Although it was little more than a whimper, the noise seemed loud in the quiet night. The cry was quickly stifled, and Timo felt a stab of anxiety about Rosa. No, surely she was okay,

Jorge was with her, and he came from a big family, he would know what to do. All the Tiburones wanted to help him out, Jorge had told him. We're your family now, he said.

Yeah, right. Timo rubbed his burning eyes. He wasn't as naïve as an American. He knew what the Tiburones were all about, especially after he'd seen them burn down that house. Yeah, he'd seen the fancy cars and big-screen TVs that came from selling drugs. But he'd also seen the pools of dark red mud left behind after the bodies had been removed from the dusty alleys of his village. His father had been one of those casualties, killed just for refusing to reveal the whereabouts of a cousin the drug lords had sought.

There was the whimper again. Rosa, crying for him. Jorge wouldn't be able to stop her now. He pushed himself to his feet and stumbled through the rows of plants toward the fence.

An hour later, when Jake rose to get the wine, Elisa stretched languorously across the tangled sheets and admired his tight buttocks as they disappeared through the doorway. A few seconds afterwards, she heard the pop of a cork. He returned with a glass in each hand, the bottle tucked under his arm. She propped herself up against the headboard, giggling. "A naked man serving wine. I love it."

"Next time I'll wear a bow tie, like the classy waiters."

"And I know just where you can hang your little linen towel."

"First things first." He handed her a glass. "Does madam approve of the vintage?"

She took a sip. Cool, dry. Perfect. "I could get used to this."

He knelt on the bed next to her. "I could get used to *this*," he murmured, sliding a hand over the silky skin of her bare hip. "I've dreamed about you, about us, about this, since I was fifteen."

She raised an eyebrow. "That's a disturbing thought, little Benjie lusting after me way back then."

His hand slid up to cup one breast. The delicate friction of his fingertips launched a ripple of electricity that spread throughout her core. "How do you feel about big Jake lusting after you now?"

"Infinitely more intriguing." She pressed her lips to the smooth hard muscle just above his left nipple for a long moment, then looked into his eyes as she stroked a finger along the scar that radiated from his left eyebrow.

He gently pushed her back down onto the sheets. A few drops of wine spilled onto her breast from the glass he held. Leaning forward, he licked them off her skin. She gasped at the warm slick wetness of his tongue followed by the rasp of whiskers.

She dribbled some of the wine from her glass on his ear. "Whoops! Let me clean that off." Her lips nibbled at his earlobe for a few seconds, then she let her tongue play down his neck to the hollow beneath his Adam's apple.

"You didn't get quite all of it," he moaned. "Some trickled down lower."

"Really?" She slid her hand down between their bellies. "Oh, yes, I see what you mean. Would you like me to fix that?"

"Yes, ma'am." He crushed his lips against hers. "Ummm-hmmmm." The vibration from his hummed response traveled from his mouth to hers and all the way down to her toes, heating up everything in between.

Then came the explosion.

Chapter 14

The shockwave rocked the camper, followed a fraction of a second later by loud impacts against its metal sides. Several chunks of lumber flew in through the open window, landing on top of the sheets. Instinctively, Jake flattened himself on top of Elisa to shield her. When the rain of debris stopped, he scrambled out of bed.

"What in the hell?" He quickly pulled on his pants and shoes.

Elisa sat up, glanced out the window. "That came from the barn."

"Stay here," he told her.

"Like hell I will," he heard her say as he galloped for the door. Throwing it open, he leapt over the steps and dashed into the shadow of the shed. With his back to the wall of the building, he quickly surveyed the area. No movement as far as he could see. Nobody running from the scene.

The back of the barn sported a large hole in the cedar siding, through which a geyser of water spouted up from the ground. Jagged pieces of white ceramic, wallboard, and two-by-fours splayed out from the fountain in a fan pattern. The security light above the back door had shattered. The gushing water was silvery in the moonlight, almost pretty.

Elisa joined him, now wearing jeans, a sweatshirt, and one boot. "Watch out for your foot," he said, nodding toward the bare toes sticking out of her cast. "Some of this stuff is sharp."

"My new bathroom!" She disappeared inside the barn and must have located the shutoff valve, because the fountain of water ceased. It seemed extraordinarily quiet all of a sudden. She slogged back to his side through the muddy wreckage. "Damn Gremlin," she moaned, surveying the damage. "Was it a firecracker in the toilet?"

He bent over to retrieve a scrap of curled cardboard from the ground. "This is usually a kid's trick."

"It wasn't Timo," she responded immediately.

Part of a label was still readable on the shred he held in his hand. He straightened, passed her the scrap of paper. "It wasn't a firecracker."

She checked the scrap, then glanced at him, her eyes round with surprise. "Dynamite?"

"This kid has access to some serious explosives." If the Gremlin had planted the dynamite under the camper, only twenty yards away, he and Elisa would be in shreds similar to those littered all around them. He pointed to the back door of the barn, which now hung unevenly from one remaining hinge attached to the splintered frame. "Was this locked?" His voice sounded distant. His ears still rang from the explosion.

"I locked all the doors before I came to bed." Elisa rubbed at her own ears as if trying to clear them, too. Moonlight glinted from her lustrous black hair as her fingers twitched through it. He felt the urge to take her in his arms again, carry her off to someplace safe. *Focus*, he scolded himself. "Who has keys to the barn?"

"I keep mine in my desk in the main building, I mean, in the greenhouse. Which is also locked. Peter and Gerald each have a key."

"Go call them both, right now," he told her. "I'm going to get a couple of things out of my car and have a look around. So if you see a guy skulking through the shadows out there, don't shoot him with that imaginary gun of yours."

She gave him a look. "Funny."

"Go make those calls. And after you've talked to them, call the police."

She snapped a salute. "Yes, master. Right away, mein general." She hobbled back toward the camper.

Oops. He should know by now that Elisa Langston would not take kindly to orders. Well, he'd have to remedy that later. He headed for his Rover and his pistol.

Peter Nguyen answered in Vietnamese. His hoarseness told Elisa that he'd been asleep. He verified that his key was on a ring hanging from a hook in the kitchen. "Do you need me to come?"

"Thanks, Peter, but I'm all right and I'm not alone."

"Oh?"

She wound the cord of the office phone around her finger and debated what to tell him. Finally, she said, "That insurance investigator, Jake Street, is already here."

"I see," he replied. She hung up, guessing that there was a reason they called Asians inscrutable. Or maybe the right word was diplomatic. It was hard to tell.

After dialing Gerald's condo, Elisa let the phone ring ten times.

"What?" Gerald finally yelped.

"It's Elisa. Sorry to call so late, but we had another incident at Langston Green."

"Need me to come over?" He sounded eager. "I can be there in ten minutes." In the background, Elisa heard a woman's voice saying something unintelligible.

"No, thanks, Ger. It's all over now, I think. Nothing too dramatic." She told him about the toilet blowing up.

"You don't consider that dramatic?" he said. "You shouldn't be there alone."

Should she admit to Jake's presence? Gerald had already

seen him earlier in her camper. But there were some things a business owner shouldn't share with her partners. "I've called the police," she lied. "They'll be here any minute."

Gerald's keys to Langston Green were accounted for, right on the dresser where he always left them. "Sure you don't need me?"

"I don't want to interrupt you and Tiffany any more than I already have."

"Tiff's at her place."

"Oh. I thought I heard a female voice in the background."

"I fell asleep with the television on." After a short pause, he added, "It's not like Tiffany and I are joined at the hip or anything, Elisa."

Odd comment for an engaged man to make. She said goodnight. As she placed the phone back into its receiver, Jake walked into the greenhouse office, still bare-chested. In one hand he held a flashlight; in the other, a pistol.

"Nobody out there," he told her. "Did you know you have a loose board in the fence at the far end? Your Gremlin could be slipping in and out that way."

"I'll fix it tomorrow." Actually, she was planning to trap the vandal by allowing him to use the same route, but she wasn't about to tell Jake that. She was having a hard time keeping her mind on fences and vandalism with a muscular half-naked man waving a gun in front of her. She placed her hands on the smooth warm skin just above the waistband of his trousers. "Gerald and Peter are at home, with their keys, *mi general.*"

He blinked several times, but refused to be distracted. "Did you ever loan Timo Martinez your keys?"

Of course she had, but she wasn't about to admit that, either. "It's not Timo, Jake. He'd never do this."

He tucked the pistol into the waistband of his pants. "He belongs to a gang, Elisa."

She dropped her hands from his waist and took a step back.

"He doesn't have time. He worked nearly every daylight hour this summer."

"He's listed in police reports as a member of Los Tiburones."

"Even if he knew them before, Timo's not associated with them now."

"But they may still be associating with *him*."

"Right," she said, her tone sarcastic. "Well, let's have a look, shall we?" She turned to the bank of recorders and monitors, extracted a videotape from a new surveillance camera, and thrust it into a VCR.

"Set it up," he told her. "I'm going to get my shirt and jacket. I'll be right back." He disappeared in the direction of the camper.

She inserted the videotape into the player and rewound it to the beginning. The tapes were eight-hour loops that continuously recorded. Up close, the screen revealed dark vegetation swaying in the breeze. In the background was the wooden fence, and beyond, the looming shapes of Baker's townhouses. Elisa fast-forwarded, watching for movement. There. She pressed Pause. A small figure, shrouded in a dark hooded sweatshirt and jeans, slipping though the fence. The face could not be seen.

Jake came back in time to see the figure move out of sight. "Anything?"

Elisa's eyes were still on the screen. "I can tell you that the Gremlin is small and favors dark clothes. Other than that—" She stopped talking as gloved fingers appeared in front of the lens, then the image dissolved into blackness. "What the heck?"

"The lens was covered with duct tape," he told her. "I didn't take it off. The police will want to dust for prints."

She turned toward him. "I saw gloves."

He shrugged. "He might have laid down a print on the roll of tape before he gloved up." He struggled with the collar of his shirt, rolled under the sweater. Elisa reached up and, curling her fingers around his neck, pulled it out for him. The feel of her body pressed against his, the caress of her small warm fingers on his neck, made him want to rip off her clothes all over again. He bent his head and inhaled the scent of her hair. He tucked a strand of hair behind her ear, thought about kissing her there, right below her velvety earlobe.

She smiled and stepped back, turned and exchanged tapes, rewound again. "This is from the new camera I aimed toward the buildings."

The scene was dark, but with the aid of the security light, they could make out the edge of the barn, the shape of her camper and rows of plants, leaves moving in the breeze. Then a shadow cleaved in two, revealing the shape of a man.

Jake's heart skipped a beat. "He's got something in his hand."

"A wine bottle," Elisa commented.

"Oh yeah." It was embarrassing, the trouble lust could get a man into. He'd completely forgotten about the cameras. He watched the two of them battle in the moonlight, saw himself being attacked by the cat, observed the three of them staggering to the door of Elisa's camper.

She placed her thumb on the fast-forward button and cleared her throat before saying, "Maybe the cops don't need to know about this videotape." A smile played across her lips. "I think I forgot to put a tape in that particular camera. Silly me."

"Thank God you're a dufus." He put a hand on her shoulder.

At that moment, a hand appeared in front of the lens and then the screen went black.

"So now we know he's observant and thorough," she said, turning off the video player.

"The cops can still recover the duct tape," he told her, "Even if a camera had no videotape inside."

"Good idea," she said. "We'll tell them when they get here."

Jake experienced a flare of panic. "Are they on their way?"

"I was just about to call them."

He shifted his weight from one foot to the other. "They don't need to, uh, know I was here."

Less than an hour ago they were making love, and now he didn't want anyone to know he'd been with her? If that wasn't insulting... In the next second, Elisa realized what he was thinking. If the police knew she was having a fling with her insurance investigator, it wouldn't look good for either of them.

"I understand," she told him. "I won't volunteer any information they don't ask for."

"After you talk to them, get yourself over to your mother's house."

Stay put. Go make those calls. Get yourself over to your mother's house. Did he have to sound so mandatory? She shook her head. "This is home now. I'm not afraid."

He groaned. "Elisa, you should be afraid."

She put her hand on his chest. "Look, Jake, if the Gremlin wanted to get *me*, he would have put the dynamite under the camper, wouldn't he? And now that he's gotten away with this, he won't be back tonight."

"You think you know what's in the mind of this nutcase?" He sighed dramatically. "Well then, get back in the camper as soon as you call. I'm going to cruise around a little right now."

"Baker's Acres?"

He nodded. "Then I'll drive by Baker's house." He turned on his heel and headed toward his Land Rover.

He had Baker's home address memorized? Jake Street, passionate lover, had morphed back into Jake Street, detective. She didn't even rate a good-bye kiss?

"Close that window by the front door," he yelled over his shoulder. "And don't come out until you're sure it's a cop knocking on your door."

Frowning fiercely at his retreating figure, she picked up the phone to call the police. So much for romance.

It was two A.M. by the time the police left, after searching the property, attempting to lift prints from the back fence and the doorknob on the barn's back door, and removing the duct tape pressed over the camera lenses. After they, too, failed to convince her to sleep elsewhere, they promised to make a couple of sweeps through the property during the night.

When she finally returned to her bedroom in the camper, she discovered Simon had taken Jake's place in the bed. The cat lay on the pillow, switching his tail defiantly.

"Don't fret, old man." She scratched him just above his tail, his favorite spot. "I'll always have room for you."

He narrowed his green eyes.

"Do you know who our Gremlin is?"

"Rrrow." His triangular face took on a wise look.

"And how about the winning Lotto numbers?"

"Rrrowrr." Simon closed his eyes and stretched out his front paws, his claws retracting and withdrawing now. His purr was loud in the quiet night.

"Just as I thought. Males pretend they know everything when they want to get their itch scratched." She sank back onto her pillow.

Sleep was long in coming, and fitful even after it did. At four a.m, she was startled by a man shining a flashlight on the camper. When he saw her at the window, he directed the beam onto his own shoulder, and she recognized the badge of the Woodinville police. She waved and nestled again into her pillow, falling back into a restless unconsciousness. Images of Jake Street, both naked and clothed, kept intruding into nightmares of fires and explosions and financial ruin. In her dreams she could run swiftly and wrap both legs around her man.

She woke at first light, disappointed to find herself alone, the cast still on her leg, and the back corner of the barn still in ruins. Just once in her life, she'd appreciate opening her eyes and discovering that her bad dreams were only figments of her imagination.

Chapter 15

When she entered the office area in the greenhouse, she found Beth, Peter, and Gerald bent over the morning paper. Gerald was clipping out an article on the front page in preparation for preserving it in a glass-lined frame.

"Do I get to see?" she asked wearily.

"Wait for it." Gerald finished the last snip, pressed the newsprint onto the glass and inserted the cardboard backing. He held up the finished product.

Langston Green Back on Track was the headline over a photo of Elisa in front of the class yesterday. She gesticulated at a sagging plant held by Jake. Her mouth was open, and one strand of errant hair made a mockery out of what otherwise would have been a straight part.

"Oh jeez," she moaned.

"It looks great." Gerald took the frame from her. "And it's wonderful advertising."

"Enjoy it while you can. Wait until you see what they print about Langston Green tomorrow morning."

Gerald placed the frame on the desktop. "I'll do my best to keep the Great Exploding Toilet Episode out of the news."

Beth raised a hand to the side of her face. "Exploding toilet?" she asked, as if she hadn't gotten the English quite right. Turning to Peter, she asked in Vietnamese.

Peter quickly explained last night's event to her, ending with the word "ka-boom." Beth looked at Elisa with wide eyes, torn between a desire to giggle and a need to express her horror. "Oh," she finally got out, patting Elisa on the shoulder.

"People!" Gerald tapped a fingernail against the glass over the article. "Since it says right here in print that we're reviving Harvest Fest one month from yesterday, we need to leave that mess to the police and work on our game plan right away."

"One month." Peter pressed his hands to his head as if it ached.

"Four weeks." Beth chewed a knuckle, looking around her at the disorder of their makeshift office.

Elisa was wondering just how embarrassing it would be to print a retraction of the party announcement when Gerald again hissed, "Team! We've done this before; we can do it again."

Peter dropped his hands and straightened. "No problem."

"It will be fun," Beth offered.

"Just like the Good Old Days," Gerald said, gesturing toward the champagne-toast photo on the wall. "By the end of the day, I want each of you to come up with a list of things that need to be done."

Beth and Peter turned to Elisa for confirmation. "What he said." She pointed toward Gerald.

Peter and Beth retreated to the greenhouse, chattering in Vietnamese.

Gerald pushed her into a chair and slid it up to the desk. After pouring a cup of coffee, he handed it to her. "You need this."

"It's that obvious?"

He slid into the chair on the other side of the desk and pulled out a lined notepad. "Elisa, keep the police, the fire department, and that annoying insurance guy out of my hair, and I'll take care of the rest. And try to keep anything else from exploding or burning down, okay?"

"I'll try." She took a swallow of the hot coffee, wondering how she could keep that vow. Her passionate hours with Jake seemed like a distant dream.

As she worked throughout the day, she kept looking over her shoulder, half expecting to see a shadowy figure creeping up behind her, half expecting Jake to show up. Neither happened. After depositing the insurance check, she scheduled repairs for the greenhouse, as well as for the damaged barn. She could hardly believe she had to get the workmen back, had to go through the construction process all over again. Gerald didn't improve her mood when he mentioned filing yet another insurance claim for the dynamite damage.

This felt like some sort of time warp—the Gremlin destroyed a piece of Langston Green, she repaired it, and then it was destroyed again. How long could they file insurance claims before Atlas Security dropped them cold? Or until the police jailed her for insurance fraud?

Jake entered his supervisor's office with some trepidation. He expected a lecture about spending too much time on the Langston case. He mentally prepared a response about how all the other cases were minor, while the Langston Green investigation had to be solved because the crimes were continuing and were bound to cost Atlas even more in insurance claims—

"Is this you?" Steven Swain tapped an index finger on a grainy photo of the front page of the Valley News.

Jake took the newspaper from him, blinked at the photo of himself holding a pot for Elisa. He looked like a subservient goofball. "I can explain."

"I certainly hope so." Swain sat down behind his desk and gestured to the guest chair beside Jake. "This looks like a conflict of interest to me."

Jake swallowed against the tight knot of anger gathering in his windpipe. His FBI physical results weren't back yet; it was too early to tell Swain that he could shove this job. He sat down and made an effort to unclench his fists.

~

With Gerald's help, Elisa installed a new motion-sensor security light a hundred yards from the back fence and replaced the one at the back of the barn. She was not going to wait like some helpless damsel for Jake or the police to solve this case. The Gremlin was her problem. She was going on the offensive. At nightfall, she gathered up a sleeping bag, a thermos of coffee, and a flashlight. After leaning a ladder against the equipment shed, she climbed to the flat roof.

Simon insisted on accompanying her, riding to the top of the ladder on her shoulder. He stood guard at the edge of the eastern gutter, scrutinizing the fields with the attitude of a cougar surveying his domain from a mountain ledge. Elisa chose the southern flank, facing the fence that divided her property from Baker's. She'd purposely not repaired the loose board, hoping to catch the Gremlin on his habitual route.

At ten o'clock, a police cruiser stopped in the parking lot. The officer jumped when the security light came on as he passed beneath it, yelping "Police!" and leaping back into the shadows with his hand on his gun. After he ran a flashlight over Elisa's camper and walked the perimeters of the greenhouse and barn, Elisa heard his car door close and the crunch of gravel as the patrol car drove away.

By twelve thirty A.M., the thermos held only enough coffee for one last cold cup. Elisa was pinching herself to stay alert, trying to remember the names of the constellations that gleamed brilliantly in the autumn sky. The nightly dew was already condensing. She shivered. Why hadn't she thought to bring a waterproof tarp? Not to mention more coffee.

It was dark in the alley. The Gremlin had a head start. The ground was uneven, and the alley so cluttered with debris and weeds that Jake could barely find his way. The toe of his shoe caught on something—a burlap bag?—and he stumbled and nearly fell. When he straightened, he found himself looking down the barrel of a Glock. Behind the pistol, barely visible in the fractured moonlight, were a boy's dark eyes, rounded with fright.

Jake's own gun was inches away from the boy's chest. He could hear the teenager breathing, smell his sweat.

"Don't do it, Jake." Elisa materialized beside him. The barrel of the boy's gun changed targets, now aiming at her. Jake tensed.

"No, Jake," she said. "He's just a boy."

She sounded so sure. Maybe he could shoot him in the leg or shoulder instead of the torso as the department regulations stated. As Jake was trying to decide the right thing to do, the boy's Glock went off, sending a bullet straight into Elisa Langston's heart.

The sheets ripped from beneath the mattress as Jake sat bolt upright in bed, gasping for breath. He hadn't dreamed of the shooting incident for nearly a year now. Was his subconscious trying to send him a message? He pulled his legs from under the covers, stood up in his quiet bedroom. No matter what his boss said, he couldn't leave Elisa alone out there. He was the streetwise one, not she. What the hell had he done leaving her all alone tonight?

Elisa had dozed off, but was instantly awake when she heard Simon utter the chirping noise he reserved for prey. He stood, twitching his tail. Then Elisa heard the scratch of gravel between the greenhouse and the barn. She crawled to the northern edge of the roof.

Another cop? She couldn't see the parking lot from her position. She didn't hear the static of a police radio in the background. The intruder tripped the motion sensor, but silently stepped out of the light too quickly for her to identify him.

When the shadow figure approached her temporary home, Simon growled. Elisa put a hand on the cat's hunched back in hopes of silencing him. The man disappeared behind the camper. Elisa held her breath. What was he doing back there? When she caught sight of him again, he was bent over, peering beneath the camper. He switched on the flashlight he held in his hand. Not a cop. Jake Street.

Delicious. Jake at her home two nights in a row.

Simon growled again. Jake looked over his shoulder in their direction. Elisa pressed herself flat against the damp roof. She counted to ten. When she raised up again, she could see Jake meandering through the rows of plants toward the back fence. He apparently hadn't seen her or the cat. He was coming in her direction, but he'd miss the shed by a good ten yards on his present course.

Simon flicked his tail back and forth, more relaxed now. Elisa grinned. She really should call out, let Jake know where she was, but this was too much fun. He no doubt assumed she was asleep in the camper and he was protecting her by roaming her fields. She heard him coming close.

Unscrewing the lid of the thermos, she dumped the last of the cold liquid into the plastic cup. She waited until the footsteps stopped a short distance away, sat up, and flung the coffee at the dark figure below.

He stumbled backward a step, let out a surprised "What the—" before stifling himself and turning toward the shed. She flashed her beam onto his face before he could raise his to illuminate her. "What are you doing out here, insurance man?"

"Nature walk." He quickly found the ladder and climbed up.

"Found much nature so far?" She extended a hand, helped him climb around the top of the ladder onto the roof.

He kept her hand in his as he crouched beside her. "An opossum, under your camper."

"Roberta. She's a regular."

"And just now, a rare night-flying coffeebird pooped on my head."

She ran her fingers through his wet hair. "In some cultures, that's considered a supreme honor."

He held up his pistol. "In other cultures, the coffeebird gets blown away. I don't suppose it would occur to you that a strange man wandering around your property in the dark might be carrying a gun."

"So you admit that you are a strange man. *I've* always thought so, but it's so rare to hear a male member of the species—"

"Elisa!" He shoved the pistol into a holster at the small of his back and captured the fingers she was stroking through his hair. "Your hands are freezing."

"I've been out here a while."

He sat down behind her, placing a leg on each side of her, then wrapped his arms around her. Simon came over, rubbed against them both, purring.

"Cops come by?" Jake's breath was warm on her right ear. The heat radiating from his body was heavenly.

"Like clockwork. Last night, at three and six A.M.. Tonight, they cruised through at ten and one. You just missed them."

"Oh, great. Three hour intervals on the dot." She could almost feel him rolling his eyes. "What did you intend to do if you spotted an intruder?"

Good question. She still hadn't purchased a cell phone. "Identify him," she said. "So I can nail him later."

"The Lone Ranger rides again," he groaned. "I was afraid of that. Guess I'll have to be Tonto."

She raised a hand and stroked the side of his face.

"Kemosabe," he breathed into her ear in a bad imitation of the masked man's Indian sidekick. "Tonto think you should have gun, or at least phone, if you want to nail bad man."

"Did you know that Tonto means 'Dummy' in Spanish?"

He snorted in surprise.

She patted his thigh. "It's okay. I'm sure it means Rides Like the Wind or Fierce Warrior in Apache. At least, I think Tonto was an Apache." She snuggled back into his embrace. "Do you always wrap yourself around your partner on stakeouts?"

He snorted again. "Valetti never seemed to appreciate it." Pulling aside her jacket and shirt collar, he applied his lips to the side of her neck. "Seen anything interesting?"

"So far only one wild turkey has tripped the light," she murmured, enjoying the sensation of his mouth, so warm against her skin.

"There are turkeys out here?" Testosterone made him a little slow on the uptake. A second later, he said, "Oh," and then applied his teeth to her earlobe.

"Yow! Turkeys with teeth!" She turned her head to kiss him. When she pulled away to breathe again, she murmured, "Suppose turkeys and coffeebirds are sexually compatible?"

"In the interest of science," he whispered hoarsely, "We should check it out. We might create a whole new species." He pulled her onto his lap, then turned and whipped her over his leg and onto her back. "Oh look, a sleeping bag!"

"How convenient. Keep watch, Simon." She busied herself trying to take off Jake's clothes as quickly as he was removing hers.

When they were well into the preliminaries, the light near the barn flashed on. Jake lifted his lips from Elisa's breast. A burly four-legged shape humped away from the circle of light. Simon growled.

"Raccoon." She tugged at Jake's arm. "Hey, I'm getting hypothermic."

"Let me see what I can do about that." He turned back to her. "I have a whole toolkit for thawing out women."

"*Women?*"

"I meant 'a woman'. Don't distract me."

"A whole toolkit?"

"This is one of my most useful gadgets." He applied his tongue to her nipple again.

"It's a start." She massaged his shoulders with her hands.

His hands slid down and gripped her buttocks. "And these."

"Whoa! You might want to warm up those tools once in a while."

"This one's warm." Raising himself on his toes, he rubbed himself between her legs.

The sensation of pulsing electricity was almost unbearable. "Oh, yeah." Elisa's breath came out in little gasps. "Let's use that one."

After they'd exhausted themselves and lay side by side, the light near the barn came on again. This time the shadow that passed through was lithe, low to the ground. Simon growled, hunched his back, and hissed.

"Tomcat," Elisa told Jake.

Simon leapt to the top of the ladder and vanished. Elisa crawled to the edge of the roof in time to see the cat bound off the ladder halfway down and hit the ground running.

"That cat descends ladders?" Jake asked.

"Apparently." Moving naked in the frigid night air was like plunging into Puget Sound. "Jeez, it's cold out here. Think we could move this stakeout into my camper?"

Jake reached for his clothes. "A brilliant suggestion. Before my own stake gets frozen."

She pulled her pants on over her cast. "Is there no end to men's euphemisms for their body parts?"

"When it comes to that particular part, we are all poets."

Elisa was fumbling to fasten her bra when the new security light in the back field flashed on. At first she saw nothing, but then a slender silhouette moved at the fringe of the illumination. Two-legged. Human. Moving toward the fence.

"Gremlin at eleven o'clock," she whispered.

"Damn it! Stay here." Jake dropped the shirt he was holding, jammed on his boots, and practically slid down the ladder. She heard thudding footsteps and breaking twigs all the way to the back fence.

She quickly finished dressing and descended the ladder much more awkwardly than he had. At the back fence, she found Jake attempting to squeeze through the gap left when the board was swung aside on its single nail. He had one leg and one shoulder through. His head and other arm, with the pistol in his upraised hand, were pressed against the fence boards as he tried to compress his chest. Elisa could see it was futile. He pulled himself out. "I told you to stay on the roof."

"Yes, you did."

He glared at her for a moment, then exhaled loudly in exasperation. "Well, he's definitely smaller than I am." He rubbed the scratches on his bare chest. "I thought you were going to fix this board." Noticing that she held his shirt, he thrust out a hand for it.

"I thought he'd be easier to catch if I let him come in the usual way." The moonlight accentuated Jake's lean muscular chest. A nice vision. She held the shirt just a little out of his reach.

He lunged for it and grabbed it away from her. Thrusting one arm into a sleeve, he said, "Was that the same person on the videotape?"

"I think so." She replayed the scene in her mind. "Slender, not very tall—"

He buttoned his shirt. "Looked like a kid to me. Timo?" Jake pressed his face to the gap and peered intently into the security lights of Baker's Acres.

She shrugged. "One of Baker's ex-cons was a small guy, too. Baker called him Wingate. A work-release guy, about the same size as Timo."

Jake put an arm around her shoulder. "If Wingate's on work-release," he told her, "He's not even an *ex*-con yet."

~

Timo huddled in the black shadow of the new building, waiting for his heart to stop pounding. If Rosa saw him now, she'd start wailing for sure. It didn't take much to set her off anymore.

He'd only escaped by inches. Those lights, they'd have to be that man's idea, too. But why hadn't the guy shot at him? He'd seen the moonlight glinting off his gun.

What would happen to Rosa if he didn't come back one of these times? He couldn't think about that. He could hear her now, crying again. Probably hungry or else she'd wet her pants for the fifth time today. Shouldn't she be potty-trained by now? He stood, reluctant to return to her fussing. Sometimes he had the urge to leave her on some church doorstep and just walk away.

He'd found another job, but the pay was half what he'd been making, and he wouldn't see a dollar until the end of next week. He missed the good old days at Langston Green, decent pay every week, respect for his skills, even sandwiches with Elisa sometimes. He chewed on a ragged fingernail. Could he get into the nursery again without getting caught?

Jake followed Elisa to her camper. He shook his head when he found she hadn't locked the door when she'd left. Would she never learn to protect herself?

"We'll get a guard to sit out there all night and catch this sucker," he told her.

Elisa shook her head. "It could take weeks for the Gremlin to show up again. I'm not paying someone to sit out there and twiddle his thumbs. I'll do it myself."

Heavens, the woman was stubborn! "You can't work all day and stay up all night. Maybe I can get Atlas to pay for the guard." Even as he said it, he knew that his boss would never go for that. He rubbed at the frown lines on his forehead. He'd pay the bill out of his own pocket. Not with a check, though, that would look bad while the investigation was still going on. He'd have to use cash.

As he was thinking through the paperwork problems, she laid a hand on his forearm. "The money's not the problem. I want to handle this myself."

He looked at her, at those bottomless brown eyes. "Not alone."

Her pretty face set into that mulish expression that he knew all too well. "It's my problem, Jake. If you want to help, check out Baker and his thugs."

"I'm doing that anyway."

"Oh, look." She pointed toward the window. A tiny frog clung to the outside of the pane. "I love these guys. They're so pretty. And they sing so wonderfully." Her expression was rapturous.

He leaned close to examine the diminutive creature. Even in the dim light spilling out from the camper, he could see that the thumb-sized frog truly was a work of art, green on its back and white on its underside, with a dramatic dark stripe through its eye. Traces of pink highlighted its lips and suction-cup toes. Elisa touched a fingertip to the glass on her side of window, as if to commune with the tiny amphibian.

Garter snakes and tree frogs. Elisa Langston was not at all what he'd come to expect from women. She did not find happiness in diamond necklaces, but in the hues of the setting sun, in the spangle of stars across the sky. In a chorus of tree frogs or the hoot of an owl.

Would that make her easier or harder to please than regular women? A man couldn't rely on the old standbys of jewelry or candy. Since flowers were the family business, those would be out, too. What could he possibly give such a woman?

"We could bring the frog inside," he suggested. "You could keep it in a terrarium."

She turned to regard him. "This frog's a wild thing, Jake. It would be wrong to keep him." Turning back to the window and the frog, she pressed a finger to the glass again. "I can only hope he'll want to stay with me for a while."

The frog twitched an eye and then leaped out of sight. Elisa stared sadly toward Baker's Acres. "With Baker converting the landscape to pavement and buildings, there'll be less room for tree frogs."

He slid onto the bench and tucked his long legs under the built-in table. "Some people call that progress. What can you do about it?"

She moved to the bench opposite his, dragging her cast under the table. "I'll tell you what I *am* doing about it. I'm making the frogs a water garden. And I'm going to teach people how to turn their yards into natural habitats." Reaching across the table, she took hold of his hands. "Thank you for the idea of classes, Jake." She pulled herself up and smacked him soundly on the lips.

He hadn't done anything. But he wasn't about to say anything that would make her stop kissing him.

A second later, Elisa yawned and checked her watch. "Jeez, it's three in the morning. I'm going to sleep." She slid out from the table and stood up. "Coming?" She held out a hand.

He stood, too, taking her hand. There was nothing he'd like better right now than to curl up with her. But he was still the insurance investigator and she was still his client. What if he was observed leaving her camper in the morning? If his bosses knew what had transpired between them already, they'd be questioning his judgment and holding up her reimbursement even longer. He said, "I should leave."

Pushing an ebony wave of hair from her brow, she gave him a searching look. "Love 'em and leave 'em?"

He felt as if he'd swallowed a rock. "I didn't mean it that way. I'll stay for a while."

She hugged him. "I was kidding, Jake. I'm not completely clueless." She leaned back to look up at him. "I know it would look bad for both of us if we were observed in *flagrante delicto*."

"I love it when you talk dirty in Spanish." Bending his head, he pressed his lips to hers.

Putting both hands on his chest, she shoved him away. "That was Latin, not Spanish. And you're going, remember?"

He wove his fingers through her tousled ebony tresses. Even her silky hair felt warm and vibrant. "I'll stay. We'll set the alarm for really early."

Reaching up, she pulled his hand out of her hair and held his fingers captive in her own. "It *is* really early, Jake." She gave him a little push toward the door.

"But the Gremlin—"

"Won't come back tonight," she said firmly. "Good night, Jake."

Simon watched from the top of the picnic table as he took one step down the stairs before he turned and gave her a quick kiss. "Good night, *querida*. I'll take a quick trot around the perimeter before I go."

"Thanks." She yawned and closed the door behind him.

He waited until he heard the click of the door lock before walking away. Then he patrolled the fence line just to be sure that nobody was lurking. The cat accompanied him as he made the rounds, and then stood in the moonlit parking lot, watching him with eyes that glowed eerily when he turned on the headlights, making him feel guilty as he drove away. When he walked into his condo and saw the FBI seal on the medical form, he felt guiltier still. He'd passed the physical with flying colors and promised to report for training in five weeks.

Elisa slid into bed. She'd forgotten how good it felt to be in a man's arms. At first, she thought that Jake was too tall for her.

But when he embraced her, pressed her head against his muscular chest, her ear over his heart, it felt right. And the sex—her toes curled just thinking about it.

If only she could tell Jake everything. She'd recognized the intruder, and it was the same one she'd seen on the video last night. She knew that distinct Mayan profile. She punched her pillow.

"Oh, Timo." She settled her head into the dent she'd made. "What are you up to?"

Chapter 16

She had to find Timo. She found out that the group's head-quarters were near Pioneer Square, just south of downtown Seattle. After thirty minutes of driving, she parked on the street among the beautiful old buildings that characterized Pioneer Square, and started walking south into one of Seattle's seediest areas. Although her leg was in a walking cast, she was supposed to use a cane, but it made her feel like even more of a cripple than the crutches, so she'd left it leaning against the kitchen cabinet at home. After several blocks, with her leg beginning to ache, she regretted that decision.

A group of dark youths clustered in front of an old wooden warehouse building with FOR SALE signs in the dusty windows. The cigarette butts littering the sidewalk around them testified that this was a regular hangout. Scrawled across the siding were slogans in Spanish, some obscene. She passed through the group once, walking quickly, her shoulders hunched defensively.

"Hey, *nena*," one of the youths hissed. "You need a shoulder to lean on?" Another added something in Spanish that Elisa couldn't quite hear, but made the others laugh. They looked like boys, most about Timo's age. All of them wore blue shark bandanas, identical to the one she'd found. These kids were trying to be tough, trying to be adult, trying to find a place to belong. Boys trying to pass for men. She could all too easily imagine Timo among them.

Sucking in a breath for courage, Elisa hobbled back. Several of the boys suddenly looked wary. Scuttling to the side of the building, they swung a loose section of siding aside to reveal a gap through which they quickly disappeared into the dark interior of the warehouse.

"Chiquita!"

A gangly youth touched her arm. She tried not to flinch. His pimpled face needed a shave. And he needed a bath. She told him, *"Busco Timo Martinez."*

He grinned and pointed toward the opening through which the others had disappeared.

"Timo's in there?" Could it really be this simple?

Pimple-face nodded, gestured toward the building.

She pushed aside the loose siding, peered into the dimness. After a few seconds, she realized that the glow she saw was not a patch of sunlight from a window, but a fire in an old garbage can. The flickering flames revealed the smooth plane of a cheek here, the white of an eye there.

Suddenly, she was shoved inside. She stumbled over the uneven flooring. At first she thought that Pimple-face's hands gripped her shoulders to keep her from falling, but then realized with a jab of panic that his grasp was much too strong.

"C'mon, boys," he urged in Spanish, his breath sour across her face.

Several of the Tiburones came forward, circling like a pack of coyotes.

This couldn't be happening! "I'm looking for Timo Martinez!" she shouted in Spanish. "Timo!" She searched among the faces in the dim light, but didn't find his. More hands were on her now, at her neckline, at her breasts, at the zipper of her jeans.

She heard her shirt rip. "No!" she screamed. "No, no, no!"

Valetti was already parked in front of the old warehouse when Jake drove up. Valetti had a list of license plate numbers in his hand and Sherry Lakotis in the passenger seat.

Valetti's window rolled down as Jake approached. "This is it," Valetti said. "Welcome to Tiburones territory. Land of liberated cars."

Jake looked toward the building. "And hideout for one Timo Martinez, I hope." The PS in Elisa's notes could stand for Pioneer Square as well as the Pacifico del Sur restaurant.

"Hi, Jake." Sherry gave him a wave. "You're going to be a feeb?"

"That's the plan." A noise from the warehouse caught his attention. He straightened. "You hear that?"

A long, drawn-out howl came from behind the dilapidated walls. "Nooooooooooo! "

"Shit!" Sherry's door opened. She had her hand beneath her jacket, drawing her weapon before she was even out of the door.

"Hold it, Lakotis," Valetti hissed. "We need backup. Who knows what's going down in there?"

Another scream from inside punctuated the air. Lakotis ran toward the building.

Jake's heart lurched. That scream sounded like Elisa. He pulled out his pistol and galloped after Sherry Lakotis. He heard Valetti yelling into the radio for backup as he slid from his seat, and then felt his old partner right on his heels.

Elisa wished she could stop trembling. Her clothes were in shreds and she'd been scratched and bruised, but her rescuers had burst in before anything worse could happen. How could she have been so stupid?

Jake's arms felt so safe. She remembered fighting until she'd realized that the arms around her were his. Then she remembered him picking her up off the warehouse floor and carrying her to his car. She had no memory of how they'd gotten into the interview room at the police station. Now she was sitting in his lap, her head pressed against his chest.

He ran his fingers through her hair. "Are you sure you don't want to go to the hospital?"

She found her voice. "I'm fine, Jake. Well, not fine, but..." She lost it again as she struggled to keep from crying.

"You never saw Timo?"

She shook her head miserably.

He kissed the top of her head. "I should have known you'd go off on your own. You always had to prove you knew best. Thank God I asked Valetti and Lakotis to show me the Tiburones' home turf this morning."

"Thank God is right; but mostly, thank you and Valetti and Lakotis," she said, shaking her head. "I can't believe I just walked in there."

"Can you think of anywhere else Timo might go?"

"No." She pushed herself off his lap and stood up, wrapping his windbreaker around her. "Obviously I'm not a natural detective."

He tried to put his arms around her once more, but she pushed him away. "I'm an idiot."

"Elisa," he said, "You're not all by yourself on some dark snowy mountaintop now. You don't have to do this alone."

Was that true? She was so tired of being alone. She looked at Jake, wondering if she could really trust him.

"This craziness is finished, right? You'll listen to the authorities from now on?" he asked. "I need to know that you'll be okay when I'm not around."

So there it was. It felt like receiving a slap while expecting a kiss. He wasn't planning on being around! She looked at the floor so he wouldn't see the tears in her eyes, and worked at summoning up anger. It didn't take long.

"Elisa, I never—"

"Made any promises," she finished for him. "And I never asked you to!"

She stomped out of the room and asked for a uniform to take her back to her van.

Jake stood by a window, watching her limp to the patrol car. He'd been about to say "I never meant to hurt you." It was true, he hadn't made any promises to her. The only promises he'd made were to the FBI, and he was determined to fulfill those. But dear God, he also wanted to wrap himself around Elisa Langston and protect her. She'd never leave Langston Green. And how in the hell could he love her and protect her from Quantico?

Valetti took the space beside him, rubbing his ribs where Elisa had landed a solid kick. Together they watched the blue-and-white drive away.

"She's a spitfire," Valetti said. "What have you gotten yourself into?"

Chapter 17

Elisa drove to the Langston house. Gail surveyed her daughter's torn clothing and bruised cheek. "What now, honey?" She drew Elisa close.

The kindness was too much. Elisa broke down. Together they stumbled to the kitchen, where Charlie was in the process of preparing dinner.

"I got mugged in Pioneer Square," she told them.

"What were you doing there? Did they get your purse?" Charlie asked. On taking in Elisa's confused expression, she added, "Don't tell me they took the van!"

Elisa shook her head. "They didn't get either."

"Then you weren't mugged," Charlie said. "You were assaulted. And where did you get that appalling jacket?"

Elisa opened Jake's windbreaker to reveal her shredded clothing.

"Oh, Elle!" Charlie rushed around the counter and hugged her.

She ended up telling them the whole sordid story of what had happened in Pioneer Square. "I've been such an idiot!"

Gail curled her fingers around the fist in which Elisa was crushing a wet tissue. "You were only doing what you thought was right. Looking out for that boy. Timoteo."

"And I didn't even guess right about that!" Elisa wailed. "And then, thank God, Jake and the cops showed up." She told them about her rescue and their conversation at the police station, leaving out the part where Jake had mentioned that he wouldn't be around.

Charlie, taking up her station behind the cutting board again, crossed her arms. "And just what would give him the notion that you might be in Pioneer Square? And that it was okay to put his arms around you like that? Could it be that Mr. Street has had his arms around you before?" Charlie pressed. "Those strong, manly arms?"

Elisa felt the blush rising to her cheeks.

"And what about those masculine lips?" Charlie continued. "Just what *have* you been doing since the reopening party?"

Elisa described how Jake had helped to make a success of her first class, and then showed up again for the tree-swinging contest in the middle of the night.

Gail was appalled. "Shouldn't you have called the police to handle an intruder?"

"Mom, will you never learn?" Charlie retorted. "Dialing 911 would never occur to Elisa. Besides, the cops probably would have shot Jake," she observed. "And then we'd never have gotten to the good part. C'mon, Elle, let's hear it."

Staring at the tabletop, Elisa segued to Jake's embraces, leaving out the intimate details. She finished her tale with the dynamiting of the new bathroom.

All that had happened in less than forty-eight hours? No wonder she was exhausted. Clubbing each other with fruit trees? Exploding toilets? And she hadn't even told them about last night's shed-top stakeout and makeout session, followed by the chase after the Gremlin.

Concern was etched into Gail's pretty face. "Let the police handle it, Elisa. I want you to move back here, where you'll be out of danger."

"That'll never happen," Charlie said to her mother. She turned back to Elisa, her eyes lit up with excitement and laughter. "What's next? Mud wrestling?"

It did sound ridiculous. Langston Green had become the set for a slapstick comedy. Her life was a joke. Then the smile disappeared from Elisa's face, and it all seemed more tragic than funny. Because it wasn't over. Nothing had been resolved. Not the arson, not the Gremlin, not whatever was going on with Timo. And most certainly not her relationship with Jake Street. How could he have gone through all that with her, and then said he wasn't going to be around?

She focused her gaze on the wall photo of the extended Langston family clan. Nana and Pop Langston, straight-backed and silver-haired; her aunt Maxine Langston, a state representative, now deceased; her father, Charlie and Gail, everyone so tall and fair and composed. She, the only short one, the only dark head in the bunch, wasn't even looking at the lens, but at something off to the left side of the group. She looked like the family mascot, the girl they'd taken home from the pound instead of a cocker spaniel.

"I can't do this!" she wailed.

"Do what?" Gail asked.

Any of it, she wanted to cry. "Run the nursery. Revive the Harvest Fest."

"Of course you can," Gail said. "You always have. You *are* doing it."

Elisa glanced at the photo again. Langstons, always successful, always well groomed, always persevering, triumphing over adversity. "I'm just not like the rest of you." She folded her arms on the polished oak surface and bent to rest her hot forehead against them. "I'll never be a true Langston!"

There was a long pause in which she imagined that her stepmother and stepsister were exchanging a pitying glance. Then Gail murmured, "That's particularly unfortunate, dear, since you're the only one here who *is* really a Langston."

Staring at the swirling grain of the oak tabletop, Elisa reflected on that. Charlie and Gail had married into the family. Her aunt Maxine, her father's only sibling, had no children. Good grief, it was true. The only Langston left was dark and short and half Guatemalan.

How very ironic. A chuckle crept up from her diaphragm, emerging from her mouth a strangled snort. The embarrassing sound made Gail and Charlie chuckle in response, which caused her to laugh harder. By the time she raised her head, she was in full guffaws.

The three of them laughed until tears ran down their cheeks. It felt good. It felt like home.

Jake let more than a week pass before he drove into the Langston Green parking lot. In phone messages, Elisa had made it clear that she didn't want his protection. He'd busied himself finalizing his other cases, making arrangements to rent out his condo, and trying to make progress on the Langston Green investigation.

He found it increasingly irritating to be a squad of one. This case was taking forever. He'd checked with all the landscaping companies and nurseries in a twenty-mile radius: none of them had employed Timoteo Martinez. If the kid was working for one of them, he wasn't using his real name. Only a clerk at Lindman's Hardware store in Woodinville admitted knowing Timo, but said he hadn't seen him lately. The police weren't having any better luck than he was. With no car, no known residence, no phone, and seemingly no friends or family, Timo Martinez was as good as invisible.

There'd been no prints other than Elisa's and Gerald's on the security cameras. The person responsible for the bathroom explosion had been wearing gloves when he'd handled the duct tape. As a manager of construction crews, Walt Baker had access to dynamite, and because he was working next door, he could easily discern when the nursery was occupied. But according to his neighbors, he and his wife had been home all evening after eight of the night in question. Ditto for Gerald Donaldson. Baker's work crew had been accounted for as well.

Jake had hoped to follow the path he found through the fence to wherever it led, but the day after the explosion, Baker's crew had laid down new sod, obliterating any footprints. Jake was stymied. This had to be an inside job; the Gremlin knew the layout of the property, the location of the security cameras, and where Elisa was at most times. It was alarming. He was working on an order to get bank account information for Donaldson and Baker, to see if they had been paying anyone for the vandalism attacks. He missed being a cop. These days, it was damn difficult for a civilian to get his hands on financial records.

Today he planned to try, for the last time, to get Elisa to come clean about Timo Martinez. She was hiding something about the kid. And then, last but certainly not least, he was going to screw up his courage and finally tell her that he was leaving town, and that whatever had been between them was over. He was down to three weeks now before he had to report for training at Quantico.

The drone of a large engine from behind the barn overpowered the sounds of customers coming and going from the greenhouse. He walked toward the noise.

Elisa sat in the operator's seat of the backhoe. She expertly maneuvered the giant machine, scooping up shrubs gently in the large, toothed steel bucket and setting them down in a row a short distance away. It was like watching a mother tyrannosaurus move her young out of harm's way.

She finished clearing a large area behind the burnt-out shell of the main building, then set the outrigger arms in place and began to scoop out a large hole in the earth. Jake revised his vision to one of a long-necked dinosaur digging a nest. Elisa looked comfortable at the controls of this prehistoric-looking machine.

He felt a little inadequate watching her dig out the new lily pond she'd designed. Carrying a gun and a badge, busting perps: that always made him feel macho, a little larger than other men around him. But here was a woman, and a tiny woman at that, who could literally move earth, create new landscapes. Scoop out a lake there, build a mountain. Send the boys to bed; Elisa Langston could take care of business all by herself. She'd been that way since he'd lusted after her in high school. Although she appeared almost icy on the surface, he now knew that beneath that dark beauty smoldered a passion waiting to erupt. Knew just how sexy her lean muscles felt under that silky olive skin, how her full lips could be so soft and so insistent at the same time—

He rubbed his chin in irritation. Testosterone was getting the best of him again. He checked his watch. Twenty minutes, that's all he had, to end this whole crazy fling between the two of them and get back to work. "Elisa!" he yelled.

She couldn't hear him over the roar of the engine. He raised the volume. "Elisa!"

He'd have to walk to the other side of the hole, where she could see him.

Elisa's new lightweight cast, only two days old, still felt ungainly. She couldn't use both feet to swing the bucket as she usually did, but instead had to shift her right foot from one pedal to the other, which made the movement more spasmodic than normal. Fortunately, the digging involved only hand controls, so scooping out a bite of earth was a piece of cake. It was a relief to be in control of something for a change, even if it was only a piece of mindless machinery.

Every time she replayed last week's events in her head, she felt more stupid. Dumb Move Number One: She knew that the Tiburones were a gang, yet she thought she could safely bluff her way into their midst just because she was half-Latina? How naive could she get? Dumb Move Number Two: Believing that Jake Street might be the love of her life. Why couldn't she just enjoy the fling and let him go? Even a fling was more romance than she'd enjoyed in a decade.

Would he even defend her to his bosses? Surely Atlas Security had to pay off eventually, even if they never discovered who was responsible for torching her building. But how was she going to pay the bills until 'eventually' rolled around?

And then there was the weird cat-and-mouse game with Timo. If only he'd come forward and clear himself, they could both get on with their lives. But she understood his reluctance. Everyone had already decided Timo was guilty.

If she came clean to Jake or the police about the Good Samaritan, they could probably stake out the place and nab Timo easily enough. But she knew in her heart that he was not the Gremlin. She couldn't give him up before she'd heard his story. She'd left him a note and money in the equipment shed. The note had been moved, but he hadn't touched the money. She'd camped out in the shed once, and in various spots around the fields, but he hadn't shown up on those nights. She could never predict when he'd come. If it hadn't been for the fields that were slowly but magically being restored to order, she would have thought that he'd left town. None of this made any sense.

The hole she was digging grew in size and depth. She used the flat backside of the bucket to press down terraces that stepped down like a miniature amphitheater. Later she'd level the shelves by hand for water plants. As she moved the bucket around, she pondered how she might make up with Jake Street. *Jake, I know you made no promises, but....* No. *Jake, I never really believed you'd stick around...*

No again. Definitely not the right tone. That sounded pathetic. C'mon, Elisa, she told herself, you want to get him back, don't you? Even a little of Jake Street was a whole lot better than the nothing she had now. *Jake, I think we have something going. We don't need to mess it up by thinking about the future?* As if she'd even have the opportunity to say any of this.

She'd burned her bridges back to him, and the man was already gone.

The bucket teeth grated on rock. She raised up to get a better view of the giant stone she had partially unearthed. She curled the bucket around the rock, gripping the stone like an octopus wrapping a tentacle around its prey, and pulled back hard on the lift lever. The backhoe dipped and bobbed with the strain for a moment. Then the stone finally broke free and the machine settled back into place. She lifted the stone to the top edge of the hole, and uncurled the bucket. But in raising the digging arm, she accidentally clipped the backside of the rock with the metal bucket teeth. The boulder thundered back to the bottom of the hole.

How apropos. She felt like Sisyphus, rolling the rock to the top of the mountain only to have it roll back down again. But she was not going to let things stay that way. She would catch the Gremlin. She was going to get the upper hand again, with Jake, with the insurance company, with this damn rock. Wrapping the bucket jaws around the boulder again, she heaved it up and jammed her right foot down onto the pedal to move the blasted thing out of her way.

Suddenly the bucket swung toward him and Jake had to slam himself into the mud to keep from being cut in two. As he hit the soft ground, the rock jumped out of the bucket, thudding to the ground only a foot away. A small chunk of stone broke off and thumped him in the forehead.

The backhoe engine rumbled to a halt. He heard the pounding of feet beside him. "My God, Jake!" Elisa's hands were on his shoulders. "Are you okay? Did I hit you?"

She knelt beside him, pulled him up into her arms, her eyes wide with fright as she searched his face. When she touched the cut at his hairline, her fingers came away bloody. "Oh no. Oh jeez, Jake, I clipped you!"

Her fingers unbuttoned his shirt, ripped it open. "Where else are you hurt?"

The sudden exposure to cool air combined with the touch of her fingers on his bare skin caused a physical reaction he hadn't expected. "Hey," he said weakly, "Don't start something you can't finish."

"Oh, God, Jake, I thought I'd never see you again." She sat back to look him in the eye. "And now you're here and I nearly killed you."

Somehow she'd managed to smear a thin stripe of his blood across her cheek. The effect was aboriginal, like the tattoo of a warrior princess going into battle. Wild. Sexy.

"What?" she said, perplexed by his expression. "Are you wounded someplace else?"

He took her small hand in his, placed it over the zipper on his trousers. "Maybe you'd better check down here. I feel a swelling."

Her gaze anxiously traveled down to his nether regions for a beat. Then she got it. Doubling her fist, she punched him in the stomach, hard enough to make him lose his breath. "Don't you know better than to approach a piece of machinery like this?" she yelled. "You could have been killed!"

"No kidding," he gasped. Stalling for time, he grabbed his head, wobbled it a little for effect, and moaned "Whoa!"

"Jake!" Elisa wrapped her arms around him again, cradling his head against her chest. "Did I really graze you with the bucket?"

If he'd felt inadequate before, he certainly felt like a simpleton now. He was covered in mud. Either he was going to have to meet his other appointments looking like he'd been dipped in chocolate, or he was going to have to spring for new clothes. He couldn't tell her now that he was going to leave her to train for the FBI. He was sprawled on the ground, wrapped in her embrace, without a shred of dignity left.

Elisa's arms felt good around him, solid and sinewy in contrast to the soft breast against which his head was pillowed. She smelled of perspiration and something green, maybe pine boughs or herbs or freshly mown grass. And by the look on her face, he knew that she'd been frightened. That she cared for him. *Really* cared for him. He'd never seen that look on a woman's face before.

"I thought I'd have to go crawling to you." Her voice was soft now. "I *should* have gone crawling to you, but naturally, being the better person, you came instead. I've been so stupid, Jake. I'm so glad to see you." Pulling up the hem of her T-shirt, she wiped blood from his forehead. "I don't think this cut is really too bad."

"Easy for you to say," he groaned. "You're a dangerous woman, Elisa."

"Not intentionally."

"Does that make it better?" he scoffed.

"You're not exactly Mr. Safe and Secure yourself." She raised her fingers to the side of her head where he'd smacked her with the root ball of a fruit tree. Had that only been less than two weeks ago?

"You know," she told him, "I don't think normal people who are in love go around bopping each other in the head."

"Then I can't wait until we fall in love. It would cut down on my aspirin bills."

Her clear brown eyes sent him the message that it was too late. They were already in love. "I said normal people. We don't qualify." She leaned down and kissed him. "Feeling better?"

His muscles suddenly tensed. Elisa Langston had him under her control again. This was not what he intended to do. This was not what he came here for, to lie in her lap in the mud and bleed on her while she kissed him. "I can't be doing this," he told her. "You're my client."

"Afraid you'll lose your job?"

"Hell, it's already gone." He pulled her down for another kiss before she could give voice to the question on her face. When he let her come up for air, he murmured huskily, "Hey, baby."

Her dark eyes narrowed. "Nobody calls me *baby*."

"Okay, *querida*," he said agreeably. "But I'm out of here in three weeks."

"Wh ... why?" Even as her lips rounded for the question, her eyes were filling with tears.

"I'm leaving town."

She pressed her lips together. She swallowed, took a deep breath, and said, "I understand."

He couldn't stand that look of injured stoicism on her beautiful face. "No, you don't understand, Elisa. I need you to marry me right away."

"What!" Her mouth dropped open and she stopped breathing for a second and simply stared at him. Then she ran her fingers through his hair like she was giving him a scalp massage. "You must have been hit harder than I thought. Hematomas can make people act crazy. I'm going to go call 9-1-1."

"Elisa?"

They both looked up. Gerald stood next to the backhoe, staring at the two of them. The papers he held in his hand—probably something he wanted Elisa to sign—fluttered in the slight breeze. Recovering, he folded his arms in front of his chest and said in a flat voice, "So it's true."

Elisa leapt to her feet, dumping Jake into the mud. She muttered something about him surprising her while she was driving the backhoe. Being injured. She looked from Gerald back to Jake, her face suddenly full of chagrin. "Oh, jeez! Does this mean yet *another* insurance claim?"

Jake pushed himself to his feet, pulling his mud-spattered shirt closed over his bare chest. His tie was twisted around his neck. He fumbled to find the ends of it.

Gerald looked him up and down. "So this is what a professional insurance investigator looks like when he's hard at work."

Jake yanked the knot of his tie around from the back of his collar, wiped the blood out of his eye. A dollop of mud fell from his ear to his shoulder. He turned on his heel, and headed for the parking lot.

When he reached the Land Rover, he turned and looked back. Gerald had disappeared. Elisa stood by the backhoe, watching him retreat to his car. She touched her hand to her head in the same spot where his own had been cut, then raised her hands, asking him in pantomime if his head was okay.

He waved and got in, turned on the engine without looking at himself in the rearview mirror. He didn't need visual verification to know that he was a total mess. He was half an hour behind schedule for the day.

This little visit had not gone anything like he planned.

Elisa stared at Jake's departing Land Rover. He couldn't possibly have meant it, could he? Not the 'marry me' part, anyway. She brushed a clump of mud from her wet jeans. She was streaked with dirt from head to foot. It had been mud-wrestling after all, just as Charlie had predicted.

She tried to call Jake on his cell phone, but hung up when his voicemail message answered. After an hour of trying, she called Atlas Security's Seattle office and asked for him, only to be told by the receptionist, "Mr. Street is out in the field. I'll have him return your call."

Well, at least she knew he was still ambulatory. She hadn't put him in the hospital. *Will you marry me?* Had he really said that? She thought about it for a moment, shook her head. She'd only received one proposal of marriage before, from her roommate's drunken boyfriend who probably hadn't even remembered it in the morning. Jake, too, could plead diminished capacity: he'd been suffering from a head injury at the time he blurted out the words.

After lunch, she dialed his cell number again, and this time left a message.

"Jake," she said, "I hope your head is better. You're not really leaving town, are you? You didn't mean permanently, did you? As for the other thing you said, well, don't worry, I won't hold you to it. We can pretend it never happened. Please don't avoid me forever. I couldn't stand that." She hung up and went back to digging out the fish pond.

Her thoughts circled all afternoon, always returning to Jake's words. By sunset, as she was installing a motion sensor connected to a hidden infrared camera near the back fence, she had come to the conclusion that the tap on Jake's head had surely knocked him off kilter.

Jake Street didn't really know her. Sure, he'd been in her bed, embraced her, and known *of* her since high school, but that wasn't the same as really knowing a person, was it? He couldn't have *really* planned to ask her to marry him. Most men did not see Elisa Langston even as a potential lover, let alone a potential spouse. When she was honest with herself, she had to admit that she'd given up the expectation of marriage and a family. But never the hope.

She finished connecting the wires and pushed herself to her feet. Another two weeks, the doctor said, and she could throw away the darn cast for good. She couldn't wait.

A faint wail drifted on the breeze. Was that a baby crying? It seemed to be coming from Baker's Acres. The sound stopped. Or had she actually heard it at all? The only noises she could hear now were hammering and the whine of a saw. Right, she thought, now I'm hallucinating babies. Was her biological clock sending her messages, turning the screech of a circular saw into a baby's cries? It was all these thoughts of romance and family. Shaking her head at her own foolishness, she slid the toe of her cast into the path of the motion sensor, which she'd positioned only two inches above the ground. The click of the shutter was faint. The small camera was nearly invisible between the leaves of a camellia bush. Hopefully the Gremlin would not even be aware that he'd been captured on film.

Back in the office, she tried Jake's number several more times. In her mind's eye, she could see his blue eyes checking the phone's readout. When he recognized her number, he'd pocket the phone without answering. The fact that he hadn't tried to call her was proof, wasn't it? The man had embarrassed himself and now he was avoiding her.

After dark, she sat on her bed in the camper, thinking about her mother and father and Jake, about how treacherous love could be. Simon languidly watched from the nest he'd made in her pillow. The framed *huipil* lay in her lap.

"This has nothing to do with what *he* said," she informed the cat. "It's just time. I've put it off too long. I've got to get this thing cleaned." She wiped a smudge from the protective glass.

A Mayan grandmother Elisa had never met had made the beautifully embroidered *huipil*. Maria Elena had worn it on her wedding day, the day she'd married Terrence Langston in her tiny village in Guatemala. And now it was Elisa's. *For your wedding day*, her mother had told her. *It's our tradition.*

When Elisa was a child, the huipil had hung in her mother's closet. She'd hidden in the closet whenever she could, pressing her face to it, stroking its rainbow threads. Then, after Maria Elena had gone away and Gail had taken her place, her stepmother had enveloped the special garment in thick brown plastic. It seemed to Elisa as though Gail was trying to hide away all reminders of her real mother.

But Terrence Langston had realized how special the *huipil* was to his daughter, because he'd cleaned and folded and framed it for her high school graduation present.

She removed the last screw from the masonite backing.

Would the smoke smudges come out? It would be horrible if the fire had irrevocably damaged the beautiful embroidery. Would the *huipil* even fit? She was a couple of inches taller than Maria Elena, and probably bigger around as well.

The skirt was folded behind the overblouse. She lifted it out carefully, pressed it to her. The hem reached a couple of inches below her knees. Just right. She stretched the skirt out on top of the bed. Simon watched with interest.

She warned him, "If I find one cat hair on that, you'll be sleeping in the barn."

Turning back to the frame, she pulled out the first fold of the embroidered overblouse, then gasped. Between the folds were more than a dozen blue rectangles. Airmail envelopes, each as light as a butterfly. All bore the brightly colored stamps of Guatemala.

Seventeen letters in all. And her father had never told her about a single one.

"Oh, Daddy, how could you?" Elisa wailed. She placed them in order. She carefully opened the one with the oldest date, mailed twenty-three years ago.

Mi querida hijita, it began. Elisa struggled to decipher the Spanish script.

> *How can I ever explain myself to you? I never learned to write English, so I must write in the national language of Guatemala in hopes that your father will read this to you.*
>
> *I cannot fit myself into a land where anything is possible, where life is so reckless. Even with your father's love, I was so lonely in the United States. Every day here I am with brothers, sisters, aunts, uncles, cousins, friends. We all know our place in our world.*

We know what each day will bring. It is a comfort.

America was like a roller-coaster ride at the fair, thrilling but frightening. I was only a temporary passenger who wanted to go back to the safety of my village. It broke my heart to leave you behind, but that is my gift to you, Elisa. You are already an American, strong and independent like your father. You can ride that roller coaster without fear, and someday you may learn even to drive it and make it stop where you want it to. You will have a wonderful life.

Forgive me. You will always be in my heart.
Mamá

Elisa laid the page on the quilt. Simon put a tentative paw on her thigh. She pulled the cat close and dried her tears on his soft fur.

"Why is it always love 'em and leave 'em, Simon?"

The cat fought to escape her grip.

"You're right, time to stop wallowing. We'll save the rest of these for tomorrow. Ready to go get that damned Gremlin?"

He twitched his tail and extended his claws, pressing their sharp points against her skin.

"Where shall we hide tonight?"

Standing at his condo window with a glass of Merlot, Jake watched the sun slip behind the Olympic Mountains. The last blush of purple faded from Puget Sound. What was Elisa doing right now? Camping out on top of one of her buildings again?

His muscles tensed at the memory of holding her slender, solid body in his arms. Her sleek ebony hair, clear brown eyes, smooth olive skin... He wrenched his mind away from the image of her naked in the moonlight and took another sip of wine. Was she safe, or hell bent on another of her foolhardy missions? He'd driven to Langston Green a couple of times in the middle of the night, cruised the perimeter, even staked out Baker's Acres, only to find absolutely nothing going on and no Gremlin sneaking around. Elisa was right, there was no way of knowing when the vandal might strike. The Woodinville cops had promised him they'd keep up the drive-bys for a while, and they'd vary the schedule: that was good. But anything could happen in between.

He'd never called Elisa back. His thoughts churned but didn't lead anywhere, like a turning propeller on a boat that was still docked. That was Jake Street all right, still docked. But not for long. He looked around him at the growing stack of boxes. He had seventeen days to finish everything here before moving on to a new life.

I won't hold you to it. There it was in her phone message. She hadn't taken him seriously. It stung a little, just like in high school, when she'd barely noticed him. On the other hand, she'd let him off the hook. He didn't have to marry her, just because he'd been foolish enough to blurt out the words.

Did he want to be let off the hook?

Chapter 18

Elisa woke the next morning with muscles stiff from sleeping in an awkward position. As she picked herself up from the pile of fertilizer bags against which she'd been resting, a canvas tarp fell away from the top of her sleeping bag. She blinked at it, uncomprehending for a minute. Then she glanced around anxiously. Someone had studied her as she slept. Someone had covered her. The Gremlin? Wouldn't he just bonk her on the head instead of placing a tarp over her to protect her from the dew? She spied a sharp-toed impression in the bark near where she'd lain.

"Timo." She could picture him standing over her in the moonlight. And there, next to her, a pot of mums, brilliant fuchsia, her favorite color. They'd discussed colors a couple of months ago while arranging a display. He favored the cream-petaled mums with magenta edges. Two-for-one, he'd said. She'd given him a potful of the bi-colors to take home. Now she reached down and fingered a tightly packed fuchsia blossom. "Oh, Timo. Next time, wake me up. Whatever is going on, trust me. I promise I won't abandon you."

It was daylight and here she was, sleeping bag puddled around her feet, talking to a chrysanthemum. She scooted into her camper before any of her employees could see her.

Last night, as she sat under the stars, she had so hoped that Jake might show up to keep her company. He was obviously still avoiding her.

Elisa checked the answering machine in the camper. The light blinked once. She eagerly pressed the button. Her heart sank as she listened to ten seconds of soft breathing followed by the click of a hang-up.

"Damn it, Jake!" She swallowed her disappointment and headed for the shower.

After making herself coffee and toast, she sat down at the tiny table and unfolded the next of her mother's letters.

> *Things I miss from the U.S. now that I am here:*
>
> *Ice cream whenever I want it.*
> *Terry's kiss goodnight.*
> *You.*

Elisa swallowed painfully against the lump in her throat, steadied her hands, and read on.

> *Things I missed from Guatemala when I was there:*
>
> *The squabbling of wild parrots at dawn.*
> *Butterflies that cover the trees at sundown.*
> *Venison stew with achiote. Mangos, ripe and warmed by the sun.*
> *The music of Maya-Quiché. Can you understand what it is like to live with a foreign language always in your ears?*

There followed a few lines that Elisa could not read, presumably in her mother's native language. The last item in Maria Elena's list brought a lump to Elisa's throat:

> *My family.*

A week later, Elisa had gone through all the letters. Timo still hadn't shown up. And Jake still hadn't come back, or even called. There had been no new incidents at Langston Green, and the whole cycle of attack and response was starting to feel like a nightmare that had finally faded away.

The orthopedist had just given her permission to go without a cast, and Elisa stopped by Gail and Charlie's to show off her newly unencumbered legs. She brought the stack of letters, too, and dumped them onto the kitchen table in front of Gail. "She did love me."

Confused, Gail picked up a letter, read the addresses on the front, then laid it back down. "Of course your mother loved you, dear."

"She sent me a letter every year on my birthday, telling me so. How could Daddy have kept that from me?"

Gail studied her own clasped hands for a moment. After swallowing, she raised her gaze to Elisa's face. "When she first left, your father thought it would be too traumatic for you to hear from her. He didn't want you to feel torn between him and Maria Elena."

"He let me think that my own mother didn't want me."

Gail grimaced. "He wanted you to be happy. That was Terry; he always wanted everyone to be happy. That was why he agreed to the divorce and let Maria Elena go home."

Elisa looked up. "He did it willingly? He *approved* of her leaving?"

"That wasn't the way he'd tell it." Gail shook her head. "He couldn't bear to see her so unhappy here. He said that loving her was like loving a deer or a hawk or some other wild thing; he had to let her go back where she belonged. And he continued to send money to Guatemala."

"The Mariposa Foundation?" Ten percent of Langston Green's profits were donated to the Guatemalan group every year. Elisa had kept up the tradition since her father had died.

"That's it." Gail scooped her hands through the pile of airmail envelopes. "I knew about the first few letters. I caught Terry reading one, and it just about broke my heart to see his face." She wiped a tear from her own cheek now. "He must have intercepted the rest. I had no idea they kept coming. I'm sorry, Elisa."

"She probably thinks I'm dead," Elisa moaned.

Gail shook her head. "No, Terry sent her pictures every year. From the family picnic."

So her Mayan mother could see that Elisa was growing up a true Langston. From Maria Elena's letters, Elisa guessed that she'd be happy about that.

Gail slid her hand across the table toward Elisa. "I really thought you'd forgotten all about Maria Elena. You never mentioned her after you were twelve or so. I thought you didn't want to talk to me about your real mother."

Elisa studied the grain of the table top. What young woman wanted to talk about a mother that had abandoned her at age nine?

When Elisa looked up, she saw her stepmother's beautiful face wracked with pain. Gail's smooth manicured fingers tightened over Elisa's work-roughened hands. "I'm so sorry, Elisa. Can you forgive me?" her voice cracked.

Elisa stared at their joined hands. There was a lot of guilt in those entwined fingers. Maybe Gail had conspired with her father, but the person who really deserved to feel guilty was herself. Maria Elena Langston had been the romantic mother, the elusive parental ghost. It had been Gail Langston who had cooked for Elisa from the age of nine, made sure she'd done her homework, bought her clothes, punished her when she was more than usually stubborn. Cherished her. Taught her how to be a woman.

Elisa pushed herself up from her chair to embrace the only mother she could really remember. "There's nothing to forgive, Mom."

After a long hug, Gail released Elisa and handed her a tissue, taking one for herself at the same time.

Charlie entered from the garage to find them both wiping their eyes. "Uh-oh," she said. "Another disaster?"

Gail swallowed and shook her head, still unable to speak. Elisa picked up her soft hand, and holding it in her own calloused one, said, "I was telling Mom that she was a great mother." She turned to Gail. "I wouldn't have had anyone else raise me."

The older woman finally found her voice. She surprised Elisa by saying, "It wasn't easy."

Elisa raised an eyebrow. "C'mon, I was a pussycat."

"Wildcat is more like it," Charlie retorted.

Gail nodded. "That *is* how I used to think about you, Elisa. I felt like I'd been given a baby bobcat to raise along with my own kitten. You were such a fierce little thing."

"And I always had to compete with that fierce wild thing," Charlie said.

"You, compete with me?" Elisa said, unbelieving. "I remember it the other way around."

Charlie put a hand on the table and leaned close. "Remember the log across the creek?"

"Well, *I* made it." Elisa narrowed her eyes. "Remember my pink sweater? You stretched it all out of shape."

"Pink has never been your color. I did you a favor."

Gail thrust out her arms. "Girls!"

After their laughter had died down, Gail poured three glasses of wine for them. "Charlie and I are really looking forward to Harvest Fest."

"I'm glad someone is," Elisa said. "Gerald and Peter and Beth seem a little crazed."

"You didn't give them much notice, dear."

"I don't want the same Bavarian-flavored celebration." Unsaid were the words 'like Dad used to put on.' She hurried to add, "We're updating it to reflect the whole community better. I want Langston Green's events to be more international from now on."

Gail smiled. "That's a great idea. Charlie and I can hardly wait to see what you come up with. Not to mention Leon and Jon. It'll be their very first one."

Of course. Gail and Leon and Charlie and Jonathan. Did everyone travel in pairs nowadays?

"The whole community's looking forward to it."

"Is there anything your sister and I can do for the party? Do you need any help now that we're getting down to the wire?"

Down to the wire—? Horrified, Elisa's glance shot to the kitchen wall calendar. The date was circled there, in bright red. The party that was supposed to re-establish Langston Green as a community fixture was only a week away. Where did she get off saying "we're updating it" as though she'd actually planned anything? Instead of attending to the business she was supposedly running, she'd been chasing after Timo, making out with Jake, bumbling into gang hangouts, pining over her mother's letters, and laying in wait for the Gremlin who never showed up. Except for during that one shed-top stakeout that had quickly turned into a makeout session with Jake. Stakeouts and makeouts—sounded like a country and western song. Her body tingled just thinking about Jake naked in the moonlight. And the way he'd felt in her arms after the backhoe incident—

Stop it. Where had she parked her brain while her hormones had taken her on this joy ride? And now she had tuned out Gail. Her hearing recovered just in time to catch "And your Jake will be there, too, of course."

"I wouldn't count on that, Mom." She hadn't laid eyes on the man for more than two weeks. He hadn't returned any of her calls. Typical male. He'd embarrassed himself by blurting out something romantic that he didn't mean, and now he'd never show his face again.

Elisa dialed Jake's home phone after her first cup of coffee in the morning. She hung up after listening to his recorded message. After her second cup, she dialed his cell phone. When his voicemail kicked in, she said, "Now listen here, Jake. Even though you're no longer my ... my ..."—she couldn't say 'lover' in voicemail, could she?—"my friend, you're still my insurance man ... agent ... investigator, whatever. Call me and tell me what's going on!"

She was staring at the old black phone on her desk, pondering placing another call to Jake's office, when Gerald came in. Tiffany was with him, talking a mile a minute. They both wore identical black leather jackets.

"Those little cocktail sausages," Tiffany unfurled a finger, then one by one thrust out a whole handful as she listed "Fruit shish kabobs, sliced French bread, cheese, maybe pâté?"

"No pâté," Gerald told her. "We don't have that kind of budget."

"So," Elisa said. "You *are* planning the Harvest Fest."

They both looked up. Gerald said, "It's my job." There was a slight hesitation before he added, "Isn't it?"

Hoping she was imagining the tinge of hostility in the question, Elisa nodded. "Of course. So, what's the plan?"

"Riley's is catering."

Elisa glanced at Tiffany, who responded with her usual cool green-eyed gaze. It smacked a little of nepotism to give the job to Gerald's fiancée's place of employment, but Riley's did make good food and they were close. "And we're getting some international dishes?"

Tiffany raised an eyebrow. "Humus and pita? Swedish meatballs? Chili poppers?"

"All good." Elisa was relieved.

Tiffany bussed Gerald on the cheek. "I've got to go." She turned and left.

Elisa turned to Gerald, who was now sitting across from her at their shared desk. "How about the music? No oompah bands, remember?"

Gerald made a face that showed what he thought of her reminder. "I booked The Good Old Boys," he said.

Not bad. The Good Old Boys were a local band that played a

little of everything from slow waltzes to classic rock and roll. But it didn't seem too international. "Did you try the Mariachi Brothers?"

Gerald took off his leather jacket and hung it on a hanger. "They're busy."

Elisa was disappointed. In her imagination, Harvest Fest had taken on the flavor of a Hispanic fiesta. Gerald was planning an ordinary American party.

"Since when do you care about food and music?" Gerald asked. "Now you'll be asking about decorations."

Which was exactly what she'd planned to come out of her mouth next. "I just thought I should find out the details," she mumbled.

"That's why *I'm* here." Gerald sat back in his chair, fixing her with a glare. "Isn't it?"

"Yes, of course. And I can see you're doing a great job, Gerald. As usual. You called the Mariachi Brothers?"

He raised an eyebrow. "How else would I know they're busy? I also tried The Fiesta Five, in case that's your next question. Also busy."

"Right." Elisa, uncomfortable in the tense atmosphere of the room, rose from her chair. "I think I'll go check on the bathroom reconstruction." She yanked her sweatshirt off the coat rack and walked out the door.

What the heck was the matter with her? Even if Gerald was a little prickly, this was *her* company; she was the boss. So why did she feel like a field hand that had been caught in the master's office? It was this business with Jake. He'd dumped her. Likewise, no doubt, Timo was off to better things as well. She'd even left him a note in Spanish, pinned next to the now-repaired gap in the back fence, but still, nothing.

The only male who seemed determined to stick with her, no matter what, was Simon. And, most likely, the Gremlin. Nothing had happened since the Great Toilet Explosion. But she had an awful feeling that the Gremlin's next big planned event might take place at the big party.

Halfway across the parking lot, she met the mail carrier. He gave her a single envelope from Atlas Security Insurance Company. She ripped it open eagerly. The letter, in formal words, gave Langston Green permission to raze the burned shell of the old farmhouse office, even though it was 'the scene of a crime still under investigation.' There was no mention of a forthcoming settlement.

Damn it! Jake had warned her that the insurance company would drag their feet as long as possible. But they'd have to settle eventually; she'd just have to hold out until they did. She'd probably need a lawyer to apply pressure. More bills. She folded the letter and stuffed it into the back pocket of her jeans. The signature on the letter had not been Jake's. The man was definitely not coming back.

She had Atlas's permission to raze the burned ruins. Good. She headed for the backhoe, definitely in the mood to destroy something.

A few days later, Jake was packing up the last of his personal belongings. He'd rented the condo to a visiting professor from Boston. Opening the carved wooden box on his dresser, Jake extracted two tie tacks and tossed them into a valet case. The wheat pennies and silver dollars could go into storage with the rest of his mementos. The blue-green rock that he'd found on the beach was his lucky charm. He slipped the water-smoothed oval into the pocket of his jeans; he'd no doubt need some luck, or at least a good worry stone, in the months of training ahead. The little black velvet box was an anomaly among the masculine items. He fingered it for a moment, then unsnapped it and studied the contents.

His grandmother's ruby ring. Old-fashioned, a little worn, but still stunning. *For your brides*, his Grandma Sara had said, as she doled out her most prized jewels. His brother Daniel, as the oldest, had received the most valuable, her diamond engagement ring. Jake had been given her second prize, her ruby. But now he knew that his grandmother had distributed the rings correctly. Daniel's wife Becky was a high-brow Harvard girl; the diamond matched her cool classic style.

The ruby, on the other hand, had color and fire. Jake knew the perfect woman to wear that ring. He pulled it from its satin nest and admired its warm glow under the lamp for a moment. His grandmother had been a tiny woman. Would her ring fit another small finger?

"*Querida*," he murmured. The Spanish word sounded so much more romantic than *darling* or *honey*. "*Te quiero. Te amo.*" He'd looked up the words in his old Spanish textbook. "I love you" came much more easily to his lips in Spanish than in English.

He had no delusions; life with Elisa would never be easy. She was every bit as smart, as capable, and as headstrong as he was; there'd never be a 'head' in any household he shared with her. On the other hand, life with Elisa would never be boring; they'd make one hell of a team. He smiled, visualizing a future with her. Why did the present have to be filled with so many obstacles? Was it so wrong to want it all—a job with excitement and honor, a woman with intelligence and passion? He pressed the ring back into its slot and then shut the velvet container.

Chapter 19

Elisa cursed Jake as she dressed for the Harvest Fest. In the weeks that had passed since the backhoe incident, he'd communicated with her only through the tape in her answering machine.

"Elisa, I'm not letting *you* off the hook," he'd said mysteriously in his one message, left six days ago. "I'll be on the case for another week, then I'm handing it over to a colleague to finish up. Watch your back: your Gremlin's still out there."

So as of tomorrow, Jake Street's involvement with Elisa Langston would be officially over. The man would be off to whatever he was leaving town for, and she could finally stop thinking about him and looking for him. Tonight would signal the return to Langston Green's 'good old days,' to a Langston in control instead of being taken for a ride. She was well aware that the Gremlin was still out there. She'd hired a security guard to patrol the party tonight.

She pushed an arm into the sleeve of her new dress. She buttoned the satin frog closings, did up the zipper under her left arm, and regarded herself critically in the mirror. The dress was Charlie's fault. Elisa had let her stepsister coerce her into a shopping trip, and now she had this blue-green oddity to show for it.

"No way," she said when Charlie had first thrust the silk Asian-style garment into her arms. They were in Worldbeat, an eclectic clothing store.

"Trust me. Try it."

The dress fit perfectly, clinging to her curves, and Elisa loved the peacock sheen of the embroidered fabric, the way it shimmered green one moment and blue the next. The slit up the right side showed off her trim calf and thigh. Fortunately, it was her right leg on display. The left, still thin from nearly two months in a cast, was pasty looking, and the scars from her surgery seemed glaringly evident.

"Panty hose. Silky black ones." Charlie advised, stepping into place beside her. "We can get 'em next door at Toes R Us. They have Petite."

"Panty hose? Yuck." Elisa couldn't remember the last time she'd worn stockings. Or a dress, for that matter.

"And those black heels you've got."

"Double-yuck. I can't possibly walk in heels yet."

"Okay. Then the black sling sandals."

How like Charlie to have memorized all of her shoes. Although, since Elisa hadn't bought a new pair for years, maybe it wasn't such an amazing feat after all. They regarded themselves in the store mirror. Charlie smoothed down the skirt of a rose-colored peasant ensemble, embroidered in beige and sea-green silk around the neckline and sleeves.

"*You* look Latina and *I* look Asian," Elisa said.

Charlie grinned. "Cool, isn't it?"

So now here she was, dressed like a refugee from a Chinese wedding. She brushed her hair, added the silver-and-copper bird barrette, and threaded the earrings Maria Elena had left behind—heavy silver and turquoise dangles—through her lobes. Taking a deep breath, she surveyed herself in the small mirror of her camper bedroom.

And found herself wishing that Jake could see her now, see that she wasn't always a grubby laborer mucking around in the mud. What the heck had he meant when he said "I'm not letting *you* off the hook"?

"Oh, for heaven's sake!" she said to her reflection. "Stop that right now. The man is gone." She'd driven by his condo, seen the For Rent sign in the window. She slipped on her shoes, forced Jake from her thoughts, and locked the camper.

At the back of the barn, she stopped to admire the light gleaming on the surface of the new pond. She pondered the extension ladder beside the back door for a moment. The electricians must have left it there: they'd completed the installation of the new sprinkler system in the barn just this morning.

Unable to put off her entrance any longer, she pulled opened the back door, flipped the switch beside the door to turn off the exterior light, and went in to her party.

The barn was packed. The Good Old Boys were playing Love Me Tender when she entered. A few couples, most noticeably Charlie and Jonathan and Gail and Leon, were dancing. Most of the crowd was gathered before the buffet table.

Gerald and Tiffany, both dressed in black and white with touches of red, held court by the front door. And next to them, forming a little impromptu receiving line, were Walt and Cissie Baker, glad-handing as if they owned the place. Elisa hurried over.

"It's about time." Gerald pulled her into place between himself and Walt Baker. "And of course you know Elisa Langston," he said smoothly to a gray-haired couple Elisa had never seen before.

She made a point of turning her back to the Bakers as she shook hands. "Welcome. Have a lovely time." After the couple had passed, she said to Gerald, "Enough with the greetings at the door. This isn't an embassy function. It's supposed to be a neighborhood party. A casual party."

Behind his glasses, Gerald's hazel eyes clouded over. He pressed his lips into a thin line, then looked down and fiddled with his red silk tie, the image of a chastised little boy.

"Sorry," Elisa told him. "I'm a little edgy tonight. But let's just keep it informal, okay? Let folks find their own way." She stepped back, the heel of her sandal coming down on the toe of Walt Baker's cowboy boot. "Oops," she said, thrusting out an elbow as she turned. "I didn't expect to find you there."

He caught her elbow in his moist hand. "No problem, Louisa," he said. "A tiny little thing like you couldn't hurt me much."

Cissie Baker reached out to finger the fabric of Elisa's sleeve. "So unusual. Daring. Like your sister's. You Langston girls are so brave."

Elisa narrowed her eyes. "Thank you."

Grasping his wife's arm, Walt Baker steered her toward the buffet.

"Your dress *is* fascinating, Elisa," Tiffany offered. Her own was a slightly retro-looking black and white cocktail sheath belted with red silk. "So, you've got kind of a Latino-Chinese fusion thing going on here? Interesting."

"It's more than interesting. It's like, wow," Gerald said. Elisa chose to believe his gaze was focused on the black silk frog fasteners rather than on her breasts.

Tiffany shot him a dirty look, then said, "I'm going to check the catering."

Gerald watched his fiancée weave her way through the crowd. "I don't know why Tiffany makes such a big deal out of the Latino thing." The lights reflected off his eyeglasses as his gaze shifted to Elisa. "I've never minded you being half-Guatemalan."

An unladylike snort escaped from Elisa. "Gee, thanks, Ger. I appreciate that."

He placed a hand on her forearm. "Really, it never bothered me at all."

A knot of people strolled past, glancing at them curiously. Charlie and Jon, now at the buffet, waved in her direction. Elisa waved back, forced a smile onto her face. "Go," she ordered Gerald, pulling away from his fingers. "Mix. Have a good time."

The party was loud. Dozens of guests came up to her and thanked her for resuming the tradition of Langston Green's annual party. But she felt awkward, not quite sure what to do with herself. Her gaze traveled over the crowd, and she realized she was holding her breath. Waiting. For what? Another explosion? Gunshots? Everything was in place. The fences were all intact, the motion sensor lights and video cameras had been repositioned and turned on, and the back door was locked; she'd checked it herself. Before the party, the rent-a-cop had done a thorough walk-through with Gerald and Tiffany, checked all the nooks and crannies in the barn. Now he was positioned outside. She couldn't actually see the barrel-chested officer through the open front door, but little puffs of steamy breath floated past the opening now and then, revealing his presence. She should close the door, tell the officer—Bartlett, that was his name—he could keep an eye on the crowd from inside.

The band started up a country western song, one of her favorites, a slow dance to a waltz beat. Maybe she could ask Joe McMahon to dance with her. He was one of her father's old friends and his wife probably wouldn't mind. She surveyed the crowd, looking for him. At the edge of the dance floor, she saw Charlie nudge Jon Park with an elbow and glance in her direction. Jon nodded at something Charlie said, then headed toward Elisa. Oh no. She turned toward the door.

He caught her by the elbow. "Could I have this dance, Elisa?" Tonight Jon looked impossibly handsome in a dark blue shirt and white tie, his black hair glossy under the lights.

Elisa shot a look at Charlie, who nodded, smiling. Oh no, not a pity dance. Not the royal couple extending charity to the poor lonely stepsister. It was unbearable.

"Please?" Jon held out a hand.

She gulped. "My pleasure." His hands were warm on her shoulder and waist, and he was a good dancer, leading gently but firmly. They fit together just as she'd imagined, the top of her head reaching to his nose, instead of only to his shoulder as she did with Jake. "It's a great party, Elisa," he murmured into her ear.

It felt so good to be in a man's arms. But they were the wrong arms, and in spite of her vow to remain professional tonight, her eyes filled with tears. To hide them, she laid her head against Jon's shoulder. If that upset Charlie, she'd deal with it later.

Then Jon stopped. Elisa opened her eyes as he let go of her and stepped away. Jake Street stepped into his place. His hair was a little tousled from the wind, and his ears and the tip of his nose were pink from the cold. Under a gray tweed sports coat, he wore the blue sweater that matched his eyes. "What are you doing here?" she asked.

Jake prayed that Elisa would not balk when he cut in to dance with her. Her cheeks flushed deep red, but she took his hand willingly enough and stepped into his arms. She looked beautiful tonight in peacock-blue satin. God, it felt so good to embrace her again. He waltzed her into the corner under a wreath of twigs and bright autumn leaves just as the song ended.

"I've been a coward. I didn't do this right the first time," he told her in a low voice. He let go of her and knelt on one knee. "Elisa Langston, will you marry me?"

She glanced at the crowd around them, and his gaze followed hers. Several pairs of eyes were on the two of them. Jon the fireman and her sister Charlie, of course. Gerald, stopped in mid-conversation with one of the white-coated catering staff, looked shell-shocked. The music started again, this time a more lively tune. Jake tried to ignore the surroundings as he dug into his pocket, snapped open the box, and held out the ruby ring in its velvet nest.

Elisa's eyes widened and her lips formed a soft "oh." She liked the ring, he could tell, but she made no move to take it. He felt like his face might crack under the effort of smiling.

"Didn't you say you were leaving town?" Her voice was soft.

"I will always come back. I can't leave you, Elisa."

She took a deep breath while continuing to stare at him with those bottomless brown eyes. This was harder than staring down the barrel of a gun. A trickle of sweat ran down between his shoulder blades. Jake thought he might have a heart attack. "*Querida*, I'm waiting. Will you marry me?"

She finally breathed out, "Maybe." She smiled at him, gave him a little shrug.

God, what now? He'd risked everything and she'd said *maybe*? He swallowed hard. "You want me to prove myself?" He rose to his feet. She hadn't said No. "I accept that challenge." He pushed the ring onto her finger, pulled her into his arms and kissed her.

Elisa had nearly forgotten how good Jake felt, how tall and solid and masculine and comforting. How his scent was clean and tangy, like a breeze off the ocean. How his lips could be simultaneously as soft as wisteria blossoms and as hard and insistent as the vines they bloomed on. How his caress took her breath away.

He leaned back and touched his fingers to her face, brushing a strand of hair from her flushed cheek. He was handsome and sexy. He was brave, he was a great lover. He made her laugh. She'd whacked him with a shovel, doused him with coffee, and nearly killed him with a backhoe, and he was still standing here. What more could she ask for? Her thoughts flashed back to being trapped under the tree, thinking about her pathetic life. Her wish for love and adventure.

Was Jake Street love and adventure? She studied his rugged face, noticed that the cut on his brow was healing nicely. Why hadn't he answered her calls? Why had he let her think that he had deserted her? Didn't he realize how much that hurt?

They barely knew each other. He hadn't denied he was leaving town. Did he expect her to go with him? Did he think that she'd just abandon her business, her family, her whole life to follow him? No, he knew her better than that by now. He'd always come back, he said. Would he?

As the song finished, she clung to Jake, afraid to look around her, wondering what came next. Obviously she and Jake needed to have a long heart-to-heart talk, but first she had to get through this party. She hoped the band would speed onto their next number, and that it would be a fast tune.

Instead, a loud hiss filled the air as the overhead sprinklers gushed on. From the back of the room, someone shouted "Fire!"

Harvest Fest changed into a stampede.

Chapter 20

Jonathan Park and Leon Maxwell threw open the double front doors and urged everyone to stay calm. Wisps of gray smoke snaked along the ceiling between the sprinkler heads.

"The loft is on fire." Elisa wiped water from her eyes. Was this really happening? She felt an urge to laugh hysterically.

"Your Gremlin strikes again." Jake held a hand over his brow to shield his eyes from the spray. "Stairs? Outdoors or in?"

"Ladder," she corrected. "In the storage closet."

"Where?" Leon Maxwell galloped up. Jon was close behind, a fire extinguisher cradled in his arms. She led them to the indoor ladder, now hidden in a storage closet next to the new bathroom. Jon hurriedly scrambled up the metal rungs. Leon shook out his cell phone and reported the fire as he followed his colleague up the ladder, climbing one-handed.

"The ladder!" Elisa suddenly exclaimed. "That's why the ladder was there!" Jake watched her in mystification, then followed as she pushed her way through the back door.

The night air was frigid against her wet skin and the ground felt slippery under her sandals. She could hear the faint whine of a siren in the distance, nearly drowned out by the clamor of shouting, car doors slamming, engines revving at the front of the building. As the back door closed behind Jake, Elisa realized that she'd forgotten to flip the switch for the outside light. Barely visible in the darkness, a black figure was descending the extension ladder that leaned against the barn.

"There!" Elisa pointed. "The Gremlin!"

"Crap!" The figure leapt the last few steps to hit the ground with a thud. The Gremlin jerked the ladder away from the building, turned, and ran.

Elisa, cursing, stopped and hiked up her tight dress to free her legs. Jake took off after the Gremlin. Out of the corner of his eye, he saw the heavy extension ladder careening down the side of the barn directly toward Elisa. Glancing up, she saw it, too, staggered sideways, caught her heel and fell to one knee.

Jake dashed back barely in time to stretch out a hand and curl his fingers around a metal rung. There was no way he could stop the ladder's downward momentum. He managed to change the angle of its arc slightly but he could see it wouldn't be enough, so he let go and leapt toward Elisa, shoving her hard. She fell forward on her hands and knees. The ladder passed over Elisa's head, missing her by mere inches, and landed beside her with a clattering crash.

She pushed herself to her feet. "I say 'Maybe' and you throw me in the dirt?"

What? "I—"

Smiling, she interrupted his explanation. "Jake, I was kidding. Thank you."

His heart was thumping heavily, not only because of the exertion but because he'd come so close to losing her. He felt a little nauseous at the thought.

"Are you okay?" she asked, her brow creased with concern.

He realized that he was rubbing his right wrist. It hurt like hell. Twirling extension ladders was not a stunt that he'd recommend. He managed to nod, still breathing heavily. As the roar of his own heartbeats and the rasp of his breaths died away, he heard splashing and muttering a few yards away in the darkness.

"Crap!" the Gremlin shouted again.

Elisa smiled again. "He found my new pond."

~

Jake loped off once more. Elisa followed more slowly, cursing her tight dress, flimsy shoes, and aching leg. This was exactly why she never dressed like this. A woman couldn't look like a china doll and fight like a ninja, could she?

Two slight figures wrestled in the fish pond. An angry shriek echoed through the field. "Get *off* me!" One scrambled out of the pond, kicking away the hand that grasped an ankle. The other stumbled behind. The two phantoms kicked and cursed their way through rows of plants, with Jake in pursuit, finally passing beneath the far security light. The bulb flashed on at the instant that Jake flew into the combatants, sending them crashing into the back fence.

When Elisa caught up with them, Jake had separated them. One he held by the collar at the end of his left arm. The other struggled in the grip of his right arm.

"It's her!" The collared figure pointed at the other squirming body.

She took hold of the boy's arm. "Let go, Jake. It's Timo."

"*You* hold onto him." Jake released his grip on the boy to wrap his arm around his other captive. "They may be in it together."

A green strip of water plant had glued itself to Timo's cheek. He eyed Jake with a wild gaze. "*Verdad que es la migra?*" he croaked to Elisa.

"What?" Elisa was stunned by the question. This was why Timo had stayed away? "No, he's not Immigration," she told him. "Jake is my ... *mi novio.*" There, she'd said it. Was it her imagination, or had Jake's expression brightened on hearing the Spanish word for boyfriend?

"Let me go, you cretin!" the figure in Jake's clutches yelped.

"She's the one," Timo said. "The *demonio*—what you call it—the Gremlin."

Jake pinned the girl's arms behind her back. Elisa peeled back her hood. Wet chestnut hair spilled out. Moonlight revealed angry green eyes.

Elisa's mouth dropped open. "Tiffany?"

Tiffany shook the hair out of her eyes. "This is all your fault! You made me do it," she spat. "What does it take to make you give it up?"

Elisa was incredulous. "Give it up?"

Tiffany stomped her black-booted foot. "Why should Cissie have everything and I'm stuck with the dregs? I deserve better, damn it!" She tilted her sharp-planed face back. "Gerald deserves better. But oh no, you're too good to sell! Even for three million dollars! Now look what you made me do!"

Jake laughed. "Interesting defense."

"Need these?" Bartlett, the security officer, appeared in the circle of floodlight, holding out a pair of handcuffs. "This your arsonist?" He took a fistful of Tiffany's sodden sweatshirt and swung her around. Elisa wondered where he'd been during the pandemonium. Probably out front directing the stampede. He flashed Elisa a chagrined half-smile over the girl's shoulder as he fastened her into the cuffs. "Is he in on it, too?" Bartlett nodded toward Timo.

"No." Elisa released her hold on the boy's grimy jacket. "He's an employee. He caught her."

"You finally got the Gremlin?" Gerald joined them. He blinked in surprise, glancing first at Timo, then at the captive in Bartlett's grasp. "Tiffany?"

"I had to," Tiffany told Gerald. "You weren't going to help yourself. You were never going to leave while *she* was here."

Gerald's mouth opened, but for a long moment, no sound emerged. Finally, he swallowed, turned to Elisa and said, "The fire's out."

Tiffany glared at her fiancé from beneath dripping strings of red hair. "You made me do it. You think I didn't know that you've always had the hots for her? That I'm your second choice?" She tossed her head. "Seven hundred thousand dollars, Gerald. Think about what we could do with that!"

Bartlett tugged on her arm. "I'm taking this little lady to the station house."

"Ger," Tiffany wheedled. "C'mon, honey. I didn't hurt anybody. I'd never hurt anybody, you know that. We love each other. We're going places together."

Gerald seemed frozen in place, his arms wrapped around himself. "I don't know you," he whispered hoarsely.

The officer frog-marched Tiffany a few steps, then paused to look back over his shoulder. "I'll need you to make the report, Ms. Langston. And your employee there." He nodded toward Timo.

"We'll follow in a minute," Elisa told him. She turned toward the boy.

Timo's eyes were huge. "I cannot go to *la policia*." He ducked away toward the fence. Somewhere near Baker's Acres condos, a baby was crying.

"Timo!" She followed into the shadows, determined not to lose him again. In the distance, she heard Tiffany yelling "Gerald!" over and over again as the officer hauled her toward the parking lot.

Timo tugged off a newly loosened board, crawled through the gap in the fence, and trotted across the soft turf on the other side. She quickly squeezed herself between the boards to follow, heard Jake's muttered curses as he tried in vain to get through the narrow space.

As they neared the condos, she heard crying. So it hadn't been just her biological clock ringing some strange baby chime. Elisa watched Timo pull open a basement window and slip through. She stuck close behind him.

Fortunately there was a wide ledge inside the window, and only a short drop to the floor. The dim light of a camp lantern revealed a mattress and sleeping bag, hillocks of clothing and groceries against the wall.

Timo sat on the mattress, rocking a little girl, shushing her sobs with soft reassurances. Two years old, Elisa estimated, at most three. Could Timo be a father?

"Yours?" Elisa gestured toward the frightened toddler.

"*Mi hermanita.*"

His little sister. "Where's your mother?"

Timo pulled a slip of paper from the floor next to the sleeping bag. He stared at it, his face crumpling. "In Guatemala."

"You're here alone? You lied to me about your mother?"

He pushed his hair out of his tear-filled eyes. "I don't lie. My mother was here, but *la migra*, they get her, send her home." He straightened. "Now it is all up to me."

Elisa pulled Timo, along with his little sister, into her arms. At first the boy resisted, but then he buried his face in her shoulder and sobbed.

"Timo," she said. "I understand."

He withdrew his head and stared at her, tears forming muddy streaks down his cheeks. "*No es posible.*"

"It's more possible than you think," she told him. "I'm half Guatemalan."

"I know. But you cannot understand. You are American."

With a gentle finger, she lifted his chin so she could look at his eyes. "My mother, too, is in Guatemala."

"*Yo sé.*"

He knew? "Gerald told you. Or maybe Peter?"

He wiped a tear from his eye. "No. By myself I know."

He handed her the scrap of paper he held. It was an old photo, worn soft and dog-eared by too much fondling. Elisa studied the image. A group of people, all ages, clustered around a young man and a pregnant woman in formal dress, mid-twenties at most, and in front of them, four children in Sunday clothes.

"This is me, three years ago." Timo pointed to the tallest child in the photo. His finger moved to the man behind him. "Papá. Bad men kill him." He made the awful throat-cutting motion again. "They think he knows something about drugs." His finger moved to the pregnant woman. "Mami." His voice caught, and he took a deep breath before naming each of the other children. "Margarita. Serena. Aguinaldo. They stay in Guatemala."

Behind them, Elisa heard Jake struggling in through the window. "Who is this?" She indicated the toddler they held between them.

"Rosa," he said. "She is at the babysitter when *la migra* comes—came—and took Mami."

"Rosa!" the little girl chirped. "Me! Me Rosa!"

Jake stepped forward. "Rosa," he murmured softly, holding out his hands. Amazingly, the toddler smiled and lifted her arms. Jake picked her up and took her to peer out the window.

Elisa concentrated on the miserable youth in front of her. She gently touched his arm. "It'll be okay, Timo. I'll take you both back home."

"You do not understand. Guatemala is beautiful. I miss my family. But there is nothing. My family has nothing. There are no jobs for Mami, no jobs for me." He leaned forward, clutching her again. "You cannot eat rocks," she heard him say, the words muffled against her shoulder.

She patted his back, feeling the tension beneath her hands. It was so unfair that someone so young felt such responsibility.

The storm of Timo's tears gradually subsided and he sat up, embarrassed by his outburst. He held himself stiffly erect. "It is up to me now. I—"

His voice threatened to betray him again, and he swallowed hard. "I took the money. The earthquake comes, and I cannot find the six men I promised, and you are gone, and the nursery is closed. And *la migra*..."

At this point he glanced toward Jake, then colored and said, "I mean, I think—"

"It's okay, Timo."

"But I work for that money. A few hours, almost every night. See?" he pulled a dog-eared calendar from the wall and showed her. Nearly every square held a digit representing the number of hours he'd worked, and on the side, calculations of his pay deducted from $370.00. So Timo had been the Good Samaritan repotting plants and repairing the drainage system by moonlight. But three hundred and seventy dollars? That was only the amount she'd given Timo for breakfast and supplies on the day of the earthquake. Twelve hundred had been missing. Her thoughts flashed back to Tiffany, to the cashmere and leather coats she'd purchased for herself and Gerald. Of course.

Timo tossed the calendar onto the mattress. "I must be here to send money back. That's why I come to you."

He said the last sentence with a certain emphasis, the same way he'd said "I know," when she told him her mother was in Guatemala. He pushed the old photo in front of her again and pointed to a row of middle-aged women standing behind the young family. The five women were all obviously of Mayan heritage, dark hair going gray, bodies thickening in middle age. Her visual analysis stopped on a central figure. She caught her breath.

Her eyes shifted to Timo. He tilted his head in a sly gesture. "You recognize someone?"

Elisa pulled the photo from his hand, staring at the familiar face she hadn't seen in twenty-three years.

"*Tía María Elena*," Timo explained, "My aunt, she teaches me English. My mother is the littlest sister of your mother."

"So, that's the bond between you," Jake said over her shoulder. "You're cousins?"

Timo nodded, his gaze fastened on Elisa. "*Sí, somos primos.* Cousins."

From Jake's arms, Rosa crowed, "Cuzzes!"

Timo rolled his eyes. Then they all laughed.

Chapter 21

Elisa parked the rental car on the rocky ground in front of the little store, scattering the rust-colored chickens scratching there. It was a good thing she'd rented the four-wheel drive with high ground clearance; nothing else would have survived the trip from Guatemala City up the primitive roads.

Two thin dogs crawled down from the wooden porch that fronted the little store. They barked half-heartedly. She opened the door and stepped down from the driver's seat, stretching.

A parrot swooped low overhead, landing on the top of a rough trellis that bordered the store. Another joined it, and they squabbled noisily for space. Even in its poverty, this village was beautiful, like the others she'd driven past since morning. Higher mountains rose in the distance, green and misty. Bougainvilleas and other flowering vines crawled over the buildings. Brightly painted pots, many in the shapes of animals, were everywhere. The air was filled with bird songs, and it was surprisingly warm for the middle of January.

She pulled open the back door on the passenger side. Amazingly, Rosa had slept through the journey, and the pink-cheeked toddler whimpered a little as Elisa unbuckled her and pulled her from the car seat. She'd bought Rosa a new dress as a homecoming present, and after picking up the child, Elisa straightened the skirt one-armed, tugged up the tiny matching socks from the little sneakers. She pushed the dark curls back from the toddler's face and swallowed against the lump in her throat. She'd miss Rosa so much.

Gail and Charlie had cried when Elisa carried the toddler

onto the plane. In the eight weeks she'd stayed with the Langston women, Rosa had become an adopted daughter.

Under a fading Coca-Cola sign, an old man sat in a rickety chair on the porch, looking as if she'd awakened him.

"*Buenas tardes, señor*." Elisa hefted the toddler up a little on her hip.

The man nodded, his eyes fixed on Rosa's curls. "*Buenas*."

"I'm looking for Veda Martinez," she told him in Spanish. "I'm bringing her daughter home."

He rose from his chair. "*Su hija? Rosita?*"

Rosa's eyes opened. Her small sticky thumb found its way into her mouth.

He ran down the sagging steps, cupped his hands around his mouth. "Veda Martinez!" he yelled loudly. "*Veda! Ven acá!*"

Elisa was instantly surrounded by dark people excitedly speaking Mayan. It sounded exotic, full of clicks and twists of consonants. Her mother's language.

An old woman touched Rosa as if she couldn't believe the child was real. She pressed her dry fingers to Elisa's forearm, giving her a toothless smile, saying words that Elisa couldn't understand, except for one: *americana*.

"*Sí*," Elisa responded, "I'm from the United States. *Me llamo* Elisa Langston."

A man said, "Langston? A familiar name." He pointed to an adobe building. A hand-painted sign near the front door read *Escuela Langston*. Then he pointed to another building across the street. *Clínica Langston*. Elisa wished her father could see the school and clinic that had been built with his money.

Three excited women joined the circle around Elisa. One, an attractive long-haired woman little older than Elisa, stood with her hands clenched in anxiety. Elisa recognized Timo's mother from the ancient photo he carried.

Veda's gaze flickered only briefly in Elisa's direction before her full attention returned to the little girl. "Rosa, Rosita! My baby!"

The toddler shrank back against Elisa, clinging to her uncertainly. Four months was a long time to a two-year-old. Long enough for Rosa to forget her mother? Elisa prayed that wasn't the case. "Rosa." Elisa patted the child on the back. "*Es tu mami.*"

The toddler turned her head and stared at the woman. "*Mami*?"

"*Sí, Rosita!*" The woman held out her hands. "*Mami.*"

Rosa removed the thumb from her mouth. "*Mami!*" she chirped, and leaned outward to fall into her mother's arms.

Clasping the toddler tight, Veda Martinez looked over her daughter's curls, her dark eyes—Timo's eyes—shining. "Thank you, Miss Langston," she said hoarsely.

"Call me Elisa, *Tia* Veda," Elisa said.

A smile brightened the other woman's face. "*Gracias, sobrina* Elisa.*"

Everyone insisted that Elisa come to the local café. They sat her down at a rickety table with a flowerpot shaped like a dove at its center. The proprietor brought out a plate of soft corn tortillas and a bowl of green salsa and a cool glass of scarlet *jamaica*, a drink made from flowers.

Was the whole village here? Elisa felt a little claustrophobic, surrounded by so many people. Rosa was passed about among the women, from grandmother to aunt to sister-in-law. She toddled back to Veda or Elisa every few minutes to receive a kiss or hug for reassurance. It was clearly difficult for Veda to let go of her daughter, but she forced herself to sit across from Elisa, grasping her niece's hand and thanking her over and over again. Elisa handed Veda a large manila envelope. When the Mayan woman saw the American dollars inside, she immediately closed the flap and pushed it back, shaking her head. Elisa caught only the word *caridad.*

"No, it's not charity," Elisa explained. "That's from Timo, from his job. He earned that money, and he told me to bring it to you." She handed the envelope back to the other woman.

Veda placed it carefully in her lap. "Timo," she whispered, her eyes wet with emotion again.

"Timo lives with me now," Elisa told her. Whispers of Mayan erupted around her every few seconds, the Spanish-speakers translating for older villagers.

"He works for me, when he's not in school." Assistant Field Manager, that's the title she gave him. And surprisingly, Timo and Gerald were bosom buddies now. They'd both learned to drive the backhoe, taking lessons from her just ten days ago, on Timo's sixteenth birthday. Working along with Peter and Beth Nguyen, they could practically run the nursery without her these days.

She passed around two photos: one was Timo's high school photo, taken only last week. With the latest buzz cut and a University of Washington Huskies sweatshirt, Timo looked every inch a proud American teen. In the other photo, she and Jake each had one hand on Timo's shoulder. Gail and Leon and Charlie and Jon stood behind them. Elisa identified each of them for the group. The photo always made her smile. The earthquake that had rocked the area—had that really only happened a few months ago?—had definitely shaken up the world of all three Langston women.

"Timo's already talking about going to college. He says he wants to study engineering, and come back here to build roads and bridges."

This last comment caused a hubbub of excited murmurs around her.

Veda studied the photo carefully, resting a finger beneath Jake's smiling face. "*Tu novio?*"

"We're not exactly engaged." Elisa twisted the ruby ring on her finger. *An untraditional stone for an untraditional woman*, Jake had said. Yours, no matter what. She pulled out another photo of herself and Jake and passed it among the crowd. It was a picture of them on a hiking expedition.

For now, she and Jake were weekend lovers, meeting for passionate rendezvous in Atlanta, in Denver, in Montreal. Jake loved to surprise her by making the arrangements, calling her late at night, whispering like a spy passing a covert message. "United Flight 42, leaving 5:30 Friday. Bring high heels." "American 367. Boat shoes and rain slicker." In the beginning, it was hard for Elisa to trust Jake and just go along for the ride. She was used to managing all the details of her life. But now she appreciated these assignations for what they were: romance to the ultimate degree, Jake choosing places and activities that would delight her.

Jake's classes were going well at Quantico. He'd never looked so happy as an insurance investigator as he did these days. As for what would happen after he graduated in the spring? She wasn't sure.

The photos had made the rounds and were placed in front of her. Elisa handed the two of Timo to Veda, and picked up the other. The picture always made her smile. She and Jake had identical happy grins on their faces. A snow-capped volcano rose behind them.

"Mount Rainier," a soft voice behind her said in English.

Elisa turned. The skin around her eyes had wrinkled and streaks of silver now threaded through the ebony braids that encircled the crown of her head, but otherwise the woman was much the same. The huipil she wore, although softly faded by years of washing, bore the same pattern as the one Elisa had kept all these years.

Maria Elena Alvarez, once Maria Elena Langston, held out her arms. "Elisa, my beloved daughter."

They hugged for a long moment. Elisa filled her nostrils with her mother's scent, with the feel of her soft arms. When finally they separated, she was embarrassed by her overwhelming emotions. Just like at Harvest Fest, the eyes of a crowd were focused on her again.

She broke the tension by pointing to the dove-shaped pot in the center of the table. "Mama, I have an idea for these pots."

"I know. It's a wonderful idea."

How could her mother know about the plans she and Gerald and Timo had for establishing a pottery cooperative here that would sell its wares at Langston Green and other outlets in the U.S.? They'd barely sketched out the possibilities themselves. She'd only told Jake last weekend.

"*Tu novio me dijo esta mañana,*" Maria Elena said, smiling.

Her mother had to be mistaken: it was impossible. "How could Jake have told you this morning?"

"You think an FBI agent can't track you down?"

Elisa whirled. There stood Jake Street, dressed in his familiar black windbreaker, jeans and leather boots, looking as if he hiked the mountains of Guatemala every day.

"Surely you realize by now that I'd follow you to the ends of the earth, *querida*." He held out his arms. She flew to them.

"Will you never cease to surprise me?" she asked him.

He kissed her. "I certainly hope not."

Stretching onto her tiptoes, she kissed him back. Murmurs of approval ran through the crowd of villagers.

"They say the third time's the charm, so I have to ask again." He lowered himself to one knee. "Elisa Langston, will you marry me?"

Gazing into his eyes, she caressed his cheek gently and said, "*Claro que sí.*"

Hc raised an eyebrow.

She translated. "Of course I will."

If you enjoyed this novel, you will also enjoy
Pamela Beason's romantic adventure novella,
Call of the Jaguar.

Like mysteries, too?
Pamela Beason has a new outdoor mystery series from
Berkley Prime Crime, starting with **Endangered**.

The following free excerpt is from Pamela Beason's
newest standalone mystery,
The Only Witness.

www.pamelabeason.com

Monday, 5:45 P.M.

Chapter 1

Brittany Morgan knew she was a good mother, no matter what other people said.

She parked her old blue Civic around the corner from the main entry, in the shade of the grocery store so the car would stay cool in the early evening sun, maneuvering it into the middle of three empty spaces. She couldn't get or give any more dings or she'd have to listen to her father's going on and on about the deductible again. When she pulled on the hand brake, it squawked like a Canada goose, interrupting her favorite song. She *had* to figure out a way to make her parents buy her a better car. She was, to quote her English teacher Mr. Tanz, 'biding her time.' At first she'd thought it was 'biting her time', which made a lot more sense, because you could see how people might want to bite off minutes and hours and spit out the boring parts to get to the good ones. But Tanz made her look it up. It meant, like, waiting.

She'd been biding, putting off asking for a new car for almost a year. All because of Ivy. She looked at the baby, sleeping in her carrier in the passenger seat, backwards like they said, so she wouldn't get a broken neck if the air bag went off. But then, this junkmobile probably didn't even have an air bag on the passenger side. She'd have to remember to ask her father, who you would think would show a little more concern for his granddaughter.

The last strains of *Love Was* faded away and Radio Rick started talking about the upcoming news. She turned off the engine. When the car did its death lurch like it always did, Ivy jerked in her sleep, waving her tiny butterfly stockings in the air. An iridescent bubble formed in the bow of her lips, broken almost instantly by the sucking motion her lips always made as she drifted back to sleep.

Brittany's breasts tugged in response. She pulled out her tee-shirt and inspected the lavender cotton fabric. If anyone saw her with big wet blotches over her boobs, she'd just die. But the pads were working. Plus, they made her look at least a cup size bigger. Maybe she'd keep using them after she quit nursing. Her stomach got flatter every day and she knew her boobs would follow once she quit feeding Ivy.

Everyone had been wrong about what it'd be like to have a baby. How could anyone not adore Ivy Rose Morgan? Only two months old, she was already prettier than any baby in the ads, with her long lashes curled against her ivory cheeks and her soft peach-fuzz hair. She was a sure bet to win the photo contest.

Diapers were disgusting, it was true, but she changed them herself, even at night. And here she was, planning ahead, going to the store after school to get Huggies even before she'd used the last one. If that wasn't responsible, what was? As soon as she graduated from high school, she'd work on her clothing design business but she'd also get a job at Sears, because then she'd be able to get anything she needed for the apartment she'd have. Just her and Ivy. And her friends, too, of course, whenever she wanted them to come over. And maybe Charlie would come around sometimes, too. After all, he was Ivy's fa-ther, and once he saw her, he might decide that he really wanted to take care of his family instead of staying away at college.

Before Brittany got out of the car, she made sure all the windows were down a couple of inches. Not so much that people could stick their hands in, but just enough for good air-flow. When she turned the key in the driver's door, she heard the locks click into place all around the car, but she walked around to double-check Ivy's door, like any responsible mother would.

She glanced at the tall gray van parked in the space to the right. It had those weird rock-star windows, mirrored so you couldn't see inside. It didn't look like the sort of ride that a rock star would be caught dead in, though; it was kind of faded with white lettering on the side. *Talking Hands Ranch*. Sounded like a camp for deaf kids. The mirrored windows were probably so people wouldn't make fun of the little boys and girls signing instead of talking.

Turning back to her car, she leaned down, moved her lips close to the opening at the top of the passenger window, and whispered, "Mama will be right back, Ivy Rose."

Chapter 2

Neema pressed her face close to the inside of the van window. Her broad hands fluttered in the air, signing *soft soft*. The girl's hair was red-gold, long and swishy. She wanted to touch that hair, press it to her nose to smell it, maybe even taste it just a little. But the girl walked away around the corner and then she couldn't see the sunset color any more.

Neema turned to watch the baby. It slept curled up in its chair, just like a baby cat in a basket. She wanted to play with that baby. She wanted its eyes to open and see her. She hooted softly, her breath briefly steaming up the dark glass. The baby didn't move.

Neema slapped the window with her open hand, making a hollow noise that was loud in the closed van.

The baby woke, opened round blue eyes, and put its fist in its mouth. *Hello*, Neema signed. The baby's face wrinkled. Was it going to cry? She wanted to open the window. But the window buttons didn't work when Grace wasn't in the van. Neema ducked her chin and made a rocking motion with her arms, holding a pretend baby close to her stomach. She smacked her lips, gave it a pretend kiss. She knew how to be gentle with babies and things that could break.

A shadow moved past the van. When she looked out again, a man stood between her window and the car. He watched the baby through the car window. Then he turned toward the van.

Neema backed away from the glass. The man leaned closer. His face was mean. Neema tried to look fierce. She showed him her teeth, but he didn't even see her.

He stepped back and looked around the parking lot. Next he pulled a plastic bag from his pocket and stretched it over his hand.

Glove hot, Neema signed to herself. Gloves were for cold.

He turned to the car, pulled a long metal thing from his pants.

She signed *Long knife*. What was he going to cut? Not the baby! She hooted softly, signing *bad bad*.

He stabbed the knife down the window. Then he opened the door and reached for the baby. His long sleeve caught on the seat belt. It slid up, and there was a flat blue snake around his arm, its head on the back of his wrist. A snake! So close to the baby! *Snake bad snake arm*, she signed, hooting with fear. *Snake!*

He lifted the baby in its chair and grabbed a blue bag. With the baby under one arm, he shut the door with his glove hand.

The baby cried. The man shook off the bag-glove, and holding his snake hand over the baby's face, he walked to a green car parked behind the van. Neema scrambled to the back window. Snake Arm gave the baby to a woman in the car, then got into the driving seat. The green car got small and smaller and finally disappeared far away. Neema pressed her hand to the window. *Bye baby*.

A bug crawled up the window on the other side. Neema moved her hand to watch it. She pressed her lips to the glass. How would the bug feel on her tongue? Would it taste good? Most tasted bad. She didn't taste red and black ones anymore.

The side door of the van opened suddenly with a loud screech. Neema jumped and banged her head on the roof. Grace thumped two bags of groceries into the box on the floor. When she saw Neema in the back of the van, she signed as she said, "What are you doing?"

Neema hung her head, avoiding Grace's eyes.

"Get back into your seat now, please."

Neema squeezed down the narrow aisle and climbed into the rear passenger seat, sticking her feet carefully out in front of her. She looked for bugs between her bare toes. She found a grain of sand.

After Grace closed the side door, she walked around to climb into the driving seat. She put a banana up by the window and turned to look at Neema.

Neema gestured the peeling sign and patted her own chest. *Give banana.*

"Put your seat belt on. We wear our seat belts in the car."

Neema remembered the other car. She signed *baby*.

"You're not a baby, you can do it yourself," Grace said.

Neema signed *baby* again, and then *car*.

Grace signed as quickly as she talked. "Neema, no pretending now; you're not a baby. You promised you'd be good if I let you come. Josh is waiting for us. And Gumu. Don't you want to play with Gumu?"

Neema signed back.

"Snake make baby cry?" Grace's eyebrows rose. Neema loved those thin black eyebrows. Like flying birds. Now one flew higher than the other. "Are you calling me a snake?" Grace asked.

Neema hated the word *snake*. The sound was bad. And the sign was like a snake moving. Scary. *Baby cry, bad blue snake.*

Grace looked down at her blue shirt and laughed. "That's pretty creative, Neema. Good use of words."

Give banana.

"I'm no snake and you're no baby. Put your seat belt on before the banana." She pointed to the dangling buckle.

Neema shoved the seatbelt parts together.

Grace reached back to pat her leg. "See, you can do it by yourself."

Neema breathed in. The banana smelled like candy and sunshine. It was for her, she knew it. It had brown spots, just the way she liked it. *Give banana Neema*, she signed.

Grace turned the key and reached for the stick, trying to wiggle it into its place. The van made grinding noises. "C'mon, damn it," Grace said, shoving the stick back and forth. "Reverse. Is that too much to ask for?" Finally, she seemed happy and put both hands on the wheel and turned to look out over her shoulder.

Grace backed the van out of the parking space. Neema watched the girl with the soft-soft red-gold hair come around the corner carrying a bag of food and a pack of soda. Then Grace pushed the stick to another spot and turned the van and Neema couldn't see the girl any more.

She stretched her arm as far forward as she could, making big gestures so Grace could see even while she was driving. *Give banana.* She impatiently wiggled her fingers.

Grace finally handed her the banana. Neema raised it toward her mouth. Then she remembered. She tapped her chin lightly and thrust her hand toward Grace. *Thank you.*

"You're welcome." Grace smiled at her in the mirror on the front window. "You're a good gorilla."

~ END OF EXCERPT ~